The Hide and Seek Murders

Banbury Cross Murder Mystery Series Book One
Ben Westerham

I0545127

Also by Ben Westerham

BANBURY CROSS MURDER MYSTERY SERIES
The Hide and Seek Murders
The Club of Death
The Hobby Horse Murder
A Legacy of Death
The Golf Club Murder
Death of a Scarecrow

DAVID GOOD PRIVATE INVESTIGATOR SERIES
The Strawberry Girl
Good Investigations
Good Girl Gone Bad
Too Good to Die
Smart Way to Die
The Good Con
Good and the Vanishing Act
As Good As Dead

ALEXANDER TEMPLEMAN SPY THRILLER
SERIES
The House of Spies
The Meyer-Hoffman Affair

SHORTS IN THE DARK SERIES

Published by Close9 Publishing
Copyright © 2025 Ben Westerham
First published 2019
All Rights Reserved
ISBN 978-1-911085-73-7

This story is a work of fiction and any resemblance
to people and places is purely coincidental.

Here's to you, Nick, old friend.
Last orders came too soon, but it was a pleasure and a joy while it lasted.

It's all English to me

A WORD ON THE LANGUAGE that's used in this book, so you know what to expect. The version of English that is used here is British. This ought not to present much in the way of a problem for non-British readers. If you do find the occasional word or phrase a little odd, then I hope you still understand the essence of what is being said.

Ride a cock-horse to Banbury Cross

Ride a cock-horse to Banbury Cross,
To see a fine lady upon a white horse;
With rings on her fingers and bells on her toes,
She shall have music wherever she goes.

This is a typical modern version of the popular nursery rhyme. There are numerous earlier recorded versions that start with the same opening line.

Chapter One

Eleanor Golightly was a woman of noteworthy girth. One who needed a tree of significant age and size if it was to pass muster as a suitable hiding place. The challenge was all the greater given the somewhat florid nature of her multi-coloured, ankle-length summer dress, not something really designed with a game of hide and seek in mind. Still, not being one to grumble about such things and ever eager to enjoy the opportunity for a little social engagement, she pressed on with a smile on her face.

She had rather quickly selected an enormous, spreading oak that resided in a corner of the garden; a truly majestic specimen that was sure to be two or even three hundred years old. In days gone by (by which she really meant in decades gone by) Golightly, a widow of three years, wouldn't have hesitated to clamber her way up into the immense and spectacular canopy, there to join the birds amongst the burgeoning summer leaves and nascent nuts. Nonetheless, the tree's still expanding trunk could have hidden two or three of her from view, so she considered it a respectable choice for concealment.

The sun had been out and unobstructed by a single cloud since they'd emerged from the house after breakfast, the temperature climbing steadily until it reached the point where even the most undemanding of exercise resulted in more than a little perspiration in all the usual places and some embarrassing ones too. Eleanor retrieved an already damp hanky from the cuff of one sleeve and dabbed lightly at her temples.

From the bright and burgeoning flower borders, close by the house, came the sound of voices; several of them, excitable, male and female. It seemed that a number of people must have already been found in their hiding places and then joined the one original hunter in their quest to unearth them all. With any luck the ruggedly handsome and distinctly tall Richard Dipping would be the one to lay hands on her, quite literally if he wished to. After all, there she was, very middle-aged, single and, well, eager, whilst he was no more than twenty years her junior, give or take a year or two, and unattached, more or less; that is, if you overlooked the silly little thing he'd brought with him for the weekend.

She had managed to seat herself next to Dick at breakfast. He hadn't exactly responded enthusiastically to her friendly attempts at conversation, but then how many men were properly human before noon. She had to admit, she'd been rather naughty when she'd ensured her fulsome bosoms had bobbled invitingly in front of his face as she'd risen from the table, but the man needed to know where he stood.

Oh, the heat was just too much, she contemplated wearily; so was the sun. She dabbed again at her temples as she peeked round the side of the tree, wondering how long it would be before someone came bounding across to unmask her. There, disappearing round the far side of the house, she caught a quick glimpse of Tamsin Spectacle and Richard, heading for places unknown. She began to consider where the others might have chosen to hide, but gave up seconds later, unequal to the challenge. She was, though, confident their host, the Reverend George Sixpence, would have sufficient home knowledge to ensure he would be the last of them to be located. That is, unless he chose to make it easy for the rest of them to find him.

Sixpence, was amiable enough, in small doses, but far too feeble and uninspiring for her tastes. Indeed, for most other people's tastes, come to that. Surely. Mrs Sprawling had even gone so far as to refuse to talk to the man at all after the fiasco at her daughter's wedding. The vicar seemed to forget every other line in the service and twice referred to the Sprawlings's daughter, Violet, as Veronica. The embarrassment had caused Mrs Sprawling to pass out, right there in the church. All the same, you really couldn't deny the man made an effort to fit in and went to considerable lengths to tend his flock in the appropriate manner. He wasn't, and never had been, an entirely hopeless case. He just needed a little regular guidance and the occasional firm shove in the right direction.

Golightly took another look round the side of the tree, but this time there was no one at all to be seen. She was all alone, just her, the tree and that irritating, ever-present, deep-seated desire to be ravaged by any man with the where-with-all to carry out the task. Good God, why were they so frustratingly scarce? What had happened to that spirit of adventure that had swept the country to such great heights of enterprise? She dabbed once more at her temples and sighed.

Eleanor Golightly never saw so much as a glimpse of the figure that moved up behind her, swift and silent, from the cover of the shrubbery. Indeed, she was only very briefly aware of the immense blow that came crashing down on her head. Just for a second or two, the world seemed to stop in silence, a peculiar sensation that she couldn't quite get to grips with before it had passed and she collapsed on to the immaculately cut lawn, dead as a dodo.

THE WEATHER REALLY had turned out jolly nicely, contemplated the Reverend Sixpence from his superior hiding place in the larger of the two garden sheds. There could be absolutely no doubt that the Lord had looked down kindly on him and had answered his prayers in a most fulsome manner, delivering the most glorious summer sunshine, with just sufficient breeze to lift away the worst of the heat. He must make a note reminding himself to include a reference to this in his next sermon. Indeed, he'd better scribble down something soon, otherwise he'd be certain to forget it.

However, whilst the breeze was jolly pleasant when you were outside in the open air, it didn't help in the slightest when you were cooped up in a tall cupboard in the potting shed. The temperature seemed already to have reached something more appropriate to the Mediterranean region, rather than the northern Home Counties. In fact, if he remained there much longer, there was a jolly good chance he would pass out. It might be necessary to give himself up shortly, rather than risk collapsing from heat exhaustion. Giving up such a fine hiding place would be a shame, for sure, but there really were limits to what he could be expected to put up with in the name of fun.

Someone had, in fact, nearly found him already. He'd not been able to see who it was, but the shed had been subjected to a brief and ineffective search by someone no more than five minutes after he'd tucked himself away in the cupboard, squeezed in behind a pair of all-weather gardening overalls that were hanging from an overhead bar. He had been certain they would open the cupboard doors and find him there, since it was surely the most obvious place to look, but he'd been fortunate that whoever it was had not possessed the necessary common sense and left without so much as rattling the cupboard door.

His armpits had become distinctly damp; you could even go so far as to say wet. But what was he to do, when he was already down to his shirt and trousers? He could hardly shed anything more, for fear of offending the ladies in the party. Mind you, not all of them were really worthy of being referred to as ladies. Women, yes, but ladies, most definitely not. He may be a man of the cloth, but he was hardly ignorant of the ways of the world. He most definitely could not be accused of being wet behind the ears. All the same, there really was a point beyond which a real lady would never step and someone like Marie Macron really ought to know better, especially when you took into account the education she had been blessed with. A venomous woman, absolutely impossible to engage with beyond the basic civilities. Really, why did he keep on inviting her to the vicarage for such weekends?

He groaned to himself, feeling feeble and inept. Who was he trying to fool? Only himself. She was always the first name on the guest list and every time he waited anxiously for her reply to arrive. But, damn it, why did the woman keep rebuffing his advances? Surely, he offered enough to elicit a positive response. She didn't have to swoon into his arms, not if she really didn't want to. A grateful, tear-filled 'yes' would suffice. The good Lord seemed to have abandoned him in his quest or, perhaps, it was a trial, a true test of belief. If it was, then he was teetering on the precipice.

It was no good. If he stood around in that cupboard for much longer, waiting to be found, he was certain to collapse. The heat was unbearable. Five minutes more, that was all, and then he was going to give himself up. He'd take defeat on the chin, like a real man should.

One glance at his watch. A second glance. Then a third. Five minutes were up. Sixpence swept open the cupboard doors and flopped forward in to the main part of the shed, filling his lungs with something approaching fresh air. He propped himself up on the hefty worktop that ran along one side, underneath the windows, and looked out across his splendid garden, listening to the birds twittering away madly and the wind blowing through the upper branches of the tallest trees. Ah, nature at its finest. His own Earthly Paradise, for sure. He really couldn't have asked for more, except for a wife with which to share it all.

It was tempting, very tempting, to remain there, but that was hardly the thing for a host to do. The game was still afoot and he was yet to be discovered. He really ought to make some kind of effort to remain undiscovered and to give the others a run for their money, so to speak.

Deciding to keep well clear of the house, he set off around the edge of the garden, making the most of whatever cover he found, all the while heading in the general direction of the big oak tree that dominated the far side of the garden. It was a truly magnificent specimen, one he had noticed as soon as he'd set foot on the premises for the very first time, and it must be two or maybe even three hundred years old. Imagine, he often thought, the sights and the sounds it had witnessed over the years. Two world wars, Victoria's reign from beginning to end, the coming of the steam engine and the emptying of the countryside as the Industrial Revolution did its thing.

Indeed, it had done well to survive the mass tree cutting of the Napoleonic period, no doubt because it happened to reside in a garden rather than the open countryside. Yes, he would give the tree a rather generous fondling when he reached it. If only that frigid Marie Macron would let him fondle her in the same way, he muttered to himself as he slipped behind the cover of a large hydrangea. The silly woman knew, deep down, she wanted to be with him, so why wouldn't she do the inevitable and give way gracefully to his wooing? Yes, he was right to think the good Lord above was testing his resolve, his staying power; in which case he wouldn't disappoint. His commitment was total and he would see it through, come what may.

It was as he first stepped out from behind an overly large weigela, clearly in need of a major pruning come the autumn, that he first saw Eleanor Golightly on the lawn alongside the oak tree. She was, it appeared, either taking a little nap, carrying out an excessively close inspection of the grass or, more alarmingly, had passed out, most likely from heat exhaustion. The poor woman was, after all, getting on a bit and it really was jolly warm in the open air.

Still keen to avoid detection, the vicar took a careful look in the direction of the house before covering the ground between himself and his prostrate guest. He moved, by his standards, at a fair clip.

"Eleanor, dear, what on earth are you doing down there?" Sixpence announced himself as he pulled up short alongside his friend. "A little early for a nap, don't you think?"

There being no response forthcoming from his motionless friend, Sixpence bent down and gave the woman a firm shake. "Wakey, wakey, Eleanor. Time to get up."

It was as he took hold of her shoulder that he noticed the rather unsettling sight of a substantial dent in the top of her head and a large pool of blood on the grass around it. For a moment, he froze, struggling to comprehend the sight before him. True, he'd seen many a dead body before, though not, let it be said, in his garden. There was, and always would be, a considerable difference between seeing someone dead on a battlefield, on the one hand, and in his garden, on the other.

"Eleanor, dear. Are you still with us?" He again shook his friend, this time with a more little force. "Eleanor?"

He stepped round the motionless body, bent down close once more, then placed a finger on her neck. No pulse. Not good. Very definitely not good. He pulled open her right eyelid. The diagnosis was no different.

"Oh, Eleanor, sweetheart," he whispered, cupping a hand around her podgy face. "Who on earth would want to do such a thing to you? Why?" He slumped on to the grass, his shaking head in his hands.

At the back of the house, where a large, paved courtyard ran right up to the building, a pair of French doors clicked closed, observed by no one other than an inquisitive blackbird, who stood on the rim of a flower pot, tilting its head to one side as it sought out a little afternoon snack.

Chapter Two

Detective Inspector Leslie Dykeman and his Sergeant, Stanley Shapes, had been enjoying the benefits of a game of stud poker, with a couple of gentlemen taking a sojourn in one of the police station's cells, when news of the events at the Lower Itchingbaum vicarage came through. The timing could not have been worse. The officers of the law had invested the best part of half an hour setting up the two crooks, encouraging them to conclude, quite erroneously, that their opponents were total novices when it came to playing poker. Mere moments before being interrupted, Dykeman and Shapes had begun the subsequent process of taking their victims to the cleaners. They were already a couple of quid up, their opponents having not yet clocked what was going on, and the hand in progress held out the promise of five quid more. A rather useful addition to the officers' spending money.

It took a lot of practice to pull a fast one like that, something Dykeman and Shapes were now highly proficient at. On the other hand, opportunities to make the most of said skills were sadly few and far between. Most of the criminal fraternity for miles around had already fallen victim to the officers' skilful and opportunistic money-making scheme and Banbury police station had thereby acquired something of a reputation as being an expensive place for an honest crook to find himself spending time.

"We'll just finish this hand," Dykeman told the constable who had brought them their summons.

"Chief Inspector's insisting on right away, sir," replied the hesitant newbie.

"Lanky," said Dykeman, glancing briefly at the young policeman. "There's right away and then there's right away. In this case, that means long enough to finish this hand."

"As you say, sir," replied 'Lanky' George Bunch.

Dykeman called for another card from the stubble-chinned felon sitting opposite him in the brightly-lit interrogation room. A card was dealt from the pack.

Dykeman smiled, a sickening, blood curdling smile that didn't promise a happy outcome for the two prisoners. Both instantly got an unpleasant feeling they were about to find themselves financially worse off. Fleeced was the word that came to mind.

"I'll raise you a quid," said Dykeman, going straight for the maximum they'd agreed on at the outset.

The two crooks looked at each other. They'd just been beaten three hands in a row and were in danger of taking a heavy loss. Anyone looking on would never have guessed that one of the crooks held a rather decent hand, but what he didn't have was the strength of character to stick to his guns; something Dykeman and Shapes had spotted some time before. The two hapless villains might just as well have handed over their cash right at the start.

"Too hot for me," groaned the prisoner with the stubble, who promptly dumped his cards on the table.

The other felon hesitated for a second or two, he being the one with the decent hand to play. He'd been waiting for a hand like that, one he could really make the most of; it would be a shame to give it up without a fight. He'd more or less decided to stick to his guns when he felt a heel driven into his shin, the pain winging its way at once up his leg, along his spine into his head and, finally, out through his open mouth, "Ouch!"

"Can't make your mind up, my friend?" asked Dykeman, well aware the first criminal had just delivered a clear message to his associate.

With just the briefest further moment of hesitation, the man dropped his cards on the table. "Yeah, it's too hot for me, too." He glanced unhappily at his friend.

"Go on then, boss," chirped Shapes, throwing a pound note into the pot, knowing full well he'd be getting his money back, with interest, after the game was over. "Let's see what you've got."

"That's more like it," replied a cheery Dykeman, spreading his cards on the wooden table. "King flush," he announced.

"Beats my pair of queens," sighed Shapes. "Well played, sir. Didn't know you had it in you to play like that."

"Nor did I, Sergeant. But always a keen learner. You know what they say about having an open mind and a happy life."

The two prisoners looked at each other, heads shaking, as it began to dawn on them they had been taken to the proverbial cleaners by a pair of unscrupulous coppers. The humiliation was almost too much to bear.

"Well, gentlemen, it seems we'll have to leave it at that for today, otherwise PC Lanky here is going to come out in a nasty rash," quipped Dykeman as he got to his feet, shoving his winnings into a trouser pocket. "Would be happy to pick things up again later on, if you fancy it?"

Both prisoners shook their heads vigorously and mumbled something about it being too expensive and cheaper to book food and lodgings at the Ritz. Shapes smiled, a broad self-satisfied look of triumph spreading across his face.

"Come on then, Lanky," announced Dykeman as he set off for the corridor. "Let's not have you slowing us down. The chief will be most upset with you if we're late."

IT TOOK THEM 25 MINUTES to drive out to Lower Itchingbaum in the police Morris Minor, Shapes at the wheel, while Dykeman puffed with care on a Rothmans and watched the countryside bounce by. All they knew before setting off was that some overweight old biddy, who had nothing better to do than flounce around other people's houses, had got her head staved in at the vicarage. As the station's best team, they had, of course, duly been assigned to make investigations.

"Not the kind of thing you'd expect at a vicar's tea party, is it?" prompted Dykeman, in a deeply philosophical moment as he observed a long, slender cloud drift slowly across the top of a nearby hillock.

"Certainly not, sir," replied his speeding sergeant, whose hands were glued limpet-like to the steering wheel, except when changing gear, which was more often than strictly necessary, and whose right foot spent most of the time pressed hard to the floor. "You could even go so far as to say it's downright rude."

"Wonder what kind of church he runs, the vicar? Maybe they go in for human sacrifice, orgies and the like."

"Don't know about the human sacrifice bit, sir, but I have it on good authority some of these villagers go in for orgies, specially on a full moon. Goes back to olden times when we was all pagans and wild men of the woods, so they say."

They crashed through an isolated crossroads, the signage propped up against an uncut hedge, scared the living daylights out of a group of crows who'd been sitting undisturbed for ages on a telephone line adjacent to the road and hammered on along the paper-thin tarmacadam.

"Ah, there it is, up ahead," pointed out Dykeman as the first few buildings on the outskirts of the village came into view. They had about a mile left to go. "Vicarage is on the other side of the village," he reminded Shapes, who ignored his boss, fully aware exactly where they were heading.

As they reached the edge of the village, Shapes, not wishing to seem inconsiderate, halved his speed to 30 miles per hour and took a more relaxed approach to his driving, leaving just the one hand on the steering-wheel while he used the other to fiddle with the rear-view mirror. They rumbled their way past a mishmash of old houses, their limestone walls taking on a pleasingly warm hue in the early afternoon sunlight.

"Jolly nice looking place," observed Dykeman. "Not that I'd fancy living in such a backwater myself, but looks nice on a day like this, all the same."

"Not safe in a place like this, sir," replied Shapes. "Too much in-breeding. Makes 'em all funny in the head."

"Used to think I'd like to retire somewhere like this," went on Dykeman. "Always seemed so... so damned pretty and charming. They don't tell you about all the bad things until you get here and then it's too late, you're trapped. No way out. No, it's the town for me, Shapes, 'til the day I die."

A bicycle, moving at some speed, swept out of a side road and on to the main street immediately in front of them; the rider's hair and skirt flying about all over the place. The woman seemed oblivious to their presence.

"Bloody idiot," barked Shapes, blasting out a long, squealing complaint on the Morris's horn. Without looking round, the woman cyclist raised her right arm and directed two fingers towards the car, before turning off left and running quickly down a dirt track towards a small group of buildings. "Bloody cheek of the woman," stammered Shapes, disappointed not to get the chance to knock the woman off her bike and, preferably, into a hedge.

"I don't know," chimed in Dykeman. "She looked pretty nice to me. You don't get too many women with calves like that."

The vicarage was the archetypal Victorian mini-mansion. Sitting on the northern outskirts of the village, it was set back a hundred yards or so from the road and surrounded by what looked like acres of gardens. To less well off members of society, like the two approaching police officers, it looked for all the world like the kind of place a well-heeled member of the aristocracy would have as their country retreat. It was certainly the sort of property they themselves could only ever dream of being able to afford, even taking into account their illicit poker winnings. Unfortunately for those inside, it also triggered deep within the two of them a total and utter dislike for the kind of people who resided at such places, vicars included.

Shapes turned the Morris off the road and in through the large gateway, between two imposing stone towers. The car crunched its way across the gravel driveway, coming to a halt under the shade of a group of chestnut trees on one side of the house.

The two men climbed out of the car, Shapes stretching as he yawned, Dykeman casting an eye over the well maintained front garden; someone clearly had a passion for a spot of gardening.

"Can't see the squad car or ambulance, sir. Don't reckon they've gone already, do you?" asked Shapes, looking around for places where it might be possible to hide at least another two vehicles.

"No, they'll be round the back somewhere," answered Dykeman, having already noticed the driveway divided into two; one part heading down the left side of the house, towards a small group of outbuildings. "My money's on the vicar. What about you?"

"Already? We haven't even seen who's staying here yet. How can you already reckon the vicar did it?" Shapes blew his large nose into an enormous and not exactly clean hankie, causing several birds to take flight.

"The victim probably upset him, so he did the only reasonable thing he reckoned he could and bumped her off," quipped Dykeman as he straightened his tie and rubbed the toes of his shoes on the back of his trouser legs. "I do, however, reserve the right to change my mind."

"Thought you might. I'm not making any guesses yet. Want to see the suspects's ugly faces before I go having a stab at who did it."

The two men walked up to the large, Gothic styled porch at the front of the house. Shapes pulled with gusto on the cord for the door bell.

"Ought to get a decent cup of tea in a place like this," observed Dykeman, casting an inquisitive eye over the old fashioned external décor.

The door was opened, almost a full minute later, by a burly, sour-faced woman. Dykeman judged her to be in her early fifties and the apron she was wearing, along with the tea towel she held in one hand, told him she was most likely staff. How the better half lived.

"Yes? Can I help you?" she demanded, folding the tea towel into neat quarters.

"Yes," replied Dykeman, stepping forward so as to assert his authority. "And you can start by letting us in. Inspector Dykeman and Sergeant Shapes from Banbury police station. We're expected." He shoved his warrant card under the woman's angular nose.

Dykeman had expected to make his way directly into the house, but the way turned out to be blocked, by the immobile, rock-like figure of the woman in front of him. She looked stony-faced at the police officer and announced in a stiff, no nonsense tone, "Maybe you are who you say, but you'll be so good as to wait right here while I ask one of the police officers outside to confirm that's the case."

The woman, whose name, Dykeman realised, had not been forthcoming, stepped back into the house, closed and locked the inner front door, then disappeared from view as she walked off down the hallway.

"Nice pair of welly boots she's got on there," observed Shapes.

Dykeman lifted an eyebrow and sniffed, "Looked cheap to me. My own are better."

"Bossy type," said Shapes. "Bet she's the housekeeper. Probably tells the vicar when to blow his nose, how to hold his knife and fork and wot-not. I hate people like that. Reminds me of school."

"Admirable qualities in a woman, determination and authority," replied Dykeman. "So long as it's the right woman."

A few minutes later the woman and a uniformed policeman appeared on the other side of the door, their confused shapes observable through the patterned glass panel. A key turned in the lock and the door swung open. The officer recognised Dykeman at once.

"Sorry, sir," mumbled the uniformed policeman. "Didn't think you'd get here so soon. Mrs Itchington here is the housekeeper. She thought you might be imposters."

"Where's the body?" asked Dykeman, ignoring the bleating of the junior officer.

"This way, sir."

As the three men marched off through the house, the housekeeper closed the door with care, wiping the handle and the glass panels until every hint of a smudge was gone, then turned, took a deep breath and told herself, "Well, no point in worrying about things, Florence. You might as well get on. There's lots to be done." With that, she walked off in the direction of the kitchen, thinking it a good idea to put the kettle on, for the umpteenth time that day.

THE BODY OF ELEANOR Golightly was covered from head to foot with a single white sheet. It made quite a considerable mound. It was watched over by a second uniformed policeman. He was young, inexperienced and had never previously seen a murder victim, let alone one that involved the spilling of so much blood. All that had been on his mind for the previous half an hour or so was the overwhelming desire to keep himself together long enough to be able to leave the scene without having made a fool of himself. Now that Dykeman and his sergeant were there, that time was almost at hand. He sighed with relief and straightened up.

As Dykeman and his small entourage made their way across the sun drenched lawn, the two men who made up the ambulance crew watched every step from the relative comfort of a wooden bench sited in the shade of a sizeable copper beech. They were in no hurry to get on with the business of loading the woman's body into their ambulance, thoroughly enjoying the afternoon sun.

"It's a bit of a mess, sir," warned the uniformed policeman.

"I'm sure we've seen worse," replied Dykeman as they stopped next to the large, white mound. "Let's have a look, then."

The sheet was pulled from the body, exposing it in all its gory glory. The two new arrivals dropped down on their haunches to take a closer look.

"Big old bird," said Shapes, as much to himself as to his boss. "And that's a nasty looking hole she's got in her head."

"She'd have died instantly, I reckon," observed Dykeman. "Would have taken a pretty ferocious blow to make a dent like that. And would have taken a pretty beefy weapon."

Shapes lifted Golightly's nearest hand and inspected it at close quarters. "No signs of skin or hair under her fingernails. Doesn't look like she got a chance to defend herself."

"Could have been someone she knew. They'd be able to get right up close before delivering a blow. Either that or someone used all this cover to sneak up on her unawares."

"Well, from what I've heard, we've got plenty of suspects here. And I bet half of them aren't as squeaky clean as they like to make out. Can't trust these sort of people one inch."

"Has this part of the garden been searched, Fry?" Dykeman asked the nearer of the two uniformed policemen.

"Yes, sir. We didn't find anything. No murder weapon and no clues. We were waiting for you to arrive before we spread the net wider."

"Well, you'd best get on with it then," ordered Dykeman, as he clambered back to his feet. "Leave it any longer and it'll be dark as Hades by the time you finish. Off you go. Take a look at the rest of the grounds. Any outbuildings and wot-not. Then get yourselves inside the house. Start with the bedrooms. Oh, and chase all the residents, guests and staff into one of the downstairs rooms while you're about it. I'll be needing to speak to them."

"Come on, Fry" ordered Shapes, clapping his hands energetically. "I'll help you out."

Turning to face the two waiting ambulance men, Dykeman gave them their own instructions. "You two will have to wait for the pathologist. Might as well get yourself a nice cup of tea."

The two men did as they were told and made for the house, happy to waste away their hours of paid employment doing absolutely nothing in particular.

Dykeman took a long, careful look around the part of the garden he was standing in. It really wouldn't have taken very much at all for someone with just half a brain to work their way into a suitably well-hidden position amongst the shrubbery and then launch their attack when the opportunity presented itself. All they would have needed to do was wait until they'd seen the direction the victim had taken, then creep unseen into place. There were most likely other entry and exit points into the garden, which would make the job even easier.

A little patience, along she comes, then wallop! They'd be in and out in a moment, minimal chance of being seen. After all, given what they'd been told before leaving the station, everyone was supposed to be hiding and just one of them seeking. Only, for the dead woman, it had turned out to be less a case of seeking and more like one of hunting. But now he was to become the hunter. The tables were about to be turned.

Dykeman smiled and reached inside his coat to a pocket where he kept a small packet of cigarettes and a lighter. As he lit up, a large crow landed on the lawn some twenty feet away. It squawked, its beady eyes trained on the substantial carcass it had spotted from its look-out point.

"Nothing here for you, sunshine. This is Oxfordshire, not the Serengeti," said Dykeman.

Chapter Three

Rounding up the various parties staying at the vicarage took rather longer than Dykeman was happy with, but at last the task was accomplished and he made his way back inside the house, slipping on an authoritative persona as he did so. He needed to make an impact; make it clear who was in charge. Get off on the wrong foot and their job would end up twice as difficult as it was already likely to be. People of the sort they would be dealing with needed firm handling.

The room that Dykeman entered, without fuss or announcement, was a substantial affair, about the size of the entire ground floor of his own house. He took a look around. It was furnished in the usual putrid middle-class fashion, none of the furniture matching and floral decoration on every surface, whilst the ugly rose patterned paper that covered every inch of the walls was broken up here and there by various boring paintings, some landscapes, others portraits. It felt like someone had tried to bring the place up to date but didn't have much of a clue and had messed up the job badly. You'd have thought they'd have the money to bring in a professional to do it for them.

Clustered round a large, unlit fireplace was a group of settees and armchairs, every one of which was occupied. Excellent. It seemed Shapes and Fry had done their job well.

Shapes was already present and correct, standing with his arms folded a little way in from the doorway, as if he wished to make it clear no one was going anywhere, not for the time being. He gave a little nod as his boss entered the room, as if to suggest they were all ready and waiting for him. The little sparkle in his eyes did not escape Dykeman's attention. The man took great satisfaction in his work, especially when it involved inconveniencing people he didn't much care for, which included the sort clustered around the fire-place.

Dykeman stepped into the middle of the room and gave a deep, bass-heavy cough, which elicited a pleasing response, as eyes turned towards him and an expectant air of silence fell over the room.

"Well, quite a party we have here," observed Dykeman, looking from one face to another as he spoke. "I'm Inspector Dykeman and, as of now, I'm in charge round here. As you'll no doubt already be aware, there appears to have been a murder on the premises. One Eleanor Golightly has been bashed over the head and the best part of her brains are spread all over that nice lawn out there," he nodded in the direction of the garden. "We don't like to jump to conclusions, of course, but I think we can safely say she didn't do that to herself and, personally, I can't see any of the wildlife managing such a feat."

He paused, conscious he'd made an assertive start to proceedings, as intended. There were several open mouths, though, disappointingly, no one had the nerve to say anything. Perhaps they realised that any list of suspects would include each and every one of them. It was, though, probably best to make that clear, just in case anyone present hadn't worked it out yet.

"All of which means that someone else did it and that, ladies and gentlemen, makes all of you suspects, until I say otherwise. I imagine that doesn't come as a shock to any of you but I wanted to make it clear just so you all know where you stand."

Another pause, to soak up the pleasing ripple of apprehension and mild shock. Some parts of the job were always more satisfying than others. Toffs got up his nose, with their jumped-up sense of superiority and entitlement, and their lack of respect for the ordinary folk of the world. Here he was now, standing in a room full of 'em, with a dead woman lying on the lawn outside. Irritation bubbled away inside him.

"Surely not, inspector," piped up a brown-haired, slender woman sitting on one of the settees. "I can hardly see why anyone here would want to bump off Eleanor. It must have been someone else. A thief, perhaps."

Dykeman looked at the woman, trying to work out where the remnants of her accent came from and whether the dishevelled and tired-looking man next to her might be her husband. She appeared to be in her mid-forties and the accent seemed to be Scottish, though it was hard to be certain as she appeared to be doing her level best to hide it.

"We'll be looking into all the options," replied Dykeman, careful to address the room as a whole, rather than the individual who'd asked the question, concerned she might otherwise feel emboldened enough to come back with a further enquiry. "But, in my opinion, casual murders of that sort by passers-by are rare. In the majority of cases I've investigated there's been an element of premeditation, even if plans have needed to be changed to fit in with events. Which means there's a very good chance, ladies and gentlemen, it was one of you who killed Eleanor Golightly. And, be under absolutely no illusions, we will identify you and you will pay for your crime."

Again, Dykeman paused so his message could sink in. He found the resulting murmurs of concern and fidgeting most satisfying. A little casual intimidation often went a long way to unsettling the guilty party in these cases. Yes, things were off to a sound start. A little too much, perhaps, to expect someone to make a run for it there and then, but the guilty party would, he hoped, already be feeling a lot less comfortable. He glanced at Shapes, who had a satisfied expression on his face.

"You've met Sergeant Shapes already. He will be assisting me in my investigations and I expect you all to make the Sergeant's job an easy and rewarding one. All you need to do is obey his commands when he delivers them and the sooner you do, the quicker we'll resolve this case."

Shapes gave the room a little nod and straightened his back.

"Goes without saying, but I'll say it anyway, that none of you are allowed off the premises. If any of you take it upon yourselves to go for a little wander, we'll make sure you can't do so again. If you're lucky, we'll lock you in your room, though we might decide to let you get acquainted with the inside of a cell down the local station."

Dykeman took a couple of deliberate and slow steps towards a nearby sideboard and ran a finger along its surface, as if checking for dust. There was none. One gold star for the housekeeper.

"We'll be speaking to you all individually and, take it from me, any inconsistencies in your statements will stand out like a stripper at a branch meeting of the Women's Institute, so take care what you say."

"How long do you think this will all take?" asked a skinny, blond-haired young man with a big, aquiline nose.

"As long as it needs to," replied Dykeman in a deliberately assertive tone. "I'm sure no one here would expect us to do anything other than a thorough job. Wouldn't want the guilty party to get away, would we now?"

A short-lived murmur arose from those seated around the fireplace. Dykeman took that to be an affirmative response. He looked at his watch. The pathologist would likely be on site very shortly and he wanted to pick her brains as soon as she'd completed her preliminary assessment. It was obvious what had resulted in Golightly's death, the big hole in her head, but there might, all the same, be something useful the doctor could tell him.

"Now then," he said, re-engaging with his attentive audience. "I will be needing to speak to the pathologist.

She'll be here any moment now. In the meantime, Shapes will sort out the arrangements for interviewing you all. Just sit tight for now and we'll start the interviews as soon as we can."

"I've already told them both my jokes, inspector. But I guess I can tell 'em all over again," replied Shapes, relishing the prospect of irritating a roomful of self-important, toffy-nosed types. It was manna from heaven for a salt-of-the-earth man like him.

Dykeman turned to leave the room when a middle-aged man with grey, watery eyes and a large nose stepped in through the doorway. On seeing the two policemen, he stopped and clasped his hands together as if he was expecting something exciting to happen.

"And who might you be?" demanded Dykeman. "The butler?"

"No, not quite," replied the other man in a soft voice that required the inspector to listen carefully. "I'm the Reverend George Sixpence, current resident of this rather delightful house." His thin lips formed a smile, of sorts, and he held out his right hand.

Dykeman looked at the proffered hand, concerned that if he grasped it he might break the thin fingers; but he went ahead and shook the vicar's hand anyway, taking great delight in squeezing a little harder than usual.

"And where have you been? Making us all a nice cup of tea, have you?"

"Er, no," hesitated Sixpence, temporarily put off balance by the pain in his fingers. "I had to, erm, attend to the call of nature."

Dykeman became very self-conscious of the hand he had just used to crush the other man's fingers.

"These all friends of yours, are they?" the inspector asked, nodding in the direction of the gathering.

"Yes, quite so," replied the vicar. "You will find the person who did such an awful thing to poor Eleanor, won't you? Such a terrible thing to do to another human being. And I can't for the life of me think why someone would want to do such a thing to Eleanor."

For a moment, Dykeman thought the vicar's watery eyes were getting yet wetter and he felt the briefest hint of sympathy for the man. But, keen not to look in any way soft in front of the others, he swatted the emotion away.

"Don't you worry, sir. We'll find whoever it was did it. Of that, you can be sure. However, as I've just said to everyone else, for the time being you are all suspects. I want to be clear about that."

Sixpence's watery eyes opened wide. So too did his mouth, though no sound came out other than a short, barely audible gasp.

"Well, I'd best be getting on with things" announced Dykeman. "If you'd be so good as to take a seat with the others, Vicar. I'm off to speak to Doctor Delph, the pathologist."

As he ambled out into the hallway, Dykeman couldn't resist smiling. A job well done, that was. Just the right balance of understanding, assurance and assertiveness. Should keep them all on their toes. Wondering which one of them had done it should give them all something to fill the time and, with any luck, that would ensure they were less likely to go causing himself and Shapes trouble.

Who knows, the murderer might have a lengthy list of intended victims and right this very moment could be looking for a suitable opportunity to take care of number two. Imagine that, sitting there in a room full of people, knowing you were the one what done it and right there, practically no distance away, sat your next victim, not a clue they were living on borrowed time. What a thought.

Anyway, over-indulged toffs like that lot were always looking down their noses at the likes of him and Shapes. It made him smile to think they'd soon have to admit to themselves, their very lives could be in the hands of two working men they wouldn't normally condescend to speak to. Yes, he had indeed pitched things just about right and a day filled with promise opened up before them.

With that thought, Dykeman threw off the last vestiges of the awkwardness and inferiority that usually lurked about him when he was in the presence of money and entitlement. He hated himself for such feelings when they thrust themselves upon him. Why should he behave any differently towards such people than he did ordinary men and women, just because they'd been lucky enough to be born with a silver spoon in their mouth? No, he wouldn't have it; they were going to get just as hard a time as any other suspects would do.

Chapter Four

"Hello Leslie. We really should find time to meet in more convivial circumstances."

"Might have people talking behind our backs," replied Dykeman, through a warm smile. "How you doing Sheila?"

Doctor Sheila Delph was the pathologist for the northern half of Oxfordshire, a large and almost entirely rural area. She had known Dykeman for a few short years, but the two of them had got on like a house on fire right from the off; a happy situation built, in no small part, on the policeman's rather dark and sometimes cynical view of the world. It helped that the two of them enjoyed the occasional flutter on the horses. Dykeman had also turned out to have quite a well-developed understanding of women, something which, in Delph's experience, was a distinct rarity amongst the male population in general and, more specifically, the ranks of the Oxfordshire police service. He had become a firm friend and she always looked forward to working with him whenever the opportunity arose.

For Dykeman's part, his deep sense of admiration for Delph was matched by a peculiar and unwelcome feeling that the woman, several years older than him, acted somewhat like his surrogate mother at times, often there with a word of encouragement or a helpful suggestion when things seemed not to be going too well. He was lucky to have the chance to work with someone whose company he enjoyed and whose professional abilities he'd never had the slightest reason to question. Maybe, under other circumstances, their burgeoning friendship might turn into something rather more intimate. It was a shame they'd had to keep things at arm's length. Anyway, the woman was a whole lot better at her job than her predecessor, James Truffle, who seemed to know more about dogs and cats than he did human beings. Utter waste of space, that man had been.

"I am well, thank you, Leslie. And grateful to you for arranging this little outing for me on such a glorious day. I'm tempted to set up a little picnic table here in the garden after I've finished with this unfortunate lady."

"Help yourself, Sheila. You won't get any complaints from me. Probably rain tomorrow, so best make the most of things. What d'you reckon, then? Large blunt instrument etc etc?"

"Trauma to the head, as you've already seen," answered Delph, looking down at the partially-covered corpse. "However, I suspect it wasn't a large blunt instrument. More likely a slim, blunt one. Something like a steel bar, perhaps. The impact is confined to a small area. I would imagine the woman died almost instantly. Small mercy, I suppose."

"Strong blow, you'd say, then? More likely to be a man than a woman?"

"Come along, Leslie. You should know better than that. Working out who did it is your job. Mine is to tell you how the unfortunate victim died."

Dykeman didn't miss the little sparkle in his friend's eyes, nor the hint of a smile that took up residence on her fulsome lips, clear signs that she was, once again, teasing him. Ah, a woman of so many talents.

"Although, if you wanted me to hazard a guess," added Delph. "I would agree it is more, rather than less, likely that a man delivered the fatal blow. Either that or it was a woman with a strong arm. Oh, and it was a single blow, by the way. No need for a second."

"I thought it looked like just the one blow. Interesting that. Not a frenzied attack by some sort of mad man. More precise. Careful, you might say. And they must have been sure the one blow had done the job," observed Dykeman, tucking part of his shirt back in to his trousers.

"Either that or they were interrupted. Maybe they were just fortunate the one blow did indeed kill the woman," suggested the pathologist.

Delph's Home Counties accent seemed to Dykeman to be entirely appropriate for the setting they were in, although he also chose not to associate it with the somewhat similar accents of the house guests, who awaited his return. They were posh snobs. Sheila was nothing of the sort.

"Couldn't rightly see any of the female guests having the strength to deliver a blow like that," said Dykeman. "They don't look like they've got the build."

"Appearances can be deceptive. A little skill in delivering the blow could make up for a lack of outright strength and, anyway, people can sometimes be stronger than they look," replied Delph.

God, she was good. And she was right, it went without saying, mused Dykeman. He really shouldn't go jumping to any conclusions. Maybe one of the women had a part-time job as an all-in wrestler. Until he had established otherwise, anything was possible. All the same, the men still seemed the more likely suspects. And they all looked like they were physically capable of delivering the single, fatal blow."

"Yes, you're right about that," he said.

"I know," smiled Delph.

"Don't suppose you've found anything under her fingernails? Shapes took a quick look, but couldn't see anything there." Dykeman rubbed his nose as a sneeze stubbornly refused to unleash itself.

"Not a thing. What were you hoping for? A little piece of paper with the killer's name on it, perhaps?" Delph's smile was teasing.

"She'd more likely tuck that in her knickers. Have you checked? Maybe I should. There again, maybe not," added Dykeman, surveying the bulk of Eleanor Golightly.

"She isn't wearing any," replied Delph, straight-faced.

"Wearing any what?" asked the inspector, before realising what Delph meant. "Knickers? She isn't wearing any knickers?"

"Oh dear, Leslie, you really are so easy to tease," laughed the pathologist.

"Thank God for that. Thought I was going to have to add a missing pair of knickers to the case notes."

Dykeman sneezed. Delph shuddered. Birds evacuated the area in panic.

"You taking the body away, then?" asked the inspector.

"If I have your permission, of course, Leslie," answered Delph. "It will be a shame to spoil the ambulance crew's leisure time. They seem so happy in their deckchairs."

"Don't need to keep it here any longer on my account. Best shift it before the crows start getting at it. You can see them waiting in the tops of those trees over there. Like damn vultures, they are. Let me know if you find anything useful once you've had chance to take a proper look at the body. And don't forget about that note," grinned the police man.

"Of course," replied Delph, pulling her glasses out of a pocket in her long white coat then slipping them on. "And don't leave it long before you invite me round to another one of your card evenings. I could do with picking up some winnings. I'd like to book a holiday in the south of France."

"Steady, you'll upset Shapes. He hates losing money, especially to you," replied Dykeman.

With that, Delph turned in the direction of the snoozing ambulance crew and barked out an order for them to jump to it. Dykeman, admiring the natural authority in her voice, turned on his heels and made his way back towards the house.

"ANYTHING USEFUL, SIR?" asked Shapes, responding to Dykeman's summons to meet him in the hallway.

"Yes, turns out the dead woman is really a bloke," replied Dykeman with a deadpan face.

"You're kidding me," said the startled sergeant, his mouth wide open.

"You're right, I am." Dykeman pulled the living room door open, before leaning in close to his Sergeant and continuing in little more than a whisper, "It was a single blow to the bonce. One wallop and that was that. Most likely take a bloke to do that. Certainly can't see any of the women in there having the strength to do it. What d'you reckon?"

"Could have been a lucky blow from a woman, I suppose," replied Shapes, after a moment's thought. "But most likely a bloke, as you say. Takes a lot to do someone in like that, in one go."

"Agreed. That makes the men in the party our most likely suspects," whispered Dykeman.

"Well, that helps narrow things down," observed Shapes, peering into the room.

"It does. I want to start interviewing that lot right away, before they have time to start conveniently forgetting things, like where they've been all day or who they were drinking tea with," said Dykeman.

"D'you want me to keep them locked in here? Might be a bit hard to keep 'em in there all day."

"I'd like to lock 'em in a shed," replied the inspector. "Make them as uncomfortable as possible. But that might give them an excuse to complain. No, keep two or three of them down here and let the rest out, on strict orders to stay inside the house, you understand."

"Got it, sir. I've been nosing around. There's a little office over there," said Shapes, pointing towards a door on the other side of the hallway. "Thought we could use it as our interview room."

"Comfy chairs?" asked Dykeman.

"Yep. And a nice, hard one with a straight back for the suspects," replied Shapes.

"Excellent work, Shapes. Now then, you go and find that odd-looking housekeeper and get her to make us a fresh cup of tea, while I get myself all settled in. Then we can make a start on interrogating this lot."

Shapes placed their order for tea and biscuits with Florence Itchington, in whose assertive company he felt entirely uncomfortable, before returning to the living room to commence the process of interviewing the house guests. He was looking forward to this part of their investigation.

Ah, the joy of it, deciding which one of the self-righteous bunch they were going to put through the meat-grinder first, he mused. Victim, was the word to use. It had a nice ring to it. Which one of them was going to be their first victim. Stick them under a spotlight and give them a good grilling. If he was being honest, it was the pleasure of the chase he enjoyed most, especially, the feeling of unbridled power that coursed through his body like an electric current. And he loved it whenever he or Dykeman threw a question at a suspect which they found particularly tricky to answer; watching them trying to get creative could be deeply rewarding and, occasionally, even funny.

It was a bit unfortunate that, so far, they knew next to nothing about any of the many suspects. A little knowledge would have gone a long way in helping him decide who to pick on first. But such is life. It's not always a bed of roses.

The good news was, there were at least two rather attractive women amongst their number. Seemed as good a place to begin as any. He and Dykeman could ease themselves into things by enjoying the company of an attractive bit of totty. Give him something to look at while Dykeman asked the questions.

Yes, the men and the old bags could wait 'til later, despite what Dykeman had said. And why not start with the blonde bombshell, Tamsin Spectacle. Nice pair of legs she'd got there and it was obvious from the way she dressed she didn't mind showing 'em off to all and sundry. He'd be doing her a favour by getting the questioning out of the way sooner rather than later. She might appreciate that. Yep, she'd do very nicely.

Dykeman had parked himself on the wood-framed chair that went with the enormous oak desk in the study, which was to be their centre of operations for the duration. The chair was lined with padded leather on the seat and the back, which made it very comfortable; an important consideration given they were facing several hours of questioning. He did his best to strike an imposing posture, but wasn't altogether sure he'd achieved anything of the sort.

It was odds on Shapes would show up first with one of the two younger women he'd seen in the living room. Probably the blonde one, if prior experience was anything to go by. The lecherous old git wouldn't be able to resist. Thus, it was absolutely no surprise when the door opened and in walked said blonde, Shapes following along several yards behind so that he could admire the woman's slender, shapely legs and delightfully curving hips. If she had been able to see the smirk on his sergeant's face, she would most likely have slapped him round the chops.

"Take a seat please, miss," instructed Dykeman.

He watched the woman seat herself with care on the hard-backed chair in front of the desk. She ran the fingers of one hand over the hem of her skirt, straightening an apparent fold in the material, then looked up at the inspector from under perfectly shaped eyebrows. It was, no doubt, the sort of thing she'd done many times before. Dykeman couldn't suppress a moment's admiration for the woman's skill and sure-footedness.

Shapes, the grin now gone from his face, sat on another chair, to the side of the desk, and picked up his pad and pencil, adopting a posture he liked to think made him look properly professional. Appearances mattered, sometimes.

"Your name?" asked Dykeman, unwilling to waste time on pleasantries.

"Tamsin Spectacle," came the reply, in a soft, feminine voice.

Dykeman felt a little tempted to soften his approach. That voice was capable of weakening the hardest resolve. He'd best keep his guard up.

"Age?"

"Twenty-five, if you can believe it," she replied, a gentle smile lighting her face.

The inspector paused momentarily, almost caught off balance by this brazen attempt at softening him up. But she'd have to do better than that if she wanted to leave her mark on him. He was determined about that; his mind made up. Mostly.

"Marital status?"

"Available."

She was good, noted Dykeman, if only begrudgingly. Confident too. Still, it was early days yet. It would be more telling to see if she managed to remain so sure-footed and confident once they got on to more meaningful questions. For now, playing a straight bat seemed the way to go.

"Is that single and available or married and available?"

"The single variety."

"Home address?"

"Oh, here and there. You know how it is when you're a single young woman intent on having a good time. You spend a little while here, then a little while there. I suppose you could say this house is my residential address at the moment."

"I would prefer," insisted Dykeman, "that you provide a permanent address. I would have thought that's hardly a difficult question to answer."

"Well... I suppose that would have to be Allington Mansions, Battersea. Flat 15. I share the place with a girl friend. That is, I share it with her whenever I'm there, which isn't very often. Do you mind if I smoke?"

"I do."

"Oh." She couldn't stop the hint of a frown from besmirching her previously blemish-free face.

"So, where were you when Eleanor Golightly was murdered?"

"Well, I can't be very precise about that, inspector, because I don't know exactly when dear Eleanor was killed.

But I suppose you mean where was I while we were playing hide and seek?"

Dykeman felt a little deflated at his failed attempt to catch out his suspect, but there was a long way to go yet, so no need to start feeling down. He'd do better next time.

"I do."

"Well, when the kerfuffle started, I was hiding in the pantry with Dick."

"Really?"

The two men exchanged glances, no words needed.

"And just who is Dick?" asked Dykeman.

"Richard. Richard Dipping. He asked me along for the weekend. A girl can't really pass up an opportunity like this when they're so few and far between."

"So, would I be right to think you are Richard Dipping's girlfriend?"

"Well, I suppose most people would see it like that. People do so like to jump to conclusions."

"And how do you see it? Asked Dykeman, wondering if she would go so far as to own up to being Dipping's paid floozy, which, he had a suspicion, was pretty much right on the mark.

"I always think boyfriend sounds so formal, almost as if you are married. I prefer to think of us as friends, very good friends."

Here was his second chance to knock the woman off balance. A little tingle of excitement raced up his spine. Yes, this ought to do the job very nicely. A little discomfort would do the woman a world of good. He never did like it when a suspect was overly comfortable. Here was an opportunity to knock her off balance and thereby leave her more prone to making a mistake, perhaps saying something she would rather not mention. It was harder to maintain a lie when you were flustered.

"And does this being friends involve sexual relations?" he asked.

Tamsin Spectacle looked at Dykeman for a moment, her face impassive. For him it was rather like opening a present on Christmas Day, keen as could be to find out what what was inside.

"That's a little personal, inspector, I must say. Is it really relevant to your enquiries?" came the reply, with just a hint of irritation in her voice.

Not bad, Dykeman thought. She's managed to keep her composure. All the same, she was clearly no longer as sure-footed as before, which was good.

"No idea, yet," replied Dykeman, without a hint of concern in his voice. "But I'm supposing I ought to know who is sleeping with who, otherwise I won't know who might be covering up for someone else. Who's to say you and Dipping aren't in on this together? Bumping off the old woman, having already arranged for her to write a new will in favour of your boyfriend, perhaps."

Though Tamsin Spectacle knew she might still be considered young, she certainly didn't see herself as naive or anyone's fool, least of all the ignorant, overweight policeman sitting opposite her. She'd made an effort to be civil and helpful and, in return, all he'd been was rude. It was bad enough being subjected to an interrogation by the police, without being expected to answer such personal questions.

A little ball of anger began to glow deep inside her, but she held it in check, unwilling to give the horrible man and his drooling sidekick the pleasure of seeing her upset.

Tamsin gave her generous blonde locks a little shake and, after briefly glancing at the fingers on her right hand, answered the inspector, in a clear calm voice.

"We have, how you put it, sexual relations occasionally. Whenever the poor old thing can manage it. He's not as young and energetic as some of us, inspector."

"And were the two of you enjoying sexual relations in the pantry?"

"Honestly, inspector." This time Tamsin Spectacle couldn't altogether stop a little flush from appearing on her perfectly smooth cheeks. "It's far too cold in there for any such thing."

Shapes took a brief break from his scribbling and adjusted his tie. Bloody Nora, what a thought. Tamsin Spectacle, in the pantry, with him. He'd never got personal with a woman in a pantry. Well, it might be cold, but he'd soon make sure the two of them generated enough heat so as not to notice. As it was, the study seemed to be getting warmer by the second. He could do with taking his tie off, but Dykeman wouldn't like that. There were standards to be maintained.

Dykeman continued to press the point. "But the two of you were in there for the whole time, from the start of the game?"

"Not quite. We took a look in the sitting room and in here, but there weren't really any places suitable for hiding two people, so we skipped across the hall into the kitchen and that's when Richard had the brilliant idea to hide in the pantry."

"And neither of you left after that? Not until word got around about the killing?"

"Oh, no. We were definitely there the whole time, until we heard the Reverend Sixpence asking everyone to go through into the living room. And that's when he told us the terrible news. Quite a shock, I can tell you."

"Did you see or hear anyone else while you were hiding?" asked the inspector.

"No. not a soul. I think we found the best possible hiding place in the whole house."

Dykeman stood up and scratched at his chin, before starting a slow, tight circuit that took him around his suspect, passed Shapes and finally back to the desk. As he went, he continued with the questions, watching Tamsin Spectacle closely the whole time.

"You and Dipping been an item long?"

"Friends, inspector, remember? Just very good friends," replied Tamsin, a hint of irritation in her voice. "We've known each other about ten months. He said he saw me at a friend's party and couldn't take his eyes off me the entire evening. Not that I hadn't already noticed, of course. I do have my wits about me. Eventually, he plucked up the courage to wander over and engage me in conversation. He's very good at that. I don't imagine there are many women who could resist being impressed by that slick tongue of his."

Shapes could hardly miss the suggestive tone in Tamsin Spectacle's voice. A shiver ran through him, causing him to lose hold of his pencil. It ricocheted off the hard wood floor and some seconds later came to a rest several feet away. Embarrassing, was that. But what was he supposed to do when that woman kept making suggestive comments? Would get any man hot and bothered. Pencil retrieved, Shapes focused on his notes, ignoring the look he knew Dykeman would have on his face.

"And did the two of you travel here together?" continued the inspector.

"Yes, we did. Dick has a wonderful Jaguar, in British Racing Green, so he tells me. Positively the fastest thing there is on the road. And Dick is such a fabulously impressive driver. I can't imagine I'd prefer to travel any other way."

"Who do you think did it, murdered Eleanor Golightly?" asked Dykeman.

This was it, the killer question, so to speak, and Dykeman leaned forward as he asked it, his eyes fixed on the woman and his fists pressed against the top of the desk. Let's see if she can keep her cool now, he mused. There never was a more pleasing way to ask such a question than right out of the blue. Was remarkable how often it either reduced a suspect to a blubbering wreck or else had them spouting forth on how this person or that person must surely have done it. Ah, the anticipation was delightful.

"Who do I think did it? Oh, how exciting," answered Tamsin, giving her hair a flick, before placing a finger lightly on her bright red lips. "Well, it's really very hard to say, inspector. Of course, we couldn't see a thing from where we were hiding and I don't really know any of the other guests at all well, but... well, I understand Edward Sweet is Eleanor's nephew, so might he not have a reason to bump her off? Perhaps he stands to inherit a very great deal of money."

She'd been expecting the inspector to ask her that question. If he'd hoped to catch her out, he would be very much disappointed. Who the hell knew who'd killed the old dear? She certainly didn't. But that arrogant little nephew must be the most likely candidate. After all, if Eleanor was worth a heap of money, he'd be laughing all the way to the bank. People had done worse for less. You only had to read the newspapers to see that. Bit of a disappointment, really, this inspector. His questions weren't exactly penetrating or likely to catch out a suspect. Perhaps they would be sending someone better later on.

Dykeman rubbed a hand over his podgy belly as he eyed the woman opposite him. He'd underestimated her, more fool him. Too eager to get things under way and too bothered by the behaviour of his lecherous sergeant. Words would need to be said there. This woman was not only very pretty, she was also no idiot. She was most likely too young to have yet acquired the experience and cunning that a more mature woman of her sort would possess, but she was still no pushover. There was no doubt that a fortune-seeker like her would have a secret or two hidden away and that alone made her worthy of more serious investigation. But that could wait. They were only getting to know the suspects right now and there were plenty of them waiting to be seen. He'd speak to Tamsin Spectacle again later.

"Thank you, Miss Spectacle. You can go now," announced Dykeman, sitting back in his chair.

"I do hope I've been of some help, inspector."

Tamsin Spectacle allowed a little more leg than was strictly necessary to show as she rose from her chair and she smiled inside, fully aware both men had noticed. Oh, the joys of being a woman.

As the door closed behind the rhythmically swaying hips of their first suspect, Shapes fashioned his lips into a circle and let out a silent whistle, then winked at his boss.

"Tasty dish, that one, sir. Wouldn't mind having her in the kitchen at home, washing my pots and pans, if you get my drift."

"Sadly for you, Shapes, I think it's fair to say Miss Spectacle is hunting much bigger game than the likes of you, or me, for that matter. Find yourself a million a year and I'm sure she'd be amenable to washing as many pots and pans as you like. She might even give you a peck on the cheek once a day."

"You reckon this Dipping geezer's just a stepping stone for her, then?" asked Shapes.

"Plain as mud in your eye. She's not going to stop until she's bagged herself a Lord or Duke or even made herself the Queen of England. Either that or, more likely, she'll end up all old and wrinkled and living with a bricklayer in a poky little two-up, two-down, wondering where it all went wrong," answered Dykeman.

Shapes felt his stomach rumble. He gave it a rub. A man couldn't be expected to work on an empty belly.

"I'm about ready for some grub. Past my lunchtime, it is," he said, tapping his watch.

Dykeman glanced at the clock on the mantelpiece. "Let's get done with Dickie boy first, before the two of them get a chance to go over her interrogation. We can ask that housekeeper to sort us out something to eat after that. You'd best bring him straight in."

IN THE HALLWAY, TAMSIN Spectacle stood with her back pressed against the closed door, her eyes shut and her hands clenched together in front of her chest so tightly they hurt. As soon as the door had closed, her whole body had slumped and something close to a sob had escaped her lips as she let go the effort that had been required to present a confident and unworried front. If she'd needed to maintain that effort for much longer she wasn't at all sure she would have been able to. Thank heavens it was all over.

She wanted to burst into tears, but heard footsteps coming from inside the study and they seemed to be heading towards the door. She looked around, not wanting to return to the others, and decided her best option was to head along the hallway and make her way outside via the dining room.

Tamsin stopped by a clematis that had covered a large section of wall with a mass of red flowers and pressed her back against the brickwork, closing her eyes as she tilted her head down towards the paving stones. Tears formed in the corners of her eyes and she struggled to hold back a sob.

Her attention was almost at once caught by the sound of approaching footsteps and she looked up to see the rather unkempt figure of Albert Collard walking towards her. She wiped away the emerging tears and shook out her hair.

Albert stopped right in front of her and took a moment to size her up. "Gave you a hard time, did they?" he asked, grimacing.

She nodded. "Awful."

Albert took her hand and held it softly between his own. "I would try not to take it too personally. The police need to be direct in a case like this. They need to make sure all our statements stand up to scrutiny and I'm sure we'll all be put through the wringer in the same way. I like to look on it as being somewhat reassuring they're going about it like they are, rather than tiptoeing around for fear of upsetting us."

There was a warmth and understanding in his voice that began to ease the tension and stress Tamsin was feeling. She even managed a little smile.

"Thank you," she said. "I think that was just what I needed."

"Why don't we go for a little stroll around the garden? It's a lovely day and the gardens really are rather splendid, don't you think?" asked Albert, offering her his arm.

"I think I'd like that very much," replied Tamsin, taking hold of Albert's arm. "Your wife is very lucky to have you as her husband."

"Now, I wouldn't mind in the least bit if you'd say that again when we're next within earshot of Daphne," Albert said, laughing, as they walked off towards the wide open expanse of lawn.

Chapter Five

Shapes found Richard Dipping almost at once. The sergeant had to acknowledge his boss had been spot on about wasting no time in interviewing the man, since Dipping was already on the look out for Tamsin Spectacle.

"There we go, sir," said Shapes as he ushered Dipping into the study, steering him towards the high-backed chair in front of the desk. "Nice chair waiting for you just there."

Shapes couldn't help feeling jealous of Richard Dipping and it annoyed him. Just because he was a tall, good-looking bloke, who had a fast motor, a posh suit and, no doubt, tons of cash, why should he get a woman like Tamsin Spectacle when an honest, hard-working police sergeant couldn't get anywhere near her type? The truth was, as Shapes knew only too well, it had been so long since he'd last had any kind of romantic involvement with a woman that he had started to wonder if he wasn't destined to end up dying alone and childless. It was a thought that worried him, especially in the dead of a sleepless night. What he wouldn't give for a woman, any woman, to take pity on him.

"You sitting down, Shapes, or going to stand there all day?" asked Dykeman, bringing Shapes back to the room with a bump.

"Sir."

Shapes sat down and picked up his pencil and pad.

Dykeman had watched the new arrival closely as he entered the room and took his seat. Irritating though it was to admit it, the other man was a good-looking devil. Over six foot by the looks of it, thick, dark hair and the kind of lean sculpted face most women would be attracted to. And he carried himself with a confidence that was beyond the reach of most men. Add to that the dark two-piece suit that looked for all the world like it had cost more than a police inspector earned in a month and it was little wonder a sexy young thing like Tamsin Spectacle was drawn to him.

But he had his faults. For starters, there was that thin moustache that arced across his top lip like some under-nourished slug. What the hell was the man doing with that? Surely someone had told him it looked stupid. And he wore too much aftershave. From where he was sat, it wafted over Dykeman in unpleasant and unwelcome waves.

"Good afternoon, inspector. How may I be of help?"

To Dykeman it seemed as if Dipping had just said a casual hello to an old friend he'd bumped into at his club. The man appeared not to be lacking in confidence. The inspector held off replying as he watched Dipping pull first a packet of cigarettes then a lighter from a jacket pocket. He lit up a cigarette without so much as a by-your-leave and blew a long, slender tail of smoke towards the ceiling. Confidence could easily slip into arrogance, mused Dykeman, irritated at Dipping's lack of manners. Perhaps the man needed an immediate reminder of the seriousness of the situation.

"You been sleeping with Miss Spectacle for long, have you, sir?"

Dykeman remained straight-faced, though he couldn't resist placing a little emphasis on the last word. Why waste any time testing the man? Might as well prod him right away and find out what he was really made of.

Richard Dipping found himself caught somewhat off-guard. Hardly surprising, given the nature of the question, which was not exactly the kind of thing he'd been expecting. He looked at the inspector with fresh eyes. Seemed he might have misread the policeman. Probably ought not to have given too much significance to his pushy little sidekick, who seemed to spend all his time eyeing up Tamsin. Best pay the inspector a little more attention than he'd originally thought necessary. After all, there were some things he wouldn't want the man to find out. Would only complicate his investigations. Dipping took another pull on his cigarette before answering.

"I beg your pardon, inspector?"

"Miss Tamsin Spectacle, you been enjoying intimate romantic relations with her for long, have you? Only, she says you aren't up to much in that department."

"Honestly, inspector," replied Dipping, letting out a deep laugh. "What on earth has anything of the sort got to do with your investigation? Or, are you just a little bit jealous of me, eh?" He threw a raised eyebrow at the other man.

"Like I told your fancy woman, it might have everything to do with this case," snapped Dykeman. "Seems to me it would be a damn good idea to have someone here with you who could provide an alibi, while you sneak outside to the garden and whack the old dear over the head."

Dykeman felt himself warming to the challenge in a most satisfactory manner. He had secured a response, caused some annoyance. And with such little effort. Dipping should take a leaf out of his girlfriend's note book and learn more self-control. The little twitch that had appeared in Dipping's right eye provided confirmation he was heading along the right lines with his questioning and from the look on Shapes' smirking face it was clear he thought the same. Get your suspect off balance and you improve your chances of success. Onwards and upwards, as they say.

Richard Dipping studied his cigarette before responding to the provocative suggestion. He hadn't really known what to expect from Dykeman, but it certainly wasn't this and, he couldn't deny it, he was getting annoyed. The impertinence of the man beggared belief, but, there again, it would be a damn good way of unsettling a nervous, possibly guilty, suspect. Calmness was called for.

"But why, inspector, would I want to whack Eleanor Golightly over the head? I'd never even met the woman before this weekend, so what possible reason could I have for killing her?"

Dykeman smiled on the inside. Dipping's casual demeanour showed clear signs of stress, fraying at the edges. His wide smile was gone and you couldn't fail to notice the hint of irritation in his voice. Excellent work.

"No idea. Not yet, anyway," answered a happy Dykeman. "But we've only just begun our investigations, haven't we, Shapes?"

"Long way to go yet, sir," replied the sergeant.

"And we will be very thorough in our investigations, Mr Dipping. No stone unturned. No skeletons left hiding in cupboards. No dirty laundry left in the basket."

Marvellous, mused the inspector, keen to drive home the advantage he'd so promptly acquired. Get the man off-balance, keep him off-balance and see if he doesn't trip himself up. If he has something to hide, then it would undoubtedly be best to get it out in the open sooner rather than later. And everyone has something to hide, no matter how small or inconsequential it might seem.

"Are you suggesting I have something to hide, inspector?"

Richard Dipping leaned forward, resting an elbow on the desk in front of him. His stony face was a fair reflection of how be was beginning to feel on the inside; annoyed, insulted even. If the other man hadn't been a police inspector, he would have grabbed him by the neck and made him take back his words. Who the hell did he think he was to behave like this? The self-righteous idiot even looked as though he was enjoying it. But he couldn't let himself lose control. That would only risk making matters worse. Best to go along with things as they were.

"I wasn't, but if you go around behaving like you have something to hide then I might just change my mind. Sooner or later, a guilty party starts behaving like they're guilty. Get all hot under the collar for no good reason. Make inconsistent statements. Look like they're feeling nervous and agitated. Anything I've missed there, Shapes?"

"Have a nasty habit of losing their temper too, sir," smiled Shapes, twiddling his pencil between his fingers.

Dipping felt a little of the tension in his shoulders lift and he sat back in his chair a tad less concerned. Yes, he ought perhaps to calm down a little. The inspector was only doing his job. He was bound to ask questions, some of them of a personal nature. Best to co-operate as well as he could, then it would all be over and he could move on.

"I just wanted to be clear about that. Some people do rather like to jump to conclusions. And I've always found a self-made man like me tends to attract more than his fair share of jealousy and innuendo," said Richard Dipping.

"So, you're only too happy to help us in our investigations, then?" asked Dykeman.

"Of course, inspector. Wouldn't have it any other way. I may not have known Eleanor Golightly very well, but that's no good reason for me not to feel outraged at what's happened. It's bloody appalling and I'll do everything I can to help you track down her killer."

"Excellent news," replied Dykeman, leaning back in his chair and clasping his hands together on the back of his head. "Now, Shapes here will ask you a few questions as to your whereabouts this morning and a few bits and pieces about yourself. Nothing out of the ordinary. Just routine stuff."

Entirely confident his experienced sergeant could run through the standard questions they needed to ask any suspect, Dykeman remained silent for the duration, watching and listening. For one thing, it was interesting that Dipping and the Reverend Sixpence should be friends in the first place. He might not know much about either man just yet, but it was already clear they could hardly be any more different from one another. What's more, why would a slippery man-about-town like Dipping choose to spend a whole weekend at an old vicarage in a quiet, almost comatose, rural backwater like the one they were in now? That might, of course, have something to do with Tamsin Spectacle, but, there again, it may not. Dykeman felt his policeman's nose begin to twitch as it picked up the scent of something suspect. Yes, there was more work to be done here.

He did at least get an answer to one of his questions when Dipping mentioned that he'd first met the Reverend Sixpence at the home of a mutual acquaintance about ten months previously. The invitation to spend the weekend at the vicarage had been something of a surprise, so he said, but his current visit was also very likely to be his last. Not really his cup of tea, he added. Dykeman felt Dipping was at least being honest on that point. But he wasn't fooling anyone. There was definitely something fishy about the man. Perhaps a little digging into his background might throw up a few choice morsels. Something to get Shapes working on later.

His initial interview complete, Richard Dipping was returned to the sheep pen that was the living room. Having noted the time, Dykeman decided to inform the assembled flock they could have some lunch and do what they liked for the rest of the day, just so long as they remained on the premises and were readily available for questioning. The combined sigh of relief at being released from the increasingly stuffy room was, thought the amused inspector, likely to have been audible in Banbury.

Chapter Six

Having despatched Shapes to issue orders to the housekeeper for their own lunch, Dykeman ambled outside. It was beautiful, he mused. The sun was still high and bright in the sky, unblemished by a single cloud, and the air was warm, filled with scent from the flower borders that glowed richly in the sunlight. Even the crunch of the gravel on the footpath as he made his way down the side of the house was pleasing. It was a damned sight better than being cooped up back at the station.

After a short while, Dykeman found himself facing into a large paved area that wrapped itself round the entire back of the house, buttressed for the most part up against the lawn and interrupted only by three sets of weathered stone steps. From the open French doors at the back of the house came the murmur of people talking. It was, no doubt, the assembled guests trying to find out from Tamsin Spectacle and Richard Dipping what to expect when their turn came to be put through the wringer. They wouldn't have long to wait to find out for themselves.

The inspector wandered across the paving towards the French doors until he could see the space inside was being used as the dining room and the guests, most of them at least, were busy tucking into a buffet the housekeeper must have been busy preparing even before he'd released them from their temporary cell. She must be a highly competent individual to have planned ahead like that, anticipating he would let them out for lunch.

Best leave it a while, he decided. Let them stuff their faces, then slip into the dining room and enjoy a quiet round of sandwiches and a nice hot cup of tea. Could always get that efficient housekeeper to put a fresh brew on, if needs be. Yes, a bit of peace and quiet. After all, the birds were tweeting and the cows mooing. The countryside. Paradise, if you liked that kind of thing. It was fine with him, but only in small doses.

Dykeman sat down on one of a pair of wooden chairs placed round a small metal table, as far away from the house as he could get, and closed his eyes. The sun beat down and a gentle breeze drifted across the garden, carrying with it the scent from a clutch of roses in one of the borders.

After a short while the sound of approaching footsteps caught the inspector's attention and he opened his eyes, initially a little blinded by the bright light. As his eyes adjusted, Dykeman saw two people walking towards him at a brisk pace. One of them was the fulsome and womanly figure of the housekeeper. What did she want? Ah, she was carrying two plates of food. The woman was a genius. Shame that was Shapes following her. And what was the idiot doing now, trying to impersonate the housekeeper's walking style? Woe betide him if she noticed.

"There we go, inspector. A cheese salad lunch for the pair of you. I'll bring out two cups of tea shortly, when I've made sure everyone else has what they need," announced Florence Itchington.

The housekeeper set down on the table two large plates filled with bread, cheese, pickles, tomatoes, cucumber, sliced ham and a chutney that Dykeman didn't recognise. Heaven.

"You weren't wanting to join the others then, inspector?" she asked in a tone that had more than a hint of an accusation about it.

"I didn't catch your name earlier," replied Dykeman, ignoring her question.

She looked at him for a moment. Dykeman felt uneasy, as if the woman was weighing him up, trying to work out which size roasting tin she'd need to use if she got the chance to stick him in the oven. How anyone felt safe committing a murder on the premises was something of a mystery.

"Florence, Mrs Florence Itchington. I'm the housekeeper here."

"Been here long, have you?" asked Dykeman, picking up the knife and fork that Shapes had deposited on the table as he sat down.

"After today, I'm thinking I've been here too long," she replied in an accent that Dykeman noted placed her as being from somewhere in the southern Midlands. "A week short of six months."

"The vicar's not married, I take it?" asked Dykeman.

"Not yet. Though I reckon he has his hopes."

"Really? And who might he have his eye on?"

"I reckon he fancies that Marie Macron," Florence replied.

Dykeman could hardly miss the tone of disapproval in her voice. Did she fancy the Vicar for herself? That sort of thing had happened plenty enough times in the past. Nasty thing, jealousy. Best not to let it get to you.

"You don't reckon he's made a good choice? Something wrong with this woman?" he asked.

Dykeman cut off a big wedge from the block of cheese on his plate and shoved it into his mouth in one go. Exquisite. A rich, rounded mature cheddar. Made the taste buds tingle.

"Well," the housekeeper brushed a hand over the front of the dull brown apron she was wearing. "I don't know as it's for me to be telling the Reverend Sixpence who he should and shouldn't marry, nor for me to go passing on tittle-tattle to other people."

"Very commendable of you, Mrs Itchington," said Dykeman, still munching on the lump of cheese. "But I'm investigating a murder here and I'll take all the tittle-tattle I can get about anyone in that room over there, including the Reverend Sixpence, so just you fire away."

The housekeeper mulled over the inspector's response. Well, he was a policeman and he had said it might help with his investigations, so why not tell him the truth. The horrid woman was a terrible choice for her employer and something had to be done about it. If he did ever persuade her to marry him, he'd soon come to regret it; of that there was absolutely no doubt. The inspector seemed like the type of man you could trust, but that hideous sergeant of his was another matter altogether. All the same, perhaps it was for the best. The inspector ought to have as much information to hand as possible. It was for him to work out what was true and what wasn't.

"Well, from what I've heard, she was married before and it didn't last very long. The husband was a banker and a much poorer one after she'd finished with him. Hardly takes much imagination to work out she's likely to be a gold-digger, already on the look-out for another gullible man to take to the cleaners. And I know for myself that she's a spiteful woman. The things I've heard her saying about that younger woman, the one Mr Dipping brought with him. And, not that I want to go putting ideas in your head, but she wasn't exactly complimentary about Eleanor Golightly, either."

The inspector popped a small, round pickled onion into his mouth and savoured the crunch that it made as he bit into it, then the sharp bite of the vinegar as it washed across his tongue.

"That's a wickedly good pickled onion you do here, Florence. You want to make sure you try one of those, Shapes. Will be right up your street."

"Yes, sir. Right away, sir."

Shapes didn't like pickled onions; they made him feel sick. He picked up one of the little monsters that he'd shoved to the side of his plate and made as if to eat it, then threw it over his shoulder as soon as the housekeeper looked back at his boss. The birds could have that one, if they were desperate enough.

"So, what was it, exactly, this Macron woman said about the recently departed Mrs Golightly?" asked Dykeman of the stony-faced housekeeper.

"Said she was a tiresome old bore, who was hardly likely to be missed by anyone outside her family. I also heard her say she thinks we'd all be better off if we dropped down dead the moment we reach fifty. Said there should be a law to enforce it. You'd think people would have a little more respect, what with Mrs Golightly gone fifty herself."

Dykeman couldn't help thinking the fact Florence Itchington was herself most likely over the fifty-year hurdle might have something to do with her unfriendly view of Marie Macron. The woman he was questioning with such skill was a burly individual with big shoulders and chunky limbs. She'd got her greying hair tied into such a tight bun on top of her head it looked like it was in danger of being wrenched right off. Didn't seem exactly happy in her work. Either that or she thought housekeepers weren't supposed to smile. Mind you, having to look after so many people all weekend with no one to help was likely to leave anyone in a grumpy mood.

He probably ought to go easy on her, for the time being. The staff at big houses, including vicarages, were often a very useful source of information about the rest of the household and any visitors. Yes, they saw and heard things other people didn't. No surprise there, since they had so many opportunities to eavesdrop. Must be a nosey person's dream job. Florence Itchington might be a grumpy old cow, but she could yet turn out to be a mine of useful information, so he'd avoid rubbing her up the wrong way. Best leave that to Shapes.

"Had Eleanor Golightly fallen out with anyone here, that you're aware of?" he asked.

"Well, not that I know, inspector. But I don't get to see much of what goes on round here. I spend most of my time in the kitchen, cooking and washing up. Or upstairs making beds. Or on any one of a hundred other jobs around the house. Don't have the time to spend watching others."

Dykeman bit the inside of his lip. Was the woman serious? Didn't have time to eavesdrop? And I'm the Queen of Sheba. There was no chance someone in her job would miss much that went on around the vicarage. Probably didn't want him and Shapes thinking she was a nosey-parker. Fair enough.

"Anyone else work here, apart from your good self?" he asked, as he eyed another onion.

"No, not live in staff. There's a gardener, Alf Hibbert. He comes in most days from the village. And sometimes the Reverend has to bring in a handyman to do work on the house. But I'm the only one who lives here."

"Was Alf here today?"

"No. He came in yesterday to do a few jobs. The Reverend Sixpence didn't want him around while all the others are here," answered Florence.

"And the handyman?"

"He's not been in all week," confirmed the housekeeper.

"Well, that's very helpful to know. Thank you very much, Florence. And if you do think of anything else, tittle-tattle or not, then you make sure to let me know, alright?"

"I will, inspector," she replied.

The housekeeper turned and departed, without so much as a tutty-bye, marching at a fair old tilt in the direction of the dining room. Any nearby wildlife fled before her advance.

"What d'you reckon to all that stuff about Marie Macron?" Shapes asked, leaning across the table so he could knock the remaining pickled onions off his plate and on to Dykeman's.

"Hardly the stuff of murder, I'd say. For all we know, Golightly might have been a grumpy old bore. Mind you, I still reckon the housekeeper's seen more than she's letting on. They always do, the staff in big houses like this. No time for being nosey? Likely story. I will need to ply her with my irresistible charm and tease the juicy gossip out of her."

"You mean you're going to get her drunk? Got any other plans for her after that, have you, sir?" Shapes grinned.

"Shapes, you've got a sick mind. And, anyway, you know full well I don't like bossy women, especially ones who wear wellies around the house. Now then, less talking and more eating. I want a bit of peace and quiet while I finish my lunch."

Shapes resumed munching his way through his food, glad to be shot of his pickled onions. They'd make his boss's breath stink something rotten, but that was his problem.

The two men might have been keen to get on with their lunch in a little peace and quiet, but the rest of the world had other ideas. Dykeman had just popped another pickled onion into his mouth when he espied a figure walking towards them. This individual strode with a spring that made his thinning hair bounce up and down in a rhythmical manner. The work of a police officer, mused Dykeman, is never done, as he contemplated an interruption to their lunch break.

"Reverend Sixpence," said Dykeman, through the crunch of an onion. "Tasty lunch you've provided here. Me and Shapes were just saying you couldn't get better at any pub we've been in and we've been in a few in our time."

"Ah, so glad you like it," smiled Sixpence, pleased his housekeeper was looking after the new arrivals. "Mrs Itchington really is such a jolly good cook. I was so fortunate to get her. No doubt she could find herself work at a far grander house than our little one, if she so chose."

"Yes, but she's also a woman with some odd habits. Shapes here has been obsessing over those wellies she wears. Makes him go all funny inside, it does."

Dykeman avoided making eye contact with his sergeant, but felt a mild sense of satisfaction at hearing Shapes choke on whatever it was he happened to be chewing.

"Er, yes. Quite so," muttered Sixpence, casting a quizzical look in the direction of Shapes. "Well, erm, I was rather wondering if you had any thoughts yet as to who might have killed Eleanor. Early days and all that, I appreciate, but, really, such a terrible, terrible thing for someone to do."

Sixpence spoke in such hushed tones that Dykeman had to concentrate hard in order to hear the man properly. How anyone in the congregation at his church managed to hear a word the vicar said from the pulpit on a Sunday was anyone's guess. Maybe he used a loud hailer.

"Nope, no idea. Might as well be the Queen Mum who did it, for all we know right now," replied Dykeman. "Lots of people still to be interviewed. But don't you go worrying, Reverend, sure as eggs is eggs, the guilty party will be uncovered before we're finished here. Only takes one little slip in their story to give the game away. We'll line up all the pieces of information we accumulate, then look for any inconsistencies. Before you know it, bingo, we'll have them."

Shapes found himself only half listening to the reply from his boss; somewhat distracted, as he was, having noticed that Sixpence was wearing non-matching socks. Indeed, they didn't even come close to being a matching pair, since one of them was black and the other one lime green. It was the kind of thing that nagged at him and left him with a growing thirst to know both why things were thus and, just as importantly, what had happened to the other two socks. Socks were meant to come in matching pairs and a failure to maintain such a basic domestic task was indicative of a shocking lapse in standards. He stifled a deep-felt desire to raise the matter with Sixpence.

"Oh, I see. Quite so. Understandable, of course, at such an early stage in your investigations," said Sixpence, who then produced a hanky from a pocket and gave his large nose a lengthy blow. "I suffer from a little hay fever," he eventually added. "Most annoying for a keen gardener, like me."

"Got any ideas, yourself?" asked Dykeman, stabbing his fork into a bright red tomato with a good deal of gusto.

"Ideas? What about, inspector?"

"Who did it. Who put an end to Mrs Golightly. You know everyone here better than me or Shapes. Anyone bear a grudge against her? Was she getting in the way of someone inheriting the family fortune, that sort of thing?"

"Oh, do I..."

For a brief moment Sixpence had no idea he'd stopped talking mid-sentence. He'd escaped the noisy throng in the dining room so he could have a quiet word with the two police officers in the hope they might have made some sort of breakthrough. Finding Eleanor like that had been such a shock. He still couldn't shake the image from his mind. It had been there, clear as a bell, the whole time. Why? The question hovered over her bloodied image, nagging at him so terribly. Who on earth would want to do that? How could his God allow such a thing to happen? He knew the Lord moved in mysterious ways, but sometimes those ways were so extraordinarily hard to understand.

He realised he was staring towards the trees at the back of the garden, not really seeing anything that was there. There was something he knew, he was sure, but what? Perhaps it was something he'd seen, maybe, or heard. But what on earth was it? It wouldn't come to him, whatever it was. Of course, it might be nothing. It really was all so very frustrating.

Sixpence looked back down to see two expectant faces waiting in silence. Both men had stopped eating. It seemed they sensed something was on his mind.

"There is something that's been bothering me, inspector, but I just can't put my finger on what it is. Probably nothing. I'm sure it won't be of any help. But, you know how it is when something just won't come to you; it causes an element of frustration."

"Something you saw? Or heard?" prompted Dykeman.

Sixpence shook his head. "No, I don't think so, inspector. I'm pretty sure I never saw anything that looked in the slightest bit suspicious. It's so difficult to recall these things. Oh well, maybe it will come to me later."

"Well, don't you go worrying about it," said Dykeman. "Take your time. Like you say, it'll probably come back to you later. Any little thing can help. Even the tiniest detail. You might think it's got nothing at all to do with this murder, but it could turn out to be crucial. Shapes and me, we'll be all ears, so to speak, don't you worry about that. Won't we, Shapes?"

"All ears, sir."

"Well, don't let me interrupt your lunch any longer, inspector," said Sixpence. "I've bothered you quite enough. Do please let Mrs Itchington know if there is anything else you need. I wouldn't want you to think we don't know how to look after our guests."

The two policemen watched Sixpence make his way back towards the dining room with the same spring in his step as before. Shapes remained bothered by the socks. Maybe he'd add a note on that to his report. Could have a bearing on things and always better safe than sorry.

"Don't know where they get 'em, sir," observed Shapes. "D'you reckon the Church of England only accepts the mad ones?"

"An endangered species, the village vicar," replied Dykeman. "He'd have been just right for the job fifty years ago, but we're not such a church-going lot these days. Makes you wonder. What if Golightly has left all her dosh to the vicar. He might have succumbed to temptation. Felt the urge to get his hands on his money now."

"Doubt he could squash a snail, let alone whack a great big club over someone's head," said Shapes, trying his best to picture just such a thing.

"Wouldn't be so sure about that, if I was you. Remember that case in Bicester last year, where that slip of a woman managed to finish off her husband with a pickaxe. Surprising what a person can do when the fancy takes 'em."

"Yes, I'd forgotten about her. Mind you, she was off her rocker. Had all the power of the insane."

Dykeman fished a sliver of ham out from between two teeth, inspected it, then popped it back into his mouth and swallowed.

"Well, we can't sit around here all day. People will talk. Start spreading rumours all we've done since we turned up is drink tea and eat the vicar's sandwiches."

"Who are we going to interrogate next? What about that Macron woman? I reckon she's the kind of person who notices what's going on around her."

"Keep your mind on the job, Shapes. You spent enough time eyeing up Tamsin Spectacle."

Dykeman stood up and brushed crumbs off the front of his jacket. His sergeant had already spent more than enough time drooling over the younger women staying at the house. If he didn't put his tongue away soon, someone was going to come along and chop the damn thing off.

"Now then, let's see." Dykeman looked at his watch. It was new, a leather-strapped number he'd picked up for a song on a recent trip to Oxford, and, so far, he'd managed to avoid damaging the face, which sparkled pleasantly in the sunlight. "It's twenty to one. You can find the uniform brigade and get an update from them on how their search is going. Then tell Sixpence we want to see him in the study at one o'clock. Now, I'm off to point Percy at the porcelain. Oh, and if those constables haven't got anything else to do once they've finished their search, keep one of them here, just in case we need him. The others can go back to the station. Don't want them lounging around twiddling their thumbs."

"Will do, sir. Shall I tell Marie Macron we'll see her after Sixpence?"

"Shapes," barked Dykeman.

"Yes, sir."

THE TOILET TO WHICH Dykeman was directed turned out to be little bigger than the average broom cupboard. All the same, he found that hadn't stopped someone from installing a wash basin the size of a small bath. As he stood there washing his hands and admiring his handsome features in the mirror, he wondered who might have need for such a vast wash basin. Maybe people who lived in big posh houses liked to wash their babies in them. Handy, perhaps, as it meant you wouldn't have to go to all the trouble of finding a baby-sized bath and a damn sight better than washing the little perishers in a cattle trough, which someone down the station had once insisted happened in all the villages thereabouts.

The mystery of the over-sized wash basin having defeated him, Dykeman ambled outside and stood for a moment in the early afternoon sun. He felt his ever-so-slightly podgy cheeks begin to warm in a most pleasing manner. Ah, the joy of the countryside. Take away all the unpleasant parts, of which there were very many, and the countryside wasn't half as bad a place to spend a bit of time as Shapes, for one, liked to make out.

As he stood watching some plump, grass-munching sheep in a nearby field, Dykeman had a little think about what they'd heard so far and where it left them. It was fair to say that no obvious candidates for the role of murderer had stepped forward thus far. A proper shame. If only the guilty party would either step forward at once to own up to the deed it would save them all a considerable amount of time and trouble.

Mind you, there was a downside to that. It would do away with most of the fun part of his job, tracking down the villains through the application of skill and cunning. OK, sometimes there was a bit of luck involved, but no one should under-estimate the skill needed to put wrong-doers and the downright evil behind bars. Wouldn't leave much to be done if you took that part of the job away.

Just so long as he got them in the end. Failure might eventually end up in his needing to find a proper job and that never had been an appealing prospect. Anyway, he liked life as a policeman. He always had.

From somewhere inside the house, the sound of music drifted out to reach his ears. What was that tune? He couldn't tell, though he was pretty certain it wasn't a death march. He checked his watch. Right, they'd had long enough to put away their lunch and have a good old gossip. It was time to put the rest of the suspects under the spotlight and see how they responded to a decent grilling. He rubbed his hands together at the prospect as he walked back to the house.

IT OCCURRED TO DYKEMAN that he ought to have realised, as he sat there waiting for Shapes to return with their next interviewee, that something was wrong. The mantelpiece clock had struck the hour three minutes earlier, which meant his sergeant was three minutes late. Shapes might have his short-comings, of that no sane person could be in any doubt, but the man's timekeeping was ruthlessly efficient. He'd once seen him bodily drag a man into an interview room at the station. Upon asking Shapes what was going on, he'd been somewhat perplexed to discover said man was the victim of a recent crime, but had made the fatal mistake of messing Shapes around to the point where they were late for their scheduled interview session.

Dykeman twitched his nose and twiddled his pencil. Perhaps he should go and look for his sergeant. The man might have fallen ill, or even been locked in a cupboard by an unhappy suspect. Dodgy-looking crowd like that was capable of anything.

As the prospect of action began to weigh upon his shoulders, Dykeman was startled from his thoughts as the door was swung wide open with some considerable force. Shapes was moving so quickly he was almost running, a rare sight to be sure. He wasn't smiling, but there again he wasn't crying either. He did, instead, look serious, even a little grim, and a dark cloud seemed to hover over him, rain imminent.

"You're late, Shapes. Not like you. Where's the Vicar?"

"He's dead, sir," came the reply.

Chapter Seven

Shapes delivered his news, Dykeman observed, without a hint of emotion. He spoke in a matter-of-fact way and his manner matched. If he was joking, and you really couldn't put it beyond him, then he was doing a damn good poker-faced job of it.

"Dead. What do you mean, he's dead?" demanded the inspector.

"Well, he's dead, sir. Gone to meet his maker, so to speak. Though I don't suppose..."

"Shapes, bottle it," snapped Dykeman. "How, precisely, has the Reverend Sixpence managed to join the ranks of the departed so suddenly? Heart attack, perhaps, brought on by the stress? Aggressive food poisoning, maybe?"

"No, sir," replied Shapes.

"Then what the hell happened?"

Dykeman paused a moment, anticipating a more fulsome response from his sergeant. When it wasn't forthcoming he realised Shapes was making the most of things, eking out the scene for all it was worth and he, like it or not, would have to play along. By God, the man could be irritating.

"Well then, what?" asked the inspector.

Shapes brought a hand up to his mouth and, with great care, coughed, just the once, then straightened his tie.

"He's had a nasty encounter with a kitchen knife, sir. Someone's used his chest as a place to store said knife. Though my guess is they won't be coming back for it any time soon."

Dykeman looked to the ceiling, then back at his irritating assistant. Why did he work with the man? Really, why?

"And why didn't you tell me this before?" asked Dykeman.

The words were delivered with a snap Dykeman hoped was redolent of a whip.

"You told me to shut up, sir," pointed out Shapes.

"Well... yes, but, well... When did it happen?"

"What, the stabbing, sir?" queried the Sergeant.

"Yes, of course I mean the stabbing."

Even before his sergeant replied, Dykeman realised with considerable disappointment that he'd succumbed to Shapes' cunning scheme. He'd been played like a sucker. Lost his temper with hardly any effort at all on the part of his sergeant. The smirk on Shapes's ugly face was growing by the second. Damn it.

"By the looks of things, I'd say very recently, sir," said Shapes. "There was blood still oozing from the victim's chest when I saw him just the other minute."

"And you're sure he's dead?"

"Well, he's not sleeping, sir, that I am sure," answered Shapes. "So, I reckon either he's a damn good actor or else he's dead as they come. Personally, I don't see him been the acting kind, but I suppose you might have your own views on that."

"Anyone else there? When you found him, I mean?" asked Dykeman.

"No one leaning over him holding on to the knife with a sickening look of satisfaction on their face, if that's what you mean, sir."

"Would have been handy. Come on then, show me where he is," instructed the inspector.

Shapes, still fuelled by a glowing sense of satisfaction at the way he'd managed to wind up his boss, showed Dykeman up the wide, ornate stairs and along the landing to a large bedroom at the back of the house. The door was still closed and it seemed safe to assume from the lack of screaming and such like that none of the guests had discovered the blood soaked corpse of their host.

The sergeant opened the bedroom door and stepped aside for his boss, who marched in without hesitation. The room was, to Dykeman's mind, pleasantly furnished, if a little too frivolous for his own tastes. In prime position against the left-hand wall was a substantial king-size bed, draped with a green and white striped sheet that was a lot more modern in style than he would have expected.

A vast landscape painting of somewhere Dykeman didn't recognise was fixed to the wall above the bed. Looked flipping dangerous, thought the inspector. If that enormous great thing should happen to come loose from its moorings and land on your head during the night, then you'd most likely never wake up. Still, not a problem the vicar had to consider any more, assuming he was actually dead. It wouldn't be the first time Shapes had got that little matter wrong.

Sunlight washed in through a pair of large windows on the far wall, giving the room a rather pleasing feel, thought Dykeman,. All really rather inappropriate under the circumstances. To their right, as they stood in the doorway, was a vast oak wardrobe and a matching chest of drawers. There was also an Art Deco standard lamp that stood guard in the far corner, to one side of the bed.

But the only thing of real interest to the two policemen was to be found towards their right, a little way in from the windows. Located there was a high-backed, leather armchair and a small, metal-framed coffee table inset with flower-patterned tiles. Sat in the armchair, leaning back against the head rest, and with his mouth wide open, was the figure of the Reverend Sixpence. If not for the irrefutable fact of the large knife that was protruding from his chest, it would have been entirely possible, thought the inspector, to believe the man was simply fast asleep, completely unaware of the two people who had just entered the room. A sad little picture that was about to complicate their investigation no end, of that Dykeman was sure.

"Unbelievable," groaned Dykeman. "It's hard enough solving one murder and now we've got two to sort out."

"No rest for the wicked, eh sir," commented Shapes.

"Lord knows what the Old Man is going to say when he hears there's been another murder and this one while we're in attendance. I've got a nasty feeling I'm going to be summoned back to the station to explain what the bugger's been going on." Dykeman rubbed the fingers of one hand across his forehead, leaving a faint red patch that slowly faded. "Who found him?"

"Me, sir." Shapes replied as he walked across the dark red carpet to the body and prized open an eyelid. "Yep, he's definitely not kipping."

"You? How comes it was you who found him?" asked Dykeman.

The inspector remained where he was, casting a beady eye around the room.

"Well, I got here first," replied Shapes.

"A race, was it?" asked Dykeman.

Shapes looked up, a quizzical expression on his face. "A race?" he repeated.

Dykeman shook his head. "I despair of you sometimes, Shapes."

The inspector stepped across the room to join his confused sergeant in front of the body of the Reverend Sixpence.

"What were you doing up here, is what I mean?"

"Well, you told me that Sixpence had to present himself for interrogation at one o'clock. When I asked round, no one had seen him for a while, so I went looking for him and, well, he was sitting here like that when I walked in."

"He can't have been dead long, we were only talking to him less than half an hour ago," pointed out Dykeman as he bent down to take a closer look at the knife. "Yep, looks like a kitchen knife to me, alright. I'd say it was just the one wound. What d'you reckon?"

"Don't see no signs of more wounds, sir. Lot of blood, though," pointed out Shapes.

"Yes, you're right about that too. It's made a mess of the carpet," pointed out Dykeman.

The inspector stepped right round the armchair, taking a good, long look at the corpse. Sometimes even the smallest of things could turn out to be the most important. Best not to be overly casual, especially when the crime had happened as recently as this one.

"No signs of a struggle, by the looks of things," observed the inspector. "And I'd say, from the angle of the knife, whoever it was stabbed him did it from in front. One plunge and they were done."

"Yes, and I bet that was a right surprise to him," grinned Shapes, bending down to take a closer look at the dead man's fingernails. "No signs of skin or hair."

"Suspect the killer took just enough time to make sure they'd done a proper job, then cleared off as quick as they could. Was the door closed or open when you got here?" asked Dykeman.

"Closed, sir. I knocked a couple of times before I entered. Hardly surprising no one answered."

"You sure there was no one else in here when you entered?" queried Dykeman.

"Absolutely, sir. What, you reckon someone might have been hiding in the wardrobe?" asked Shapes.

"Did you look? And under the bed," added Dykeman. "You might have got here before they'd had time to clear off."

Shapes half-turned to carry out said checks, then stopped. "Well, if they were, they wouldn't still be there now, would they? They'd have legged it as soon as I left the room to fetch you."

"What's that smell?" Dykeman sniffed at the air. "Unpleasant, whatever it is."

"Probably moth balls, sir," answered Shapes. "They always use 'em in these big houses. Full of moths, are these old buildings."

"Well, you'd better get on the phone and tell Doctor Delph she needs to get herself back here. When you've done that, I'll summon up the courage to call the Chief Inspector. I'd better get in there quick, before he hears a messed up version of events on the station jungle drums. Oh, and before you phone Delph, you'd best get that constable up here to keep an eye on our latest corpse," added Dykeman, with a sigh.

Dykeman had hardly finished speaking when the two men's attention was drawn to the sound of squeaking floorboards behind them. They turned just as the slender figure of Tamsin Spectacle entered the room.

"Oh, there you are inspector. I was..."

The young woman's words tailed off as she saw first the figure of the Reverend Sixpence and then the black wooden handle of the knife sticking out of his chest. Those two things alone, Tamsin Spectacle might, just might, have been able to cope with, but when she then noticed the blood that seemed to be here, there and everywhere, things proved to be a little too much. Before she could reach something solid on which to support herself, her legs began to give way and she felt light-headed. A moment later, she was in a heap on the floor, the contents of the glass she'd been holding washing across the carpet.

The two men came to her assistance at once, rolling her on to her back with great care, then propping a pillow under her head. Her eyes opened and she tried to speak, but the words were nothing more than a jumble. Dykeman told her to rest while they got some help.

"I think you'd best fetch the housekeeper, Shapes. Get her to bring along a whiskey and something to mop that mess up with," instructed Dykeman.

Shapes was gone at once, leaving Dykeman with the semi-conscious woman and a horrible feeling about this new case they were trying to get to grips with. Two murders, in the same day. Would that be an end to it? He prayed it was. Despite his dislike of the people staying at the house, he had no reason to wish death upon them. It was his duty to bring this killer to book and he'd better get his finger out before they decided to add to their toll by killing for a third time.

Chapter Eight

"Pleasant conversation with the Old Man, sir?" asked Shapes, with a chuckle.

"No it damn well wasn't. And you don't need me to tell you that. He blew a gasket. Enquired as to my professional competence and told me to stop swanning around making the most of things here. And don't think you didn't get a mention, because I made sure you did."

"Thank you, sir. Very generous of you, was that," said Shapes, the smile gone from his face. He held back a sudden urge to kick his boss hard in the shins.

"My pleasure. I don't like to take all the glory. Now then, where have we got to?" asked Dykeman.

"The doc's on her way. Said we should stop being so careless."

"Everyone's a critic when things go wrong," observed the inspector.

"The housekeeper wasn't any too pleased either when I told her the carpet had got a bit wet. Reckons it's genuine Edwardian. Expensive stuff. Surly old woman, she is," added the Sergeant.

The two men were back in the study, neither of them in a remotely good mood. Shapes had at least been able to take out some of his frustration on the truculent Florence Itchington, but Dykeman had, as yet, enjoyed no such outlet for his own growing irritation, something his sergeant was all too aware of. Anxious to avoid becoming Dykeman's punch bag, Shapes decided to take the initiative and propose their next course of action.

"Shall I bring in another of the suspects, sir? We might as well get on with things while we wait for Dr Delph to show up." He inched towards the doorway as he spoke, ever hopeful.

Dykeman was busy stabbing a pen into a half-eaten apple, his thoughts temporarily elsewhere.

"Mm? Oh, yes. Might as well get on with it. Bring in someone sensible." He picked up the apple and dumped it in the waste basket next to the desk as Shapes turned to leave. "In fact, make it that young fella, whatever his name is. Reckon he might be easy pickings and I fancy some easy pickings right now."

Shapes made a prompt exit, not keen on hanging around when it was clear from the tone of Dykeman's voice that he was feeling grumpy. In his experience, the inspector's mood could shift from grumpy to volcanic in little more than the blink of an eye. Best to make sure he wasn't anywhere nearby when that happened.

As he stood waiting by the window, Dykeman found himself irritated now by the beautiful, sun-drenched view of the garden he looked out on. It had all appeared so wonderful barely half an hour earlier, but now it clashed with his rapidly declining mood. Maybe a whisky would perk him up. There was sure to be a half-decent selection of single malts in the vicarage; there always was in such a place. But he'd best not. Probably a bit too early for that. And there was always the danger that one drink would end up becoming two or three and that might very well make matters worse. He kicked the skirting board and then wished he hadn't; it made his toes hurt.

Things were getting messy. Killing the old dear in the garden was bad enough, but the vicar. What did he have to do with things? And so soon after the first murder. At this rate, there'd be practically no one left alive in the vicarage come bed time. It was, he had to admit, worrying.

The second murder had, hardly surprisingly, not gone down any too well with the surviving guests and staff, all of whom had been herded together so he could update them on this alarming development. The initial shock had very quickly been followed by a torrent of questions, some of which seemed to openly question his professional competence. That irked him, but, given the circumstances, he'd decided to let such comments pass without challenge. People were worried. Like him, they were wondering if there was to be a third murder. Their happy weekend party had turned into something of a nightmare and, if he gave them the chance, every last one of the guests and maybe the staff too would be gone in the blink of an eye. But he couldn't let them go and had made that clear. Allowing your key suspects to clear off really would be a sign of incompetence.

After responding to a couple of their questions, he'd made his excuses, stressing the need to get on with his investigations as a matter of urgency, and left them to it. Interesting, all the same, to have noticed that Marie Macron and the housekeeper remained impassive the whole time, not allowing themselves to become overwhelmed by panic, unlike some of the others. Took a lot of character to remain calm under such circumstances.

"Here we go, sir," announced Shapes, as he steered the tall, skinny figure of Edward Sweet into the study.

"Thank you, Shapes," replied Dykeman.

"Take a seat here, please sir." Shapes directed Sweet to the chair in front of the desk.

Shame, thought Shapes, they couldn't get some sort of lamp angled over the suspects as they were put through the wringer. Maybe he'd be able to find something suitable in one of those outbuildings, if he could find a spare moment to go looking. Shouldn't take long to have a nose around.

"My next victim," fired Dykeman. "And what might your name be, young man?"

"Sweet, sir. Edward Sweet."

"And are you? Sweet, I mean?" asked Dykeman, not a hint of humour in his voice.

"Most droll, sir. Not heard that one in, oh, weeks," replied Edward Sweet.

Dykeman immediately recognised this young man, with straw blonde hair and a big sharp nose, had the kind of upmarket accent that only came from attending a private school. It irritated the inspector from the off. Posh idiot, he said to himself, then repeated it for good measure. Yes, this one would need bringing down a peg or several. Put him in his place, good and proper. It was really quite a pleasant prospect; someone on whom he could, at last, vent his simmering frustration. A little ripple of anticipation ran through his body.

"And just what do you do, Mr Sweet, when you're not swanning around the Oxfordshire countryside?" demanded the inspector.

Dykeman stepped a little closer to Sweet. In fact, he stood so close to the younger man it must have made him feel uncomfortable, which was just as the inspector intended. With any luck, mused Dykeman, it might even make him feel positively uneasy, concerned maybe for his own well-being. A little intimidation might work wonders.

"I'm at Oxford University, as a matter of fact," answered Sweet, leaning back. "In my final year studying Classics, don't you know. Plan to do a little travelling after that. A modern day Grand Tour. Italy. Rome, Florence, Venice. Then on to Prague and Vienna. Berlin, I shouldn't doubt, too. And I'll finish up in Paris, where I'll no doubt allow myself to be seduced by some cheap little harlot who can't resist my youthful vigour."

Sweet ran the fingers of one hand through his flat hair as he spoke, re-arranging what needed no re-arranging. If the inspector thought he'd be able to intimidate him so easily, well he'd jolly well got another thought coming. The police were public servants, after all. Mind you, the fellow could do with a bath. Shouldn't be surprised, considered Sweet, if he'd not had a bath all week. That was the kind of thing the working class did. Saved on the cost of heating up fresh hot water every day. And as for the obnoxious little rat who'd hurried him all the way to the study, well that fellow must have grown up in some kind of animal pen. He'd seen and smelled more pleasant farm animals.

"And what are you doing here? Asked Dykeman.

"Doing? I'm a guest, naturally. Were you imaging I'd crashed the party, inspector?"

Dykeman observed the other man, in much the same way a fox does a one-legged chicken escaped from the safety of the coop. His nose twitched and he felt saliva well up around his tongue. Sadly, a short survey of the room failed to identify anything he could readily use by way of a large, blunt instrument with which to put the toff in his proper place. Toffs. Their overwhelming sense of superiority got right up his nose, as did the way they talked to you, like you were some gormless idiot to be pitied or laughed at. The inspector felt his eyes narrow and it took no little effort to resist bopping the man on the nose.

"And there I was thinking you were the butler," quipped Dykeman, easing himself into attack mode.

"Most droll," smiled Sweet. "I wouldn't know the half of it. Rather skilled profession, being a butler. All the more so if you're going to be any good at it. Nothing worse than a butler who doesn't know how to do his job properly, don't you think, inspector?"

Dykeman ignored the question. In any case, it was probably meant as an insult, since someone on his meagre salary could never afford to employ paid staff. Anyway, even if he could afford them, they probably wouldn't put up with him for very long.

"Who invited you here?" asked Dykeman. "Mrs Itchington? Maybe she was hoping you'd help her wash up some of the dishes."

"I don't have the hands for washing dishes, inspector," replied the younger man, casually lifting his left hand in the air and twirling it around, so Dykeman could see for himself. "I was invited by my aunt, as it happens. Seeing how we're not so very far away from Oxford, she rather thought it a good opportunity for me to spend some time with her."

"Your aunt? Which one of the women here has that burden to bear?" snarled Dykeman.

At last, something interesting to get his teeth into, considered Dykeman. An avenue of investigation that might just be worth pursuing.

"Why, dear aunt Eleanor, of course. Has no one told you? I would have thought they'd make sure to let you know that. You should find yourself some more superior constables, inspector," suggested Sweet.

The young man felt a modest glow of triumph fill his veins. The inspector was proving to be something of an idiot. He might be the one with the authority of the law behind him, but he was clearly no match for an Oxford educated mind. Ought not to be too much of a challenge to fend off his jabs and lunges. Really, it was bordering on the incompetent for the man not to already know he was related to Aunt Eleanor. Surely it made him something of a prime suspect, one who ought to have been interviewed as a priority, not left to wander the premises at his leisure for a good part of the day.

"Eleanor? You mean Eleanor Golightly is your aunt?" asked Dykeman.

"I believe that is what I just said, yes. She's been my aunt since birth, naturally. We had got on rather well ever since. I think she always found my sense of humour and natural charm a little too much to resist. Rather spoilt me, I fear. But one mustn't complain about such things, especially now poor Aunt Eleanor has passed away and under such terrible circumstances," added Sweet.

Dykeman remained silent, unruffled by the taunting. It seemed he needed to re-assess the young idiot sitting in front of him. At last he'd been dealt a decent set of cards. Shouldn't go rushing in and betting the house, of course. No, hold back and weigh up the other runners. Look into their eyes. Watch for telltale signs they might be trying to pull a fast one. Only go for the jugular once you're certain. He wasn't certain of anything yet, but at least now there was something to go for.

"If you don't mind me saying so, you don't seem all that upset by the murder of your aunt. Maybe you didn't care for her as much as she, apparently, cared for you?" suggested Dykeman.

"Not the least of it, inspector. It was quite the shock to see Aunt Eleanor lying there on the lawn, her skull smashed in. I do believe a tear or two welled up in my eyes. But I wouldn't want to let down my aunt by allowing my emotions to get the better of me in public. What would she think about all those years I spent at Bressingham, learning to be a proper gentleman? She paid me a modest little allowance and I'd hate for her to think her money had been wasted."

Shapes sat in silence, taking down notes, the whole time wondering at what point in proceedings his boss would take hold of Sweet by the throat, before hurling him straight through the window. He could recognise the familiar signs with one eye shut and the curtains drawn. The twitching nose, the narrowed eyes and unbroken stare. And the way Dykeman rubbed the thumb on his right hand over the ends of his fingers. They were, each one of them, entirely predictable precursors to a growing annoyance that was sure to result in a violent and highly entertaining explosion.

Yep, things were looking promising. Another stuck-up toff would be put to the sword, just like that time at the Green Man pub in Banbury when some self-centred snob had bowled in well after lunchtime closing and demanded to be served. Told the barman he ought to recognise his betters and get on with pulling a pint, if he wanted to keep his job. Didn't take too kindly to Dykeman stepping in and insisting on his leaving the premises. Got all hot under the collar. Told the inspector he was an ignorant little turd who wouldn't know which way to pass the port. Well, he might not, but he did know how to throw a toff into the canal that ran along the back of the pub. They still talked about that one down the station. Become local folklore, it had.

It was, therefore, a proper old let-down when Dykeman's mood clearly changed at the news Eleanor Golightly was Edward Sweet's auntie. Poor old bird. Was bad enough getting your head smashed in, let alone having to put up with this Sweet as a nephew. Maybe he could intervene and re-ignite his boss's frustration and anger. Might be worth a go.

"Do the rest of the guests know she's your aunt?" asked Dykeman.

"I would have thought so," responded Sweet. "Though I can hardly be expected to go marching right up to all and sundry and announce our family relationship. I know the Reverend Sixpence was aware. He and my aunt were old friends. And the Collards know, I'm certain, because I did mention it to them. You'll have to ask the others yourself, I'm afraid, though I imagine Aunt Eleanor would have mentioned it. She was so proud, you see, of my getting into Oxford. Only the second member of the family to manage the feat."

"Did you kill her?" demanded the inspector.

Dykeman had chosen his moment with care, waiting for the other man to relax into things, and it was obvious he now had. He delivered the question, he liked to think, as he would a rapier towards an opponent's heart. But would it prove a fatal blow?

Sweet's eyebrows reached for the ceiling and his head rocked back a little.

"I say, inspector. That's a little off piste. Why on earth would I want to bump off Aunt Eleanor? She was everything a young man could have asked for in an elderly aunt. I grant you, she was a little eccentric at times, but aren't they always, these elderly aunts? And, really, when would I have had the opportunity?"

Sweet tried to brush away his sudden discomfort with a little smile and a shrug of the shoulders.

"So, where were you hiding while this game of hide and seek was under way? And who saw you there?" pressed Dykeman.

"Me? I wasn't hiding at all, inspector. You see, I was the one doing the seeking. I had to wait in the sitting room, counting to one hundred, while the others scampered around like little sheep, looking for some suitable hiding place."

"Did you find anyone before the news of your aunt's murder broke?" Dykeman asked.

"Oh, yes. Marie Macron didn't make it any too difficult for me to find her. I do believe she was rather unenthusiastic about playing the game, but the Reverend Sixpence did somewhat insist. Told her not to be a party-pooper. She was sitting in a corner of the dining room, smoking a cigarette. I asked her if she would like to join my pack of hounds, seeing how there was just the one hound, me, at that point, but she told me to run off like a good little boy and find the others on my own."

"That all? Just Marie Macron?" persisted Dykeman.

"Well, I did see someone run off round the side of the house when I trundled out into the garden," answered Sweet. "But it was just the most fleeting of glimpses and I couldn't make out who it was. When I arrived on the scene some moments later, they were already gone."

"Male or female, can you at least tell me that?" Dykeman asked.

"Oh, a chap, most definitely," came the reply.

"You're sure you didn't see anyone else?" asked the inspector.

"Absolutely. After all, that was my objective in the game, inspector. I was the hunter, don't you know."

Edward Sweet scratched an itch on the side of his nose. To Dykeman it seemed a person could hardly have appeared more relaxed, even if they'd been injected with a sleeping drug. But was it, he contemplated, a case of being too relaxed? And the irritating little idiot seemed to have regained his composure with annoying ease after it looked for a moment as if he was all at sea. Maybe he was a more slippery customer than first appeared. The inspector rapped the fingers of one hand on the desk as he considered his next question.

"She have any enemies, your aunt? Upset anyone enough to cause them to take their revenge by bumping her off?" he asked.

"Hardly, inspector. Aunt Eleanor seemed to make a special thing of it to get along with anyone. Can't even think I've heard a single person say a bad word about her. Well, apart from my mother. She's always felt Aunt Eleanor over-indulges me, but isn't that just what an elderly aunt is for? I jolly well know I'm not complaining."

The self-satisfied smile that appeared on Sweet's face had a similar effect on Dykeman to that of poking a pig with a sharp stick. The older man felt the contempt rise within him, like an over-flowing toilet. It took some effort to fend off an explosion.

"I wouldn't know," grunted Dykeman. "I never had a rich aunt to spoil me. Did you, Shapes, have a rich aunt to shower you with money and turn you into a stuck-up little moron?"

"Sadly not, sir. I turned into a stupid little moron all on my own. Mind you, I did have an aunt who used to run a brothel. Reckon she must have made a bob or two, but we never saw any of it. She spent most of her illicit earnings on booze, betting and fellas way younger than she was."

Dykeman nodded, then picked up where Shapes had left off, aiming to apply a little more pressure to Sweet. "When I was a spotty teenager, I used to dream about bumping into some spoilt rich brat down a dark alleyway or in the middle of some gloomy, lonely woods. I looked forward to being able to smash the self-satisfied smile off his ugly face, then steal his bulging wallet. Sadly, that little dream hasn't ever come true, not yet."

Edward Sweet fidgeted in his chair and raised a hand to cover a feeble cough. Excellent, thought Dykeman. That's made the jumped-up idiot feel less comfortable. He's probably had the same dream himself, only to him it's always been a nightmare, being cornered by some hard-nosed working class lad keen on relieving him of some of that slush fund his aunt lavished on him. Those,like Sweet, who get it all served up to them on a plate, never have any idea how much work goes into creating all that wealth in the first place. The hard, repetitive graft. The sort of thing his parents spent their lives doing.

"So, Sweet, where were you when the Reverend Sixpence had a fatal encounter with a large, pointy kitchen knife? Got an alibi for that one too, have you?" barked Dykeman.

"Well, inspector, I really can't be sure, of course. Not knowing precisely when the Reverend Sixpence was stabbed to death, it's hard to be certain where I was," pointed out Sweet.

Shame, thought Dykeman, that's the second time that particular trap has failed to come up with the goods.

"How about telling us what your movements were following the murder of your aunt? I'm particularly keen on the bits that involve other people, so we have some means of confirming what you've told us is true," added Dykeman.

"Absolutely, inspector. Well, you'll know we were all summoned to the lounge after Aunt Eleanor was killed. After that, I read the newspapers on the terrace for a while. Marie Macron was there for a time and Mr and Mrs Collard. As it happened, the Reverend Sixpence put in a brief appearance. He wanted to speak to Marie Macron, but she seemed disinclined to engage in conversation. So he retreated back into the house, looking, I must say, rather glum. Seeing how we were heading rapidly towards luncheon, I popped upstairs to spruce myself up, then came back down to the dining room, where Mrs Itchington was already busy laying out our meal. I think most of the other guests were there by then, though I'm afraid I can't be certain who was and wasn't. And, well, that's it, really. Shortly afterwards your man brought me in here."

"Did you see anyone else when you went upstairs?" asked Dykeman.

"Absolutely not."

"You're sure about that?" persisted the inspector.

"Inspector, I have the most marvellous twenty-twenty eyesight. If there had been anyone else wandering around, you can be sure I would have seen them."

"Got any questions for this boy, Shapes?" asked Dykeman, turning to his Sergeant.

Shapes shook his head. "None, sir."

Dykeman remained silent for a moment, deep in thought. By his own admission, Sweet had gone upstairs, alone. It may have presented him with an opportunity. One he decided not to pass up. It was a possibility, but the problem still remained that of motive. It might make sense for Sweet to murder his aunt, but what had Sixpence got to do with it all? It seemed unlikely they would find the answer right there and then, more's the pity.

"Off you go, then," said Dykeman to the young man opposite him. "But don't go far. We'll have more questions to ask you later."

"Are we really not to leave the vicarage, not even to go for a walk?" asked Edward Sweet.

"That's right. Leave the grounds and when we catch up with you, we'll have you locked up. And, take it from me, the cells at Banbury nick aren't anywhere near as plush as the bedrooms here."

"Oh, well, suppose we'll just have to do our best to make the most of things," smiled Sweet.

As soon as the door closed behind Sweet, Dykeman turned to his Sergeant. "I want to know more about him, Shapes," barked Dykeman. "Got right up my nose, he did. Reckons he's smarter than the likes of you and me. But we'll soon put him right about that. In fact, I want to know everything there is to know about every single one of the guests here. They'll all have things to hide; dirty little secrets they do their best to keep under wraps. Richard Dipping is a shoe-in for someone with a dodgy past. Probably a dodgy present and future too. But I'd take a bet the rest of 'em are a long way from being the squeaky clean middle class members of the establishment they'd like us to believe. Get some of those lazy bleeders down the station to start digging and make sure they don't stop until they've dug right the way through to the Antarctic."

"With pleasure, sir. One of my favourite parts of the job," grinned Shapes.

The eager Sergeant snapped his notepad shut and stuffed it into a jacket pocket. It was the little things that gave him the most pleasure. He wasn't a man with grand expectations of life or a greedy need for more than his fair share of the good stuff. Give him a decent case to get his teeth stuck into and he was like a pig in muck.

"Go on, then, you can bring that Macron woman in next. But don't sit there gawping at her like some goggle-eyed schoolboy. Makes you look like a half-wit," complained Dykeman.

Shapes couldn't stop a grin from appearing on his face. As he struggled to keep a lid on it, he straightened his tie, stood up and fiddled with his jacket, before marching out of the room in search of his next quarry.

Chapter Nine

Dykeman rubbed the fingers of one hand over his chin, his brain picking through the slim offerings they'd heard so far from those he'd questioned. Whilst it might be fair to say that no one had done much to make an entirely positive impression on him and Shapes, neither had they done anything to suggest they'd murdered either Eleanor Golightly or the Reverend Sixpence.

As ever, it all came down to motive. Somebody in the vicarage had, or believed they had, a good reason to kill, and to kill not just once but twice. Or maybe it wasn't one killer. There could be two on the loose, especially when you thought about the murder of Sixpence. That seemed downright peculiar. It must have been riskier than the first killing. For one thing, there were several police officers on the premises and anyone in the house could have walked into that bedroom and caught the killer there, red-handed.

Maybe they wanted to be caught. Some people liked to gloat about these things. An odd thing to do, to be sure, but he'd met the sort in his time, so why couldn't it be the case here? Would have saved a bit of time, though, if they'd chosen to hang around with one of their recently deceased victims long enough to be caught in the act. But maybe that was all a part of things too. They wanted to be caught but only after everyone had enjoyed an amusing game of deadly hide and seek. After all, they'd been playing that very game when Eleanor Golightly had been murdered.

Where to look next, that was the question. What might their best options be? Tricky situation. One that required a cool, calm analysis. Good thing he was just the man for the job.

Dykeman's ruminations were interrupted by the sight and sound of a beaming, chattering Shapes leading the sour-faced figure of Marie Macron into the study. If his Sergeant's tongue had been hanging down any lower it would have been licking the floor. It was ridiculous, thought Dykeman. There was no denying it, Shapes needed help, of the professional kind, before something drastic happened. Quite how drastic that might turn out to be was not entirely clear in the inspector's mind, however it was not a happy prospect.

Marie Macron walked with an elegance that couldn't fail to catch the eye of any man and probably a fair few women too. It helped that she had a slim, shapely figure and a beauty few of her sex could match, but she had no doubt put in the required hours of rehearsal to ensure she made the very most of these natural advantages. Dykeman might have been most impressed with her slim, tempting calves or her rich, brown, shoulder-length hair. Maybe even her high, Classical cheekbones, to which she had applied just the right amount and shade of face powder. But it wasn't any of those things that held his attention. No, it was her eyes that did that. They were deep, dark pools of utter self-confidence, into which it would be all too easy to fall, helpless and willing. It left him a little unnerved and uncertain of himself. Maybe Shapes wasn't the only hopeless one in need of help on this occasion.

Marie Macron stopped in the middle of the room and looked Dykeman full in the eye.

"Inspector," she said.

"Pleased you could join us, Miss Macron. Do take a seat."

Dykeman tried to sound as if his was the voice of authority, but he had an inkling it hadn't come across as anything of the sort. Shapes hadn't noticed. He was too busy staring at Macron's legs. He guessed his sergeant had also noticed the lack of a wedding ring on the woman's left hand.

Marie Macron looked at the chair she had been directed towards as if she had just been asked to sit on a cactus. After a pause she eased herself on to it, crossed one leg over the other and brought her hands together on her lap.

"Wouldn't want you getting too comfortable," said Dykeman, in response to the unspoken complaint. "This is a formal affair, not part of your weekend's entertainment."

Marie Macron made no response; indeed, she didn't so much as raise an eyebrow. The temporary silence in the room was broken by a rather feeble cough from Shapes.

"French name, is that?" asked Dykeman.

"It is," came the curt reply.

"Recent arrivals, your family, are they? Or been here a while?" enquired the inspector.

"I believe my ancestors arrived in the 17th century. They were fleeing religious persecution in France," answered Macron.

Marie Macron spoke with little emotion and her face remained expressionless. She was well aware such an attitude sometimes resulted in people accusing her of being cold and unfeeling, but on this occasion she wasn't much bothered by that. In fact, she was keen to keep as much emotion out of the exchange as possible, since she felt it would help her to maintain control of both herself and the situation she was now in.

"Me and Shapes, we're persecuted down at the station," commented Dykeman. "Him for being ugly as sin and me for being a bit on the podgy side, aren't we Shapes?"

Shapes tried to speak, but found his mouth so dry that no sound could escape, so he nodded his agreement instead and felt his cheeks begin to warm. Marie Macron remained silent and impassive.

"Cat got your tongue, Shapes?" asked Dykeman.

The inspector did his best to appear relaxed and composed, but the truth was he had to acknowledge the woman facing him really was remarkably beautiful and it wasn't just her physical looks; her whole demeanour had an appeal he found difficult to resist. This really wouldn't do. Just because she was pretty, that was no reason to go soft on her. No, he needed to get a grip.

He decided her marital status was as good a place as any to kick things off. Would help him get back on track. Might even knock her out of her stride.

"You're not married, I see," announced Dykeman. "Would have thought a pretty little thing like you would have been snapped up ages ago. Not found Mr Right?"

There was an unmistakeable, if brief, burst of fire in Marie Macron's eyes and her raised foot turned a single circle, then stopped. Neither sign of annoyance escaped the inspector's notice.

"I fail to see what my marital status has to do with your investigations, inspector. Though if it particularly bothers you, I was once married. We were divorced two years ago. No doubt your pet here," Macron glanced at Shapes, "can confirm that for you. Shouldn't be difficult to do."

"We like to know where we stand, on all fronts," replied Dykeman, feeling a mild ripple of satisfaction at eliciting some form of emotion. As much as anything, it made him feel a bit more sure of himself. "And who knows yet whether or not anyone's marital status has got anything to do with the two murders we're investigating. It might have everything to do with them and, there again, it might not. Known the vicar long, had you?"

The brief feeling of irritation that has flared within Marie Macron began to subside. The man's opening question had been so personal and so irrelevant to the investigation; nor did it help matters that he seemed to take pleasure from the obvious annoyance he'd caused her.

But there was nothing to be gained from losing her temper. In fact, doing so would more than likely just make matters worse. Besides, there were things in her personal life she would very much like to keep away from the prying eyes of the police and anyone else, for that matter. Better to go along with things, then it would all be over and she could get back to her life. And she needed to do that. Above all else, she needed to do that.

"My parents were friends of the Reverend. My father met him during the last world war, where they served in the same regiment. Apart from that, they never seemed to me to have a great deal in common, but that didn't stop them from keeping in touch after being demobbed."

"You been here before, then?" enquired Dykeman.

"Once. We stayed with him at his last place quite often, usually in the summer. It always makes for a nice change to spend a few days in the countryside every now and again."

Dykeman could tell the woman was trying to be more engaging and a little less the ice queen, but it wasn't a whopping great success. For one thing, there was an almost total lack of emotion in her voice. She had the same public school intonations and vocabulary as so many other middle class women, but even by their standards she was cold. Hard to imagine her reading a romance or kissing a baby. No, she was a cool, calculating individual who would, no doubt, be hard to break down.

It was easy to imagine that if she did ever commit murder then she would be very good at subsequently giving little away. Such a notion might cause some coppers concern, but it didn't him. No, he liked a challenge. He'd need to show some skill and maybe some cunning, of course. Best not be too predictable, for one thing. Fortunately, he had just the right question to ask her next.

"He fancy you, did he, Sixpence?"

Dykeman delivered the question casually, but he was confident it was his ace in the pack and he was primed to take in every little facet of her response.

Marie Macron's nose twitched, her eyes widened and she felt her body tense. He'd caught her entirely off-guard, despite her best efforts to ensure she was prepared for anything and everything. The rudeness of the man was quite appalling, but he was also very perceptive.

Before she realised she'd done it, her hands had formed into little fists, her fingernails digging into her palms, and her mouth had already set about a response she would have preferred to frame in her mind before speaking it.

"What on earth makes you think that, you rude little man?" She snapped.

Dykeman purred inwardly, delighted at the result of his expert probing. Not such a hard nut to crack after all, he decided. Now they might be able to make some proper headway.

"Bit of a sore point, is it? His feelings towards you weren't reciprocated, I'm guessing? Must have got a bit wearing, all that wooing. Probably also got in the way of your own attempts at finding yourself a new husband," suggested Dykeman.

Marie Macron stood up, as if jumping to attention. The fire within had been well and truly stoked. She stared down at Dykeman, eyes ablaze.

"How dare you drag me in here, then start making such impertinent accusations. What do you take me for? I will not remain here a moment longer if this is what I can expect from you. You have two murders to solve and instead all you can do is make groundless accusations and dish out the most appalling insults. I suggest your sergeant puts his tongue back in his mouth, you stop behaving in such an ignorant manner and the two of you actually get on with some real police work."

God, these men were idiots. Rude, disgusting, obnoxious idiots. If she'd had the strength, she would have thrown a punch at Dykeman. Maybe more than one punch. Her heart was racing and her cheeks were warm. Enough, she decided, then turned and took a step towards the door, stopped as she contemplated adding to her last remarks, then changed her mind and left the room.

"Nice pair of legs," observed Shapes, grinning. "Bit of a temper, though. Shall I bring her back?"

"No, I think we got what we needed to out of her, for now. Didn't deny it, did she, that Sixpence fancied her? I think we can take that as a given. And, as you've just observed, we now know she's got a right old temper."

"The sort of thing that could end up with someone dead, you mean?" suggested Shapes.

"Exactly. I wouldn't have any trouble at all imagining Marie Macron smashing someone over the head nor, for that matter, burying a knife in their victim's chest. But believable though that might be, it doesn't mean she committed either murder. What we still lack is a motive. If it was her what did it, then why? Get to the bottom of that little conundrum and we're on to a winner."

"Maybe Sixpence gave up on her and turned his attentions elsewhere. Who knows, it might have been the old bird, Golightly. Marie Macron finds out, blows a gasket when she decides she fancies being a vicar's wife after all, so takes out her revenge on the pair of them. Sounds good to me," commented Shapes, slipping his notepad back into his pocket.

"Very creative of you, Shapes. As plausible as anything else we've come up with so far."

"So, who we putting through the wringer next?" asked Shapes. "What about the Collards, we've not seen them yet?"

"Yes, suppose we might as well speak to the pair of them now," answered the inspector.

As he spoke, Dykeman found his attention drawn to the sound of a vehicle crunching across the gravel drive outside. He walked across to the window and peered out into the sunlight.

"Ah, it's Dr Delph. The Collards can wait. I want to have another word with Sheila, er, Dr Delph. You can get on to the station and tell 'em to get a move on with those there background checks. I want to know more about this lot. Oh, and you've got my permission to leer over that Macron woman as much as you like. Let's see if you can't annoy her so much she ends up letting slip something she regrets."

Dykeman grinned at Shapes, then turned towards the door and made off for his second rendezvous of the day with his favourite doctor, hoping that, on this occasion, she could tell him something useful about the corpse that was waiting for her.

"HONESTLY, LESLIE, YOU really do need to take more care of these people. At this rate there won't be a single one of them left alive come tea-time."

Dr Sheila Delph couldn't resist the chance to have a little laugh at her friend's expense. He was man enough to take it on the chin. Besides, she wasn't far off the mark with her observation. It wasn't every day of the week she was called to the same location twice in less than twenty-four hours to cast her eye over the corpse of a murder victim. Perhaps she should enquire as to the availability of a bed for the night. It might save on a good deal of travelling.

"Very funny," replied Dykeman. "Anyway, my standards must be slipping, because I was sure there'd be half-a-dozen of 'em dead by now. They're a right suspect bunch, I can tell you. You wouldn't trust 'em with the family silver, that's for sure.

"Where is this new victim?" asked Delph.

"Upstairs, in his bedroom. Come on."

Dykeman had met Delph in the downstairs hallway, keen not to waste a minute. As he led his friend up the stairs, they were watched, he noticed, by the skulking figure of the housekeeper, who lingered in the kitchen doorway, from where she was just able to see out into the hallway. Just like he'd told Shapes earlier, the woman was very unlikely to miss anything that went on around this house, despite her claims to the contrary.

"You are sure he's dead, I take it?" asked Delph as she approached the motionless figure of the Reverend Sixpence.

"Yep. No more sermons for him. At least, not in this world. I checked his pulse myself."

"All the same, I'll check for myself, just to be on the safe side," smiled Delph.

There was a light-hearted warmth in the Doctor's voice that Dykeman found, as ever, lifted his spirits. True, he'd enjoyed himself with Macron and Sweet, but he was still smarting from the swiftness with which the second murder had taken place, and right under his nose at that. Anyone who possessed the wherewithal to cheer him up was very welcome.

"Watch that knife, though. It's flipping sharp," he quipped, as Delph leaned in over the corpse.

Delph glanced up, an ironic smile on her face, before taking hold of the vicar's left wrist. Several seconds later she pronounced her official verdict that Sixpence was, indeed, dead. She then set about examining the corpse in the limited way possible while it remained in situ. Dykeman watched her as she worked, wondering, as he had done several times before, why she had taken on such work. The answer Delph had given him, when he'd put the question to her one afternoon after she had briefed him on a particularly brutal demise, was that it paid well, but he suspected there was more to it than that. It might even, he once contemplated, be indicative of a morbid fascination with the dark underbelly of mankind.

Delph straightened up and stepped back from the corpse, having completed her initial assessment.

"Well, foul play or natural causes?" asked Dykeman.

"I can't be certain," replied Delph. "Though I'm inclined to the view the Reverend Sixpence didn't stab himself with this knife."

"Damn, and there I was hoping he'd simply fallen over while he was peeling an apple and been unlucky enough to land on the pointy end of a very large fruit knife," quipped the inspector.

"And I suppose he then sat down for a little rest before deciding what to do next?" proposed Delph, taping a finger against her cheek.

"Ah, we think so alike, the two of us. That's exactly what I had in mind," replied Dykeman.

"I can tell you there are no obvious signs of cuts or abrasions elsewhere, though I'll only be able to confirm that once I've done a full postmortem. It seems likely a single stab with that large knife was enough to finish him off. By the looks of things, I'd say the knife has pierced the heart," observed Delph, in more serious tones.

"Who the hell goes around killing vicars?" asked Dykeman, rubbing the back of his neck. "It's not exactly your common or garden murder."

Dykeman stifled a yawn. He liked to take a little nap in the afternoon, business permitting, and missed it when he couldn't. To his mind, if it had been good enough for Churchill when he was running the country and fighting a world war, then it was good enough for him too.

"Keeping you up, am I?" teased Delph.

"Need my afternoon nap. Can't function properly without it. What d'you reckon then? Could a woman have done that?" He nodded at the corpse. "Knife's in pretty deep."

"I don't see why not. A knife as sharp as that will go in easily enough, whether it's a man or woman using it. Does that make things a little more complicated for you?" enquired Delph.

There was a little sparkle of mischief in Delph's eyes as she spoke. The poor man really did have his hands full this time. She probably ought to be offering support, not taking the mickey, but humour was such a key part of their relationship. It was such a shame they hadn't met earlier in life. Things could have turned out so very differently.

"As a matter of fact, yes it does," answered Dykeman. "I'm a simple man and I like to keep my investigations nice and simple too. If all the clues point in one direction then I'm very happy for it."

Delph stepped across to the window and looked outside. It was a very pleasant view.

"A lovely day and a lovely house. Such a shame people keep dying here. Are they giving you much trouble?" The tone in her voice suggested she already knew the answer.

"Typical toffs. Reckon they can pull the wool over our eyes, they do. Seem to think me and Shapes are a couple of raw recruits, too stupid to recognise their lies and their little games. But I've got Shapes digging into their pasts. He'll soon start uncovering their secrets, then we can begin properly knocking them into shape. Mind you, we know one juicy bit of gossip already," he added with enthusiasm. "Seems the Reverend Sixpence here fancied one of the women guests."

"Really? Which one?" asked Delph.

"Marie Macron, the attractive one with brown hair and a decent figure. Shapes is drooling over her now," replied Dykeman.

"And did she reciprocate?"

"She didn't say. Got quite shirty about things when I tested the waters," added the inspector.

"I take it you were your usual tactful self?" prodded the doctor.

"Me? I'm always tactful. Win awards for being tactful. Well, I may have been pretty brief about it. Got a lot to do, what with two murders on the go," answered Dykeman.

"I can imagine. I do so hope I never have to be subjected to one of your more tactful interrogations," smiled Delph.

"I do too. But what about you, would you take to sticking a knife in a man if he kept trying to seduce you?" enquired Dykeman, looking once more at the brooding, silent corpse of Sixpence.

"It would be rather a drastic step to take," responded Delph. "Perhaps I'd prefer to put something unpleasant in his tea."

She smiled again at her friend, pleased he seemed able to see the lighter side of things in what was, of course, such a horrid situation. It was good he'd chosen to share with her something of what he'd unmasked so far. It was those occasions when he kept things entirely to himself that bothered her most. That was always a sign that he was under stress. Her job could sometimes be rather unpleasant, but she had a clear notion her friend's occupation could occasionally be even worse.

"Must remember that," said Dykeman, joining his friend by the window. "Shapes has this idea Sixpence had given up on Macron and turned his attentions to Golightly. In a mad rage, brought on by being abandoned by Sixpence, Macron took her revenge on the pair of them. Not his worst ever idea. What do you reckon?"

"I've heard sillier suggestions. Love and jealousy have been the cause of a good many murders," answered Delph, as she watched a huge crow launch itself from off the top of a large chestnut tree.

"Well, don't tell Shapes, he might be on to a good thing. It'll give him ideas; make him think he needs a promotion or a pay rise or both. You done?" asked Dykeman, gesturing at Sixpence.

"I am."

"Come on then. I suppose you'll be wanting to get the vicar's body back to the mortuary?" enquired Dykeman.

"I will, assuming that's alright with you," replied Delph.

"It is. No need for it to remain here."

Delph took a moment before speaking again. "Leslie, I hope you'll not think I'm interfering when I say this, but do try to remember the people here are very likely frightened. They've seen two of their party murdered and are probably scared out of their wits they might be next." Her voice was gentle and re-assuring and she let a hand rest on Dykeman's arm as she spoke.

Her friend wrinkled his nose and took a moment to consider what she had just said.

"I can't help it, Sheila. People like this lot get right up my nose. They're so arrogant and self-centred."

"They maybe, but they still deserve your support and understanding, don't you think?" asked the doctor.

She was right, of course, he realised. She usually was.

"I'll try to go easier on them from now on. So long as they don't wind me up," added Dykeman.

Delph smiled at him. "Good."

The two of them began walking towards the open doorway.

"What happened to that French fella your sister was seeing?" asked Dykeman. "Shapes was telling me the other day, he's disappeared."

"Well, there's a story," replied Delph. "Though not exactly a mystery."

Chapter Ten

Outside the whole world remained a blaze of bright, warm sunshine, the sky a seemingly endless expanse of deep blue, unblemished by so much as a single cloud. With the temperature having reached the high seventies, most of the wildlife was minded to rest in silence, with only the occasional call from a startled or bored bird interrupting the near silence. For anyone who cared to contemplate the matter, it seemed as if the high point of summer had been reached; the countryside a burgeoning, scent-filled Arcadia.

On the sun-drenched terrace outside the dining room, two women sat round one of the small metal tables. Both were wearing wide-brimmed hats to fend off the glare of the sun and these tipped backwards and forwards in some peculiar dance as the wearers' heads moved during the course of conversation.

To anyone who might have seen her there, the younger of the two women, Tamsin Spectacle, would have been barely recognisable behind the over-sized sunglasses that struggled for purchase on the ridge of her nose. But the bright red lipstick, a near perfect match for her hat, might have been a sufficient clue to her identity. In one hand she held a tall, slender glass, half-filled with gin and tonic, its rim stained red.

The other woman was middle-aged, wearing a sharply cut, expensive dress she had purchased especially for the weekend; something her husband considered a luxury, rather than the necessity it was to her. Although she spoke for the most part in the same Home Counties tones as the other women staying at the vicarage, she couldn't quite manage to hide entirely the hint of a Scottish accent, which poked its head above the parapet every now and then. She was the one doing most of the talking; something any onlooker would have noticed she appeared to be entirely at ease with.

"I suppose you know that cheap, desperate divorcee, Marie Macron, is angling to take your man away from you?" said the older woman, who then paused, as if to ensure her question had settled properly in Tamsin Spectacle's mind. "I've been watching her, though it hardly takes a detective to see what her game is."

Tamsin Spectacle smiled inwardly. She was curious to hear more of what her fellow guest had to say, though she was wholly confident as to where she stood with Richard Dipping. She had the man wrapped entirely round her little finger. So she should, because it had taken a great deal of work to get him there. He wasn't, she knew, the most reliable of men and he certainly wasn't the one on whom she had set her sights, but men of all sorts almost always found her an irresistible temptation and, in any case, she knew very well how to string a man along. She'd had plenty of practice. It would be amusing to hear what more her drinks partner had to say on the matter.

"Really? What makes you say that?" asked Tamsin.

She raised her glass to her mouth and let the cool lemon-scented alcoholic tingle of her drink run across her tongue.

"It's hard to miss. From the moment she arrived, she's been watching him like a hawk. I'm sure she believes no one has noticed, but she'd be a fool to think I'm so inattentive. Little escapes me." There was a pause, before the older woman added, "Do you mean to say you hadn't noticed, my dear?"

Tamsin might have laughed, but that would only have risked causing a scene, since she had already worked out her companion had a rather high opinion of herself. She was reluctant to cause a scene, given the current situation at the vicarage, and decided to let things go. Besides, she was enjoying this silly gossip and suspected there was more to come. There wasn't anything much better to do.

"Richard's quite a catch, I know,W she replied. "I'm not so silly as to think other women don't find him attractive. That's why I'm with him, after all."

"Well, take my word, she's made her mind up and I doubt someone like that gives up easily," persisted the older woman.

There was more than a hint of malice in the woman's words, noticed Tamsin. Interesting, she mused. What could possibly have prompted such a dislike? Perhaps the two of them had history. If that was so, it would certainly be amusing to find out what she could about it.

"Quite appalling behaviour, of course, but then what could one expect from such a person," added her drinks partner, dismissively.

Tamsin wondered if she could in some way turn the tables, perhaps by implying something about her companion's husband. That might be wickedly funny. Oh what a temptation. But what to say? That was the tricky part. Before Tamsin Spectacle could decide, their conversation was brought to a halt by the sight of an approaching figure.

"Oh no, it's that terrible policeman, the one who was so rude to us earlier and he appears to be heading this way. I do hope they replace him with someone more competent and the sooner the better. I think he's too stupid to ever find the killer," observed the older woman.

It seemed to Tamsin as if her drinks partner was making a pretence at keeping her voice low enough for Dykeman not to hear, while all the time trying her best to make sure that he could.

If Dykeman had indeed been able to hear the insult, he chose to ignore it, arriving at the women's table full of the joys of summer, or so it appeared to them.

"I ought to get one of those for myself," he said, nodding at Tamsin Spectacle's gin and tonic. "Just the thing for a hot summer afternoon."

The two women said their hellos, Tamsin Spectacle sounding by far the more enthusiastic of the pair, noted Dykeman.

"Mrs Collard?" he asked, addressing the older woman.

"Yes, that's me."

"Sergeant Shapes and I would like a word please." He half-turned towards Tamsin Spectacle. "Alone please, Miss Spectacle."

"Message received, inspector," she replied. "Apparently I need to go and check on my man. It seems he may be the quarry in a big game hunt."

Tamsin Spectacle wore a thin, suppressed smile as she walked away. What a shame, she thought. Just when things were about to get so very interesting. Still, there was always later. Perhaps, in the meantime, she could tease Richard about the accusation that had been made about Marie Macron. He was bound to find it funny.

As Tamsin Spectacle left, she was replaced by Shapes, who was disappointed to see the woman leaving. He wondered for a moment if Dykeman had sent her packing so that he wouldn't have the chance to engage her in witty conversation, but settled on the realisation they couldn't have her hanging around while they questioned Daphne Collard, more's the shame.

Dykeman sat down opposite Daphne Collard. She was wearing what he could clearly see was an expensive gold and emerald-studded necklace, hanging in a long loop around her slender neck. On her left wrist she wore an equally pricey looking watch. This, decided Dykeman, was a woman who had a taste for the finer things in life and he wondered how well equipped her husband was when it came to financing such luxuries. Another line of enquiry was added to his mental notepad.

"Poor Shapes, you'd think he'd never seen a shapely pair of legs before," quipped Dykeman as he watched Tamsin Spectacle make her way towards the house.

Daphne Collard laughed. It was such a loud and deep laugh that Dykeman, caught for the moment off-guard, flinched.

"Your sergeant is hardly a geriatric, inspector. You'll give the poor man a complex," Daphne Collard announced.

She cast an eye over the unappealing figure of Shapes, hoping her gaze would make it clear to the little man that she was, in a modest way, offended by his presence. He was, she had already concluded, the type of man who did menial little tasks for others; the sort of things she couldn't possibly be expected to do for herself. He certainly wasn't the kind of man with whom she could possibly be expected to have dealings on anything remotely like an equal footing. For one thing, he appeared to be wearing someone else's suit; someone taller and wider than himself. And he kept picking at his ears as if there was something wrong with them. Best to keep him at arm's length. A fully-stretched arm's length.

"I reckon I can safely say he's too old for that one. He should be looking for a model with a few more years on the clock. Put your tongue away, Shapes, you'll have Mrs Collard here bringing up her lunch. Now then," Dykeman turned his attention back to the pale-skinned, thin-lipped woman sitting opposite him. "Mrs Collard, how long had you known the vicar?"

"Oh, quite some time, inspector. We're neighbours, actually. We have a modest little house on the other side of the village. Just a half-dozen bedrooms and five acres of gardens. I'm afraid it's all my dear husband, Albert, could stretch to at the time. But we've become so attached to the place over the years that we've never felt able to drag ourselves away to something more... suitable."

If the tone in her voice or the look on her face had been any more arrogant, thought Dykeman, he would have lost his temper and, no doubt, have said things he'd soon regret. It was exactly the kind of behaviour that made him dislike people like her so much. They had too much, too easily and reckoned, as a result, they were superior to everyone else. It was no wonder he'd been so hard on those he'd interviewed and why he was tempted to carry on in just the same way with the rest of 'em. But Sheila Delph's words came back to him and he made an effort to control his annoyance.

"Never could do with any less than six bedrooms myself," quipped Dykeman.

"Oh, really, inspector? I wasn't aware the salary of a policeman allowed for such... essentials."

"Essentials is the word for it," remarked Dykeman. "That's one for each of my wives. They can't be expected to share a bedroom as well as their husband. I'd get complaints."

Dykeman winked at Shapes, who grinned, then grabbed the opportunity to add an embellishment of his own.

"You need to add another bedroom and wife, sir. Then you'd have one for every day of the week," he said enthusiastically.

"Sound idea that, Shapes. Bit of a squash in the house right now. Maybe I can stick a bedroom in the barn."

"Am I supposed to find this amusing, inspector?" Daphne Collard's face had taken on a stern appearance and her voice, thought Dykeman, was that of an irritated school teacher. "Under the circumstances, with two people having been so horribly murdered, I would have thought this was hardly the time to go making what you both seem to believe passes for a joke. Perhaps we should continue this conversation another time."

Honestly, what awful, ignorant men. She would like to say so, to their faces, but she was far too well-mannered to do any such thing. No, she told herself, don't go lowering yourself to their level, Daphne. You need to remain calm, well-mannered. All the same, she should make her displeasure clear. It was important to do that. She pushed back her chair and stood up, as if to leave.

"Sit back down, Mrs Collard," insisted Dykeman.

He fired out the words with a degree of authority Daphne Collard had not been expecting. She sat back down, in silence, and looked away in the general direction of the house, careful not to resume eye contact with the inspector until she had adjusted to the abruptly changed circumstances.

"There are one or two questions we need you to answer. Now then, apart from Sixpence is there anyone else here you know?"

Daphne Collard patted the side of her hat, as if attempting to reposition it, though, to Shapes, it didn't appear to actually move at all.

"Yes. Eleanor Golightly and I have been, were, friends since our school days. Mind you, we hadn't seen each other for quite a few years."

"Any reason for that?" asked Dykeman.

"We just went our separate ways, as one does. I suppose I was a little surprised we hadn't bumped into one another before. Then one day, over tea, the Reverend Sixpence mentioned Eleanor still lives, sorry, lived, in Warwickshire, not far from here. She always was such a delightful woman, full of the joys of life. It really is so utterly awful she should die the way she did. Very upsetting."

"She have any enemies you know of? Fall out with anyone over money or men, perhaps?" asked Dykeman.

Daphne Collard fiddled a little with her expensive watch. A hint of a frown appeared on her face.

"Not that I am aware of, inspector, but, as I say, it had been rather a long time since we had last met. I think I'm not really the best person to answer such a question."

"You say you knew her when you were girls, so what was she like at school?" asked Dykeman.

"Oh, much the same as she was as an adult. Always the life and soul of the party. You could never stop her from talking, or not for very long. I'm afraid that sometimes she could be so talkative it would get rather tiresome, but then I imagine we all have our little flaws, don't you think?"

You should know, thought Dykeman. The cheek of the woman.

"Shapes here has enough for the both of us. I prefer to see myself being as near to perfect as a human being can get." He grinned broadly.

"Shall I write that down, sir?" asked Shapes, poised with his pencil and pad.

"Absolutely. Let's make it official. But enough about me," the inspector turned back to Daphne Collard. "A smarty pants, was she, at school?"

"Eleanor? Oh no, inspector. Eleanor was definitely not one of the brighter students. Something of a dunce in some classes. Her Latin teacher made her attend extra lessons for an entire year, she was such a hopeless case. She was always more suited to the domestic lessons. Cookery and needlework, that sort of thing. Oh, and horse-riding. She was quite proficient at that and absolutely adored it."

"What about the Reverend Sixpence?" asked Dykeman. "What can you tell me about him? I hear the man was desperate for, er, sexual relations."

Daphne Collard's face went crimson and her back straightened as if an electric current had been fired into her. She looked, contemplated Dykeman quite happily, as if she was ready to explode at any second. Excellent. Let's see how Mrs prim and proper gets along responding to that one.

"The Reverend Sixpence was a wonderful man. Something of a simpleton, it is fair to say, but he never had a bad word to say about any other human being and was always willing to lend a hand to those in need."

Daphne Collard felt herself on the precipice, teetering on the verge of a major fall. The man's rudeness seemed to know no bounds. He was quite disgusting. He may think he'd got the better of her, but she wasn't, she absolutely wasn't, going to give in. No, she'd play his puerile little game now, but he could be sure she would be making a most vociferous complaint to the Chief Inspector. She was sure her husband could bring enough influence to bear to ensure the man lost his job. The public shouldn't have to put up with men like him. But she would hold back her true feelings for now and press on, in a most heroic manner.

"I have to say, inspector, I really cannot think of two people less deserving of being murdered. It really is most perplexing," she declared, careful to avoid answering Dykeman's question.

"That's one word for it, you're right there," observed the inspector.

Whilst he had no intention of admitting it to her, Dykeman had to acknowledge that Daphne Collard had a point. As far as he had been able to make out thus far, the two murder victims had damn all reason to have been bumped off. He and Shapes had interviewed a majority of the surviving house-guests and so far they'd managed to come up with pretty much nothing of substance. But, he knew, there had to be something out there, waiting to be unearthed. Neither of the victims had been sent to an early grave without a reason, no matter how twisted that might turn out to be. They just needed to work out what the hell that was.

"Have you identified any suspects yet, inspector?" asked Daphne Collard. "Not that I want to go muddying the waters, but that horrid woman, Marie Macron, looks rather suspicious to me. She seems to be under the, mistaken, impression she's better than the rest of us. And you hardly need eyes in the back of your head to see the way she looks at Richard Dipping. I know it's not for me to say, but I would have thought she should be the person to focus your enquiries on, don't you think?"

"No need to worry on that score, Mrs Collard. I've asked Shapes here to give the woman his undivided attention. By the time he's finished, we'll know everything there is to know about her, won't we, Shapes?"

"Certainly will, sir. No stone unturned or cupboard unopened," replied Shapes enthusiastically.

Shapes's reply reminded Dykeman there was another question he needed to ask.

"Where were you hiding, Mrs Collard, during this game of hide and seek? I know..."

Dykeman didn't get to finish the question. Standing in the open doorway to the dining room was the figure of Edward Sweet. He appeared to be most anxious to get their attention, waving his arms in a passable impression of a windmill.

"Inspector," he yelled. "A phone call for you, from the station."

"What do they want now?" barked Dykeman. "How are we supposed to sort out the mess here when I spend half my time on the phone? Finish up with Mrs Collard here, Shapes, then join me inside. No doubt I'll have news to share."

Dykeman climbed to his feet, making little effort to hide his irritation, and set off towards the house at a fair clip, muttering something about Chief Inspectors with nothing better to do than pester their officers.

Shapes directed an unsettling smile at Daphne Collard, twirled his pencil between his fingers and started to probe the woman as to her whereabouts earlier in the day. It was an experience Daphne Collard was to remember for a very long time to come.

Chapter Eleven

"Someone's blabbed, Shapes. Don't know who, but that doesn't matter. The papers have got wind of what's been going on here at the vicarage and you know the old man, he can't bear to face a battery of questions from reporters when he doesn't have a full set of answers for them."

"So, we've got to go back to the station, then?" asked Shapes.

"Yes. Tout suite, and all that. I strongly suspect it will be me what gets nominated to face the press. Nasty little leeches. Suck you dry then leave your carcass rotting at the side of the road, if they get a chance," complained Dykeman.

"You fallen out with Tom Gently again, sir?"

"I have," grumped Dykeman, rubbing his nose.

"What happened this time?" asked Shapes.

"It doesn't really matter, Shapes. He's in my bad books and that's that."

"The newspaper editor do better than you at the Warwick races last week, did he?" suggested Shapes, unable to stop himself from smirking.

"He might have done. Can't say as I was particularly keeping score," muttered Dykeman, strangely unable to look his sergeant in the eye.

"And I suppose he's been reminding you about that all week? Getting right under your skin."

Shapes was keen not to miss an opportunity to wind up his boss. It didn't happen often, so when it did it should be grabbed willingly with out-stretched hands.

"You should just take it on the chin, sir, like a man. When you're beaten, you're beaten," snickered Shapes.

"Shapes," snapped Dykeman.

"Sir?" An angel couldn't have sounded any more innocent.

"Shut it," insisted the inspector.

"Yes, sir."

"Now, go and tell those constables that I want at least two of 'em here at all times. That means overnight too. I'm not supposing we'll get back here until the morning and I don't want any of the guests doing a runner. If that happens, we'll be joining the ranks of the unemployed, you can bet your last penny on that," declared Dykeman.

"And we don't want any more of them dying of unnatural causes, sir. We'll start getting a reputation if that happens," added Shapes.

"Mm," mused Dykeman, thinking things over. "Maybe I could throttle the lot of 'em, then claim it was this unknown killer."

"Shall I get the car when I've spoken to the constables, sir?" asked Shapes.

"Yes. Think I'll drive," replied Dykeman. "Will help relieve the stress. Off you go then and get a move on."

As Dykeman dropped his backside into the high-backed, leather armchair in the study, Shapes set off in search of his uniformed colleagues, already worrying about the drive back to the station. Dykeman's idea of decent driving left a lot to be desired. Still, if he kept his eyes closed most of the time then he could probably get through the worst of it without feeling sick.

"I RECKON THAT WENT pretty well, sir. All things considered. The old man didn't invite us back to his office for a ticking off afterwards."

Shapes was sitting on a standard issue wooden chair opposite his boss in the office they shared. He'd already mulled over the disaster zone that had been the press conference and decided to make a stab at cheering up his harassed boss. What a joke it had been. It had been so bad the old man might well not ask Dykeman to do another one, which would be a definite bonus for his boss.

"Pretty well? Who the hell are you trying to kid, Shapes. The only reason the old man didn't haul us in for a mauling is because he legged it when things started getting tricky. Funny how 'important business elsewhere' can crop up at such short notice whenever it suits him. Try that one ourselves and we'd be bent over this here desk and given a right good spanking," complained Dykeman.

Shapes wondered if the old man would use a cane or his hands and if it would make any difference. It was always a cane at school. Damn thing left you red raw for days.

"Well, how were you to know the newspaper editor had been best friends with Sixpence? If he'd had the manners to tell you that in the first place then you wouldn't have said those things about the vicar. Gently can hardly complain about you being rude and obnoxious when he'd fallen short in the manners department himself," added Shapes.

"Stupid idiot. Him, not you," replied Dykeman.

He was most definitely still smarting and sulking from the mess that had been the meeting with the local press. His chubby features were overwhelmed by an upside-down smile that had appeared on his face almost as soon as the questions had started. The Chief Inspector was supposed to be running the show, only asking Dykeman to chip in with the occasional comment to confirm what he had himself already said. And that was exactly the way things should be. The Chief Inspector, who got paid the big fat salary, should get the crappy job of talking to the hounds from the press.

"I should have known something was up when we saw it was the editor himself who'd come along, not one of his lackeys," observed the depressed sounding inspector.

Things had gone down hill pretty much right from the off. The Chief Inspector was an old hand at spotting trouble and even better at putting someone else in the way of it. Dykeman would have grabbed hold of Shapes and stuck him in the way, except his sergeant was malingering at the back of the room, keeping well clear of any such thing. If only he'd been able to do the same himself. His stomach had begun to tie itself in knots as the questions started raining down on him. When the boss did a runner, he found his mouth drying up and his body temperature climbing.

"How comes you didn't know he was friends with Sixpence? You and Gently have been knocking around together for years," said Shapes.

"We don't go jabbering about every little detail in our personal lives, Shapes. In fact, we don't talk about our personal lives much at all, if we can help it. It's not what blokes do." Dykeman bashed the sharp end of a pencil into the heavily beaten blotting pad on his desk. "Maybe I should ask him if he's got any more friends I might bump into at a murder scene."

"Yeah, you could ask him to make a list. We could put it on file. Might come in handy," suggested Shapes.

Shapes was feeling pretty chipper, as he took a sip from his cup of too-hot tea. He hadn't had to say a word, not one, while his boss had blindly stumbled into a hornet's nest the size of a small planet. It turned out the editor of the Banbury Globe had been friends with Sixpence for some time, the two men sharing a passion for music. Indeed, the editor, Tom Gently, had been up to the vicarage many a time, most recently just the fortnight previous.

Unfortunately, this little piece of information had only come to light after Dykeman had made several disparaging remarks about the people currently ensconced at the vicarage. The narrowed eyes and furrowed brow that took up residence on Gently's face should have tipped-off Dykeman but the discomfort he was feeling, being made to answer questions his boss didn't much care for, seemed to have induced a lack of focus.

Shapes had enjoyed watching Dykeman squirm. It had made his day, his week and, quite possibly, even his month. Hilarious, it was. Better than anything you could see down the local playhouse. Shame there'd been no one there to film it.

"What a bloody mess," remarked Dykeman. "Now I'll no doubt have to do lots of 'good' deeds, like opening village fêtes and whatnot, just so I can prove I'm sorry for giving outrageous offence, bla, bla, bla."

"Could be worse, sir. The old man might order you to take his wife out for tea."

Shapes grinned like a naughty schoolboy.

"Leave it off, Shapes. I'd rather clean the bogs with my tongue than take her anywhere again. No wonder he spends so much time in that office of his. Probably thinks of it as some sort of refuge."

"Yeah, most blokes have a shed, he has an office. She's not your type, I take it, sir?" teased Shapes. He made an effort at sounding casual and curious, but he was fooling no one, least of all Dykeman.

"Shapes! Another word on the subject and I'll tell the old man myself you're just itching to take his missus out for lunch... once a week... from now until Christmas."

"Yes, sir." Shapes choked off the laughter by lifting his cup to his mouth.

The room was stuffy and Dykeman had already opened the window as far as it would go, hopeful the cooler air outside the building wouldn't be put off a little visit to the smelly, cramped confines of their office. It hadn't made much of a difference and he still felt uncomfortably warm.

"Now then, we found out anything about all these guests?" he asked. "I'm getting restless waiting. The sooner we get to shake out their dirty laundry the better. They'll soon start co-operating once they know we've got the upper hand."

"Tomorrow morning, sir, is the best the boys can do. They're on the phones now, but it takes ages working out who we need to speak to and then, half the time, they're not around when we call 'em. Though we do have got some interesting stuff on Richard Dipping."

"Ah, that's more like it," responded Dykeman, instantly perking up. "And why aren't I surprised Dipping's name is first to crop up. What we got, then?"

"Johnston got on the phone to Scotland Yard, asked them to take a look through their files for all the people up at the vicarage. They got back to him pretty quickly to say Dipping has some form."

"Bingo!" Dykeman leaned back in his chair and cupped the back of his head in his hands. He was looking forward to what he hoped would be a long and fascinating story. "Let's have it."

"Don't go getting your hopes up too much, sir. He's small fry. Turns out he got picked up in 1949 for partaking of some business opportunities available on the black market. He was supplying meat to a bunch of butchers in the Home Counties. Deliveries after dark, cash payments only, etc, etc. When it went to court, Dipping claimed he'd been dealing the meat in good faith. As far as he was aware, it was all above board and coming from legit suppliers. These were suppliers who, by some strange co-incidence, had evaporated into thin air when Scotland Yard went looking for them. Seems Dipping made a good impression in court and, what with it being his first time in the dock, the judge went all soft on him and let him off with a fine. You ask me, Dipping was as guilty as they come. Lucky bleeder got away with that one."

"And, in my experience, once you're a fly-by-night operator like that, you're one for the rest of your days. He been pulled in for anything else since?" asked Dykeman.

"No. Though that's not all. Year before last, a warehouse in Northampton went up in smoke. Insurance claim went in. Owners reckoned the place was packed with new shoes waiting to be shipped out. Well, the insurance company had its suspicions about that, but the fire had taken hold so fast the fire brigade hadn't been able to put it out until pretty much the entire place had burned to the ground, not leaving much for the insurance company to pick through. They had to make a whooping big pay out. Can you guess who one of the owners of the shoe company was?"

"Dipping," suggested the inspector.

"Yep. The company had only been set up six months previous by Dipping and two others. Didn't even have much of a trading record when the place went up in smoke," added Shapes.

"Are you going to say it or am I?" asked Dykeman.

"No smoke without fire, sir?" answered Shapes, grinning. The old ones were still the best.

"Exactly," said Dykeman. "So Richard Dipping is a long way from being an upright and morally commendable member of society. And he's the kind of bloke, I'll bet, who's rubbish at making his ill-gotten gains last very long. Cars, restaurants, clothes, women, they're all good ways for a man like him to blow the lot in next to no time."

"I'd reckon a woman like Tamsin Spectacle can get through his money like it's going out of fashion," suggested Shapes.

"I bet she can. So, he'll have to top up his funds plenty and often. Makes you wonder what he's been getting up to recently." Dykeman sat up and scratched his chin. "Anything else?"

"Not much. The usual service record. Army. Managed to keep himself in Europe. He doesn't seem to stay at the same address for long, though he does pay his bills. At least, as far as we can tell. No court summons or such like," added Shapes, sounding a little disappointed.

"We'll give him a proper grilling tomorrow. See how he responds to a decent bit of pressure," said Dykeman. " Don't know about murder, though. It's a long jump from arson and selling dodgy meat to bumping off a couple of acquaintances."

"And he'd need a motive, sir. What's he got to gain from killing two old folk?"

"That's very true, Shapes. People like Dickie boy normally like to keep a low profile. Drawing attention to themselves isn't good for business. But that's no reason to go crossing him off our list. Maybe things have got desperate for him. Who knows? At least we've got something to get stuck into now. We'll need..."

Before Dykeman could finish his sentence, the door to their office swung open and a huge, ball-shaped man with a triple chin and narrow eyes stepped into the doorway. The room went dark.

"'Ere, Dykeman, what's this I 'ear about you killing off vicars? They been trying to turn you into a good little Christian again, 'ave they?" The multi-layered chin wobbled as the enormous man guffawed.

Dykeman knew at once that his goat had been well and truly got. He didn't like Inspector Harry 'Heffalump' Houghton and the feeling was entirely mutual. It may have been necessary for the two of them to maintain a wafer-thin veneer of respect for one another where work was concerned, but that didn't stop either of them from sticking the boot in whenever the opportunity arose. And the Heffalump had made straight for Dykeman's office as soon as he'd heard about the latter's messy struggles at the vicarage; keen as mustard not to miss an opportunity to wind up his colleague.

"Isn't it your feeding time, Houghton? Better watch out or someone else will tuck into your grub while you're gone. You'll end up going short of rations. Wouldn't want you passing out in the office from lack of nourishment," fired back Dykeman.

"Too much for your boss is it, Shapes?" prompted Houghton, keen to ignore Dykeman's insult. "Bit careless, ain't he, letting a second person get killed while he's on the premises. He wants to watch out or else the Chief Inspector will start wondering if he ain't past it."

"From what I hear, sir, it's you that needs to watch your back," responded Shapes, totally unruffled by Houghton's attempt to drag him into the conversation. "Word is, the old man reckons you need to lose weight. Says you can't do your job properly carrying round all that blubber. And if you can't do your job properly... well, it don't take a brain surgeon to work out what happens next." Shapes drummed the fingers of one hand on top of his desk as he directed a raised eyebrow at the vast bulk standing in the doorway.

The Heffalump wobbled briefly and looked from Shapes to Dykeman, then back again. He'd had high hopes of seriously upsetting Dykeman. Best opportunity he'd had in ages to get one over on mister know-it-all. A sense of disappointment begun to settle on him as he saw how little impact he'd made. More to the point, however, was the snotty-nosed sergeant's accusation. The conversation he'd had with the Chief Inspector only the week before was supposed to have been private. Who the hell had found out and started blabbing? Deflection tactics were called for.

"Rubbish. The old man knows I've got a medical condition. Can't be helped," he asserted.

Shapes could hardly fail to notice the lack of conviction in Heffalump's voice.

"Just saying, sir," added the amused sergeant. "That's the word."

Houghton glanced at Dykeman, then, mumbling something about a fresh brew, turned slowly round and shuffled out of the office, now seriously disappointed at the failure of his ambush. Maybe he'd have a little slice of cake with his cup of tea. Would help cheer him up.

The shadow from the man's vast frame lingered for what seemed to Dykeman and Shapes like an eternity as he made his way down the corridor. Light, at last, returned to the small, stuffy room.

Dykeman felt a renewed surge of pride in his sergeant, impressed at this latest display of quick wits, imagination and calmness under fire. He'd like to have claimed this success for himself. The years of attentive, high-quality training he'd provided ensuring his sergeant had turned into such an impressive example of what a police officer should be. But that would be taking things a bit far. For one thing, Shapes and he had only been partners for a few years and, for another, he'd never provided any sort of training whatsoever; something Shapes might be at pains to point out should he attempt to suggest otherwise. Still, it was deserving of a little pat on the back.

"Top marks, Shapes. He'll be eating one less cream cake with his cup of tea this afternoon. Can't believe we're still waiting for him to drop dead of a heart attack," added the inspector.

"Maybe he needs a little help, sir. Perhaps we should make arrangements for him to spend the night up at the vicarage. The murder rate there is shocking; who knows what might happen," sniggered Shapes.

"You're such a wit, Shapes. You should have your own radio show."

WITH NOTHING ELSE TO go over and it being teatime, Dykeman decided to let Shapes head off home. Best to have him bright-eyed and bushy-tailed come the start of the new day. Dykeman, himself, lingered for a while, replaying the events of the day in his head, wondering if there was anything they'd missed. It was the vicar's murder that bothered him most. There was something about it that just seemed, well, odd. Quite what it was, he couldn't put his finger on, try as he might. It looked like a straightforward stabbing, but what was it that was nagging at him about it?

It was no good, his brain needed some rest. Trying to force things to happen just wasn't going to work. It almost never did. Food, a nice cup of tea and a potter in his veg garden was the thing to do.

The truth was, he was more than a little concerned he might walk into the station the following morning to find out yet another guest at the vicarage had met with an untimely and violent death, despite the presence of two constables. Perhaps both he and Shapes should have stayed there too. It was a worrying time.

Chapter Twelve

After a surprisingly good night's sleep and a hearty breakfast, Dykeman was delighted to arrive at the station the following morning to find there were no reports of any untoward events at the vicarage. New start, new day and all that. He almost felt like his normal self, not the grumpy old sod he'd become as a result of being forced to spend time with those toffs at the vicarage, everyone of whom seemed to rub him up the wrong way. Well, almost everyone; although she was a bit odd and most definitely scary, the housekeeper wasn't half so bad as the rest of 'em. He might, at a push, even go so far as to say she was alright.

Shapes was already in their office. In fact, he'd been there for over an hour, ploughing through the various reports that had been put together for them overnight. Impressive, thought Dykeman. Once he'd picked up a scent, Shapes was a determined and persistent so-and-so, not afraid to put in the hours and the hard graft. Bit of a lesson there for any constable aspiring to the lofty rank of sergeant.

"You're keen, Shapes," said Dykeman as he hung his coat up. "Or couldn't you sleep?"

"No problem there, sir. Slept like a baby. I just wanted to get stuck into these reports." Shapes waved a hand over the paperwork spread across his desk. "Loads of stuff here. The boys have done us proud."

Dykeman put his cup of tea down on his desk, then picked up one of the skimpy folders from the hoard that Shapes had been working through.

"What have we got then?" he asked, as he began leafing through the papers.

"There's plenty on the Collards," noted Shapes. "Shame most of it is boring as could be. Some stuff on the Reverend Sixpence. Useful background. A few bits and bobs on Marie Macron. And some decent notes on Eleanor Golightly. There's also a longer write-up on Richard Dipping, though nothing new there."

"You been through it all?" asked Dykeman.

"Most of it. You want a round up?" enquired Shapes.

"Go on, then," replied the inspector.

"Let's start with Sixpence, then," said Shapes, picking up a couple of sheets of typed paper. "An only child. Both parents dead. Went to Cambridge University, where he studied English and Philosophy. Got a First, so bit of a brainbox. During the war, he served as a chaplain and medical officer in the Royal Army Service Corps. Served in

North Africa and Italy. Got shipped home from Italy with a leg injury."

"No sign of that when we saw him," observed Dykeman. "Must have made a proper recovery. Go on."

"Before he was vicar at Lower Itchingbaum, he was vicar for eight years at Little Tysoe in Warwickshire. Interesting that is. It's where Eleanor Golightly was living, so looks like that's where they met," suggested Shapes.

"That it?" Dykeman sounded a little disappointed.

"Yep. Exciting stuff, it ain't."

"What about the Collards? They got a good reason to bump off Sixpence or Golightly?" asked Dykeman.

"Doesn't look like it," replied Shapes, replacing one set of papers with another. "Albert Collard is a partner in a firm of architects, James & Sheppard, based in Oxford. He takes the train from Banbury to work every day. Went to grammar school and Manchester University. An upstanding member of Banbury Conservative Party and, according to these notes, he was a town councillor here for two years. Don't remember that myself. He can't have made much of a splash."

"Anything else?" prompted Dykeman.

"Word is, he likes a drink," answered Shapes.

"Having met that wife of his, Shapes, I can see why."

"And speaking of her," continued Shapes. "Daphne Collard, born in Dundee, went to school, didn't do anything remarkable, blah, blah, blah. Got herself married to Albert at the age of 23 and had squeezed out their first nipper twelve months later. Doesn't look like she's ever done a day's work in her life. Must like a bit of attention, though, because their modest little house and gardens were featured in Splendid Homes and Gardens three years ago."

"Splendid Homes and Gardens? Bit of a society rag, is that," commented Dykeman.

"A 'must read' for all the well-to-do, so they say. That's why the likes of you and me don't read it, sir."

"Speak for yourself, Shapes. I read it every month."

"Yes, sir," responded Shapes. "Shall I go on?"

"If you must," replied the inspector, stretching his arms above his head.

"They've got two children. There's a daughter at university and a son at a private school," announced Shapes.

"That it? No dirt? No snogging with the butler and that sort of thing?" Dykeman sounded disappointed.

"Sorry, sir."

Shapes dropped the Collard's paperwork on the desk and picked up another set. "Marie Macron," he said, before clearing his throat with a little cough. "Thirty-four years old. Single," at which point there was a brief pause. "Born in Nottingham. Her dad owns a lace business originally set up by his granddad. Another one who went to a private school. Bit of gossip here. She was married for a while, to a London banker. Worth a few bob, he was. But she dumped him when she caught him having it off with an old girlfriend. She's divorced now and Macron is her maiden name. She knows Sixpence via her dad. He was an officer in the same regiment during the war. These days she lives in London, bank-rolled by her parents and the money she got from the divorce."

"I'm surprised you didn't ask for photos, Shapes. You could pin one up on the wall above your bed," suggested Dykeman.

"I did ask, sir. They arrive tomorrow," grinned Shapes, in a manner Dykeman found unsettling.

"What about the notes on Dipping?" asked the inspector.

"Bit disappointing, to be honest, sir. He didn't go to private school, which means he also didn't go to university. Born in Brighton. Youngest of five kids. Dad's a lorry driver. Hasn't had a proper job in years, though that doesn't seem to have stopped him from having a good time."

"I bet he gets through women like Tamsin Spectacle in the time it takes you and me to read a book," commented Dykeman.

"Not jealous are you, sir?"

"Looking for a clip round the ear, Shapes?"

"Not today, thanks, sir."

"Nothing to add to what we already know, then?" asked Dykeman.

"No. Real let-down there. Bit more detail on the incident with the dodgy meat. Spoken to a couple of times by the local bobby when he was a kid. But that's it."

"Damn it. After yesterday's news, I was expecting a big fat dossier with a list of arrests long enough to go all the way round Heffalump's belly," said Dykeman, puffing out his cheeks.

"Sorry, sir."

"Alright, what about Golightly? Don't suppose she was a secret agent in the war? Or happened to have been doing a bit of smuggling on the side?" asked the inspector.

"No such luck. Mind you, the family business is a bit more interesting. Golightly Explosives, based in Leamington. Was set up by her husband. It's the youngest son who runs it now. Must make a few bob, because most of her money comes from company dividends." Shapes turned over the single sheet of paper he was holding. "The husband died four years ago. Family home is in Little Tysoe in Warwickshire. We ought to visit," he suggested.

"We should," replied Dykeman, looking out of the window at a pair of starlings fighting over a scrap of food. "I don't suppose we'll find anything useful, but would be remiss of us not to call by. Let's head out there on our way back to the vicarage."

Shapes dropped the sheet of paper on the desk with all the others and scratched the back of his head. "That's your lot, sir. Might get some more stuff come in, I suppose, but that's all we've got for now."

"You get an E minus for that effort, Shapes. Must try harder. I don't reckon there's a thing in all that lot that's of any real help, more's the pity."

Dykeman got to his feet and stretched out his arms. He knew it wasn't his sergeant's fault, but he'd been hoping for a lot more. Maybe the officers doing the work weren't asking the right type of questions. They needed to be nosey if they were going to turn up any dirt. And dirt was just the thing he and Shapes needed. Something that might shake up that lot at the vicarage. He'd been doing his best with what he had, but that wasn't much, and, for his money, they were all sitting too comfortably. Someone had committed murder, twice over, and it was his job to do whatever it took to identify the killer. They needed to try harder.

"Come on then, let's get over to Golightly's place and take a look through her privates. But I want to get on back to the vicarage as soon as we can. I reckon today's going to be a big one, Shapes, because if it isn't we're going to find ourselves facing a right grilling from the old man and, after my run in with Tom Gently, he's probably not going to tolerate another slip up."

THE TWO POLICEMEN WERE forced to wait in their car for nearly half an hour, until Eleanor Golightly's housekeeper returned from an expedition to the shops, weighed down by nothing more than a pint of milk and two newspapers. The housekeeper was still deeply upset at recent events and their appearance brought on a flood of tears. What with the need to dish out some sympathy to her and have a decent rummage round all five bedrooms, three bathrooms, kitchen, dining room, lounge, study, scullery and a gaggle of outbuildings, it was over an hour later before Dykeman and Shapes were back in their car and heading out of Little Tysoe.

Dykeman was unimpressed and keen to share his disappointment.

"Right waste of time, that was. Woman couldn't make a decent cup of tea to save her life and when I asked her for biscuits, you'd think I'd ordered her to nick the crown jewels."

"Think she was upset, sir. About Mrs Golightly."

Shapes pressed down hard on the accelerator and they surged past a tractor, the enormous wheels of which were hurling great big clumps of mud all over the road and verges, as well as their car.

"Upset? It's not as if they were related and the woman's only been working there four months." Dykeman gripped the strap above the car door as they bounced their way over a stretch of particularly bad road. "Don't they ever look after these roads. Makes you wonder what we pay our taxes for."

"It's them tractors, sir. The combine-harvesters too. They bash the hell out of the road surface. Should make 'em stick to the fields. Make it easier for people like us to get around the place too."

In truth, Shapes wasn't really too bothered about the quality of the road, but he was annoyed at how often they got held up by farm vehicles when they were on police business, sometimes even in the centre of town. Should be a law against that sort of thing.

"YOU DON'T THINK IT'S a little early for a drink, do you?" asked Albert Collard, feeling rather uncertain of himself in unfamiliar company. "Only, what with the murders, it's left my nerves on edge. A little whisky would do me the world of good."

"Half-ten? Plenty late enough, if you ask me," replied the other man.

Richard Dipping smiled as he answered, then took a long draw on the cigarette he'd only just lit. He'd been enjoying his own company, parked on one of the living room chairs and wondering whether he might decide to spend a few days with a friend in Devon, when Albert Collard wandered into the room. It was obvious from the startled look on the man's face that he'd been hoping to find the room empty. In that respect, they had something in common.

It didn't bother him if Collard wanted a drink, despite the time. Why the hell not? A man's life is his own. Could even say he had a point. The atmosphere in the house was damned awful. They were all on edge, wondering if the murder spree was at an end or if another body was going to turn up, stuffed in a wardrobe, maybe, or hanging from a light fitting. Perhaps they could all do with a drink.

"In fact, I'll jolly well join you, if you don't mind," he declared.

Albert Collard was hovering next to the drinks cabinet, glancing repeatedly at the closed door while rubbing his thumbs against his clenched fingers. He'd hoped the room was empty and felt a little awkward when he saw Dipping sitting there, looking like he didn't have a care in the world. Impossible to know how the man managed it, what with the stress they were under. Dipping's response was like manna from Heaven, lifting the weight from his shoulders in an instant.

"Excellent, excellent. Always better to drink in company," replied Collard in an energetic tone. "Ice? Water?"

"A single ice cube, old man. Don't like to swamp the whisky. Robs it of most of the taste," came the reply.

Dipping blew a long, unbroken trail of smoke towards the ceiling and watched it spread in rippling plumes over the off-white paintwork.

"I'm with you there," declared Collard.

He opened the cabinet and whipped out a near-full bottle of whisky and two glasses. He poured a large measure into each glass, followed by an ice cube from the container the housekeeper must have re-filled earlier in the morning. That sort of attention to detail impressed him no end; it made such a difference to your stay when these things were so well attended to.

"Rather good breakfast, don't you think?" Collard asked as he picked up the two glasses.

"Bloody marvellous. Old Sixpence found himself a gem in that housekeeper,W replied Dipping. "If I had a need for one myself, I'd sign her up on the spot. She's so good, you hardly notice she's around most of the time. Can't stand the sort who like to draw attention to themselves all the time."

Dipping took the glass Collard offered him and swirled the drink around, admiring the rich, velvety tones, before letting a little of the warm, peaty liquid slide across his tongue and down his throat. Despite what he'd said to Collard, it was, perhaps, a tad early for a drink, but why not?

"I wish the police would let us all go home. How on earth they can think one of us killed Eleanor and Sixpence is utterly beyond me. It's obvious someone else has entered the property, probably hoping to steal whatever valuables they could find, and been caught in the act. Would have thought any fool could see that," observed Collard, his voice tinged with nerves.

Dipping had noticed the tremble in Collard's hands when they'd sat down to dinner on the Friday evening and it was visible again as he clutched his glass. He'd seen that sort of thing before, more than once, and always for the same reason. Collard had a drink problem. In which case, it was a wonder he'd had managed to last this far into the morning before getting his hands on a drink. Or maybe he'd already knocked back one from a hip flask and this was just a mid-morning top-up.

A thought percolated through Dipping's brain. There wasn't much to entertain them, what with the police having them cooped up in the house, so why not make up some fun himself. What he had in mind might not be much of a challenge, but it would be better than nothing at all. Barely able to conceal a smile, he decided he'd encourage Albert Collard's drinking and see if he couldn't get the man slurring his words before lunchtime.

"I doubt we'll be allowed out of here until they've worked out who the killer is," suggested Dipping. "Either that, or they've framed someone for it. They might not be bright enough to do the former but I suspect they're perfectly capable of the latter."

"Really, you think they'd frame someone? Wouldn't get away with it, surely," replied Albert Collard.

Albert hadn't considered the possibility of police incompetence, let alone corruption. The mere suggestion that such a thing might be a possibility gave him something else to worry about and he felt as if he had enough on his plate already. Without even glancing at his glass, he brought it up to his lips and downed most of the contents in one go, re-assured by the familiar taste.

"Never met a smart copper yet." insisted Dipping. "Certainly not one who's got what it takes to unravel a proper little crime of the sort we've got here. Think about it. It's already obvious to any dimwit, this inspector and his sidekick haven't got a clue what's going on. Sixpence was even murdered while they were here, in the house. The trouble is, they know if they don't arrest someone for the two murders, they'll end up looking like the useless bunch of idiots they really are and they don't want that, do they? What would you do in their place? Me, I reckon I'd frame one of us."

"You think so?" asked Albert Collard, filled growing increasingly concerned.

"Happens all the time," suggested Dipping. "I say, you're nearly empty. Fancy a top-up?"

"Oh, yes. I should. Only had a small one, after all," mumbled the architect, before returning to the drinks cabinet with a little more haste than he intended. He hoped Dipping hadn't noticed.

"You might as well bring the bottle over here. Save the shoe leather. I'll be ready for another myself in a bit," said Dipping.

"Splendid idea," replied the other man.

Albert Collard's face took on a happier demeanour and, to Richard Dipping, he seemed to caress the whisky bottle as if it was some kind of rare, ancient artefact, before he placed it with care on the small round-topped table next to his chair. Dipping was happy his little scheme was progressing so nicely. All the raw materials were in place, now all he needed to do was add plenty of liquid to the solid and stir to just the right consistency. And he was good at stirring things up.

"Quite a woman, that wife of yours," prompted Dipping.

"Yes, she's certainly that," replied Collard, before wondering what Richard Dipping actually meant. "I mean, she's a first class woman. Runs the house like clockwork. Landed on my feet there, I did, though I've never been entirely sure what she saw in me, except for the money, of course," he laughed.

He had sprawled across the armchair, feeling a little more relaxed as the calming effect of the whisky spread through his body. How fortunate it had turned out to be that he'd found Dipping in the room. Another man who appreciated the pleasure of a little drink, or two, and one who seemed to have a far better understanding than he did of the way the police went about their business. Perhaps he should encourage him to say more; after all, forewarned is forearmed.

"That wouldn't be the first time that sort of thing's happened," suggested Dipping, slipping into a more relaxed pose himself.

Another thought had come to him, one that had him wondering if he might not be looking at a new business opportunity, as opposed to some simple entertainment. He knew already, of course, that Albert Collard was a partner in a firm of architects and what was on his mind now was the extent of the man's hold on the company purse strings. It would be useful to find out if he carried real clout or had no more influence than what biscuits to buy to go with their morning tea. If it turned out to be the former, well then, opportunity beckoned.

"I've met a few women like that myself," he continued. "Ambitious young things desperate to move up in the world and determined to do so without the inconvenience of hard work on their part. It's best to spot them early on, then stay one step ahead. That way, when you've had enough of them, if you get my drift, you can toss them overboard before they can do any serious damage."

He took another long drag on his cigarette, leaving the other man to make up his own mind what he meant. It didn't really matter what he thought, just that it added to what Dipping hoped was a growing sense of unease. The more uncomfortable Collard felt, the more he would drink, just like every other drunk he'd ever met.

"Oh, I don't think I have anything to worry about with Daphne. She's been there for me through thick and thin. Would be a bit late in the day now to go trading me in for a new model. Mind you, she's an ambitious woman, right enough. I don't doubt there's little she wouldn't do to move us all up in the world, whether we like it or not."

Albert Collard gave a little laugh, one that sounded as hollow as it actually was, then emptied his glass in a single go. This time he didn't wait for Dipping to suggest he have a refill and he poured a measure that would have left many men unsteady on their feet.

"Always wanting to spend a chap's money, is a woman, don't you find?" prompted Dipping.

He eyed his companion with interest, pleased at the progress he was making. Really, it was all too easy, which was probably a sign of just how on edge Collard had been feeling in the first place. He wondered for a brief moment if any of the other house guests might be feeling their nerves to the same extent. He wouldn't let things get to him like that. Just keep those two stupid policemen at arm's length and he'd do just fine.

"Good Lord, you can say that again," replied Collard. "The spending never seems to end. Why, only last week Daphne announced that we need to have the dining room redecorated. It's started looking old and tatty, apparently. I can tell you, if you took a look in there now you'd think the place had only been decorated the day before. Not a thing wrong with it," he went on, not noticing that some of his words had become a little more rounded than usual. "I tried objecting, but got accused of being tight-fisted and causing the family an immense amount of embarrassment. Seems we have to keep up with the times and, more to the point, with the fashions, for when we entertain. God knows how much she'll end up spending."

Albert Collard barely tasted the whisky this time, as another half a glass slipped down his throat. My, it was good to be able to talk these things through with a proper chap, someone who understood how demanding these women could be. He'd tried, heavens how he'd tried, to understand his wife, but it always ended up the same way. She'd want to spend money on things they didn't need, he'd object and they'd end up having an argument. It didn't grow on trees, he'd say, but Daphne was a tough old boot and she always seemed to get her way. Yes, it was good to have a chap to talk to about these things.

"It's a wonder you can keep up with all the spending. I know I'd not be able to if I moved in with a woman like that," observed Dipping.

"Yes, it's a good job I've a decent income from my partnership. Not a hope otherwise. Mind you," he was talking freely now and more rapidly. "Daphne does have a little income of her own. Always seems to come up with some money when it's really needed. I say, you not having another snifter?"

"Don't mind if I do," replied Dipping, swallowing what little whisky remained in his glass, then pouring himself another, very small, measure. "Best be careful though. Too much drink during the day sends me to sleep."

"Always like to have an afternoon nap myself," replied Collard, with a little wobble of the head. "Good for the constitution." He managed to pronounce the last word only with some difficulty.

"I'm a gruff sort of fellow whenever I wake up after sleeping during daylight hours. Doesn't seem to agree with me. Must be rather handy, being married to a woman with money of her own," probed Dipping.

"Don't know about that," muttered the older man. "Gives her ideas beyond her means and you can imagine who has to make up the shortfall."

"It wasn't the money that attracted you to her then?" quipped Dipping, trying hard to sound innocent.

"I should say not. Wasn't me that bagged her, for what it's worth," Collard knocked back yet another mouthful of whisky and licked his lips before he went on. "Daphne hunted me down. Like wild game. Only she didn't have any beaters. Did it all on her own. We first met at a family wedding in darkest Shropshire. Reckon she must have thought I earned rather more than I do, which is what had her setting her sights on me."

He raised his hands so as to hold an imaginary rifle in front of him, his glass wobbling so that what little whisky remained in it sloshed dangerously close to the lip.

"Sounds like quite a woman," replied Dipping, keen to let Collard continue.

"Well, I can tell you, after that it wasn't safe for me to go out in public. Popped up everywhere, she did. I rather fancied another young filly at the time, a pretty little thing with a sweet smile and delightful brown eyes. But Daphne soon saw her off. Eventually, I couldn't stand the stress any more. Popped the old question after dinner at the Ritz."

To Dipping the word Ritz sounded more like Witz. Collard refilled his glass with such a practised action that he hardly seemed to notice what he was doing, thought Dipping.

"Very romantic of you. I take it she said yes?" suggested Dipping.

"Certainly did. Turned out she'd already started organising the wedding, would you believe," replied Albert. "Booked a venue for the reception and a honeymoon in Rome. Even had family members updating their diaries, every last one of them sworn to secrecy, of course. Took me by surprise at the time, but wouldn't now."

Collard's head was continuously wobbling by now and most of his words had a drink-infected pronunciation that required Dipping to listen more carefully than normal.

"What a woman," Dipping remarked, with a smile. "At least you've always known where you stand. Unlike some men, who seem to think they rule the roost when all the time it's been the lady of the house in charge."

"Certainly have," mumbled Collard. "Well, can't sit around here all morning. Best take a walk. Think I've got a bit of a headache coming on."

"Think I'll stay inside for a while longer," replied Dipping. "Tamsin promised to bring me a cup of tea."

A look of mischievous self-satisfaction grew across the younger man's face as he watched Albert Collard struggle to his feet, then totter across the room and out into the hallway. It hadn't, he appreciated, taken much of an effort to persuade Collard to drink rather more than he really should have, but it amused him all the same. God only knows, there was precious little else by way of entertainment to fill the day. He picked up the newspaper he'd been reading before Collard had shown up and turned to a story about the theft of several thousand watches from a factory on the outskirts of Leeds.

Chapter Thirteen

Bright, warm sunlight washed across the dining room floor, flooding in through the open French doors. It was, thought Tamsin Spectacle, an utterly glorious morning, if you ignored the small matter of the two recent murders; something she had been trying her very best to do, though without a great deal of success. The sound of birdsong seemed to fill the air as she stood by one of the open doors, slowly taking in the full beauty of the vicar's garden. For the briefest of moments she wondered who would look after the garden now that Sixpence was no longer there to do it. It would be such a shame to see it all go to rack and ruin. But not to worry, she decided, for the new incumbent, whoever he might be, would surely pick up the baton.

She had been waiting for the housekeeper to bring her two cups of tea, one for herself and one for Richard. But it wasn't Mrs Itchington she saw entering the room when she turned at the sound of approaching footsteps. It was the slender, self-confident figure of Edward Sweet, who marched into the room apparently filled with some urgent purpose. For a brief moment, Tamsin Spectacle felt a flush of unease at his approach, worried he might have more bad news.

"Ah, Miss Spectacle."

Sweet paused for a moment in the middle of the room, as if not sure what to do or say next.

"Hello Edward. Were you looking for someone?"

"I was, as a matter of fact. Rather fancied a coffee. Been looking for that slacker of a housekeeper. Don't suppose you've seen her?" he asked, looking round.

"She's making tea for myself and Richard. I imagine she'll be here shortly."

"Blasted woman. I'm absolutely certain she keeps avoiding me on purpose. Don't suppose she much cares what people think, not now Sixpence has gone to meet his maker. She can jolly well do as little as she likes and I know her sort, they'll not do a jot of work if they can get away with it," insisted Sweet.

He ran the fingers of his right hand through his blonde locks and stepped across the room to take up station next to Tamsin. The sunlight caught his hair, causing it to glow with a bountiful radiance that wasn't entirely lost on the young woman. Indeed, she imagined there were many women who would be jealous of such a wonderful head of hair.

"I'm sure she'll be along soon," replied Tamsin. "And it's such a glorious day I don't really mind waiting a little while."

"Blasted murders," asserted Sweet. "They really have made a mess of the weekend."

"I don't imagine Eleanor and the Reverend Sixpence got themselves killed on purpose, Edward. I'm sure they'd much rather still be here amongst the living."

Sweet wasn't so insensitive as not to pick up on the note of irritation in Tamsin Spectacle's voice and he certainly wasn't keen on having her think ill of him.

"Well, yes, of course. I wasn't meaning to imply they'd gone and got themselves killed on purpose. Just a shame, it really is, when everything seemed so jolly well set up for a terrific weekend, don't you think?" he asked, hesitantly.

He looked at the slim, attractive woman, whose blonde hair seemed even more vibrant than his own, and wondered if he'd done enough to sound sincere. He rather hoped so.

"I'd never seen a murder victim until now," said Tamsin, gazing back out at the garden. "And I hope never to see another ever again."

"I'm with you on that one," said Sweet. "Made my stomach turn to see my aunt's head all smashed in, I can tell you. I know it's not the done thing for a chap to seem so sentimental, but it really did leave me jolly upset. Can't begin to imagine who would want to murder Aunt Eleanor."

"That really does seem odd, doesn't it? When you try to think about who might want to murder Eleanor and the Reverend Sixpence it's just about impossible to imagine why anyone would want to do that. I'm sure it must have been someone from outside the house. A thief, maybe."

As Tamsin Spectacle continued to focus her gaze on the sun-drenched gardens, Edward Sweet took the opportunity, not for the first time, to run an admiring eye over the length of her delightfully curving body. Everything about her, from the shape of her slender calves, to her pert, jutting breasts and her full lips, dressed with a bright red lipstick, appealed to him. He might even go so far as to say that, was he to sit down and draw a picture of his ideal woman, he'd find it looking very much like Tamsin Spectacle.

They weren't so very much apart in terms of age, certainly there was less difference than there was between her and that cheap cad, Richard Dipping. What on earth she saw in a man like that, Lord only knew. Surely, she would find a properly educated, cultured man such as himself altogether more appealing. There was a natural order to things and his place was not far off the top of the pile. Dipping, on the other hand, well, he barely made it to the middle.

"I didn't think people went around bumping off vicars, anyway. It doesn't seem... natural. Rather an abomination. Still, I suppose he'll get let in at the Pearly Gates without too much trouble," he suggested.

As he spoke, Tamsin turned her gaze back towards him. He looked away at once, out at the garden, a gentle red flush warming his cheeks.

Tamsin didn't miss the fact Edward Sweet had been staring at her. She had long since become used to attracting attention from men. But she wasn't sure he was the sort of man she should be happy was taking an interest in her. For one thing, he was ridiculously young and, for another, he was, in her admittedly rather limited experience, a stuck up snob. What's more, he didn't appear to have any money of his own and what use, she asked herself, was a man without money. Even the green eyes, which she would normally find attractive in a man, looked cold and harsh. No, there were much bigger fish to be pulled from the sea. Mind you, if it turned out his aunt had left him lots of money in her will then she might view things rather differently.

"Would you mind passing me my handbag," she asked, gesturing towards the white leather bag that she'd placed on a chair behind Sweet, its polished steel edging glistening in the sunlight.

"Of course."

He picked up the bag and handed it to her, finding it rather heavier than he had expected. Still, he thought, there never is any end to the things a woman keeps in her handbag.

Tamsin Spectacle retrieved a cigarette and lighter from the depths of her bag and returned it to Sweet, who obediently placed it back on the chair. He watched her light the cigarette and blow a long funnel of smoke out into the open air with an exaggerated pose that he'd seen so many women of Tamsin's age take up, her head tilted back and the cigarette held out to one side over the back of her hand. Somehow, though, it appeared so much more natural and appealing on her than it did on most other women.

"You're at university, aren't you?" she asked.

"Indeed. I'm taking Classics at Durham. Bit of a bore, I'd say, but essential to set oneself up properly. I'm in my final year."

His fingers slipped through his hair once again, almost as if he was checking it was still there. He'd been keen to take the opportunity to make it clear he would soon have completed his studies. Didn't want Tamsin getting the idea he was younger than he was.

"I never got to go to university. My parents couldn't afford it," she blew more smoke into the air and tapped the cigarette so that ash fell in a disintegrating lump on to the outside paving. "What will you do afterwards?"

"Hadn't really given that a great deal of thought," replied Sweet.

To Tamsin, Sweet's tone was rather arrogant, as if he was trying to show a complete lack of interest in something as ordinary as finding a job. It was as if he thought such a thing was beneath him.

"Perhaps a few months touring the sights," he went on. "I've a friend, of sorts, at Durham who has relatives in the United States. He says they would be delighted to play host to us for a week or two. If only he wasn't such an unappealing dimwit, I'd give it a go."

"Won't you have to find yourself a job? Most of us have to earn a living somehow or other."

"I should jolly well hope not. Well, not so soon, perhaps," he said, affecting a little laugh that irritated Tamsin. "My father has the means to keep me well fed and watered and I plan to make the most of that for as long as I can."

"I've never been to America, though I'd like to one day. It looks such an exciting and adventurous place, not drab and rundown like it is here," commented Tamsin.

"You could accompany me," offered Sweet, in a manner he hoped didn't sound too presumptuous. "We'd start off in New York, move on to Chicago and San Francisco, then make our way down the West Coast to Los Angeles and Hollywood. If that isn't glamorous enough for you, then I don't know what could be."

Tamsin felt an urge to move a little further away from Sweet, ideally completely out of his reach. The thought of spending weeks in his company came close to bringing her out in a rash. She wondered what his friend thought about the prospect of spending so much time with Sweet.

"I think that might give people altogether the wrong impression, don't you?" She dropped what remained of her cigarette on to the paving and dabbed at it with a shoe. "Well, I really must find out what's happening with the tea. At this rate, the day will be long gone before we get to drink it."

Sweet watched her walk across the room and, as she disappeared from view, he brought the leather sole of one shoe down hard on the cigarette butt, crushing it into the ground.

"Don't say I didn't give you the chance," he growled.

He stepped out on to the paving, looked briefly around, then marched off towards the old stable yards at the rear of the house, feeling annoyed. He couldn't decide if he was more upset at himself for finding Tamsin attractive or her for giving him the brush off. Damn it, what was it about women that made life so much more difficult than it really needed to be?

"WHAT'S THE PLAN OF action today, then, sir?" asked Shapes as he steered their car through the entrance to the vicarage.

"To catch ourselves a murderer," replied Dykeman, as he slackened his grip on the door strap. Shapes had driven with considerable gusto, making the absolute most, Dykeman felt sure, of the lengthy run out to the vicarage. Fangio himself couldn't have got there any faster.

"You don't say," muttered Shapes. "And how we going to do that? Ask for volunteers?"

He brought the car to a halt right outside the front door, where it was sure to get in someone's way, then switched off the engine. For a moment there was no other sound than the twittering of nearby birds.

"Torture, if needs be," answered Dykeman, relaxing fully for the first time since they'd left the relatively safe confines of Banbury, where speed limits applied to everyone, including Shapes.

"Can I use pliers?" asked Shapes. "I've always wondered what the skin looks like underneath your nails."

"I wonder about you sometimes, Shapes."

"Thank you, sir."

"I want to have another word with Richard Dipping," declared the inspector. "I'll bet there's hardly an honest bone in that man's body. All I'm not sure about is how far he'd go to get his hands on someone else's cash."

"Well, I still reckon it's one of the women what did it. Both murders. Can't trust 'em. One minute they're all sweetness and light, the next they're sticking the knife in, and giving it a good twist," responded Shapes.

"Personal experience there, Shapes?"

"Not saying," came the reply.

"Come on, let's set up shop in my unofficial office. Then you can round up Dipping and we'll put the squeeze on him good and proper. There's more to be unearthed there, I'm sure of that," said Dykeman.

"I think we ought to interview Marie Macron again. She got off a bit lightly last time. Needs a proper going over, she does," proposed Shapes.

The sergeant couldn't entirely hide the twinkle in his eyes. As far as he was concerned, she was the kind of woman he'd be happy to spend the rest of his days with. Sexy, clever and almost certain to boss him around, just how he liked it.

"Shapes! Put a sock in it. And put your tongue back in your mouth."

"Sir."

The two men stepped out of the car into yet another beautiful sun-filled day, the cool air that had arrived with the new morning all but gone. The scent from the matching rose bushes planted either side of the doorway wafted over them as they stepped forward. Dykeman rang the bell.

The front door opened, to reveal the imposing figure of Florence Itchington, statuesque, with her hands planted on her hips. Her greeting perhaps lacked a little of the warmth they might have expected, "Oh, you two are back."

Chapter Fourteen

Richard Dipping left the study in quite a fluster, thin beads of sweat at his temples and his eyes rather wider than was usual. It was fortunate there was no one else passing through the hallway at the time, because he had little awareness of his surroundings, fixed, as he was, on making it to the lounge, and its drinks cabinet, as quickly as he could.

If there had been anyone else there to see him, they might have concluded that he looked a worried and unsettled man. And they wouldn't have been far off the mark. The twin causes of this discomfort sat happily in the study, comparing notes on the performance they had just witnessed. A performance that had been delivered almost entirely at their own prompting.

"The man's a crook, sure as eggs is eggs," asserted Dykeman, scratching an irritating itch on the end of his nose that seemed to be in no hurry to go away. "Even a one-eyed monk with little hearing and half a brain could work that one out."

"I'm with you there, sir. He didn't like it much, did he, when you started asking all those questions about where his money comes from? Got the right hump."

"He didn't like, Shapes, it because he knows damn well he'll be for the high jump if we find out what he's up to. I'd bet a month's wages he's got a whole bunch of dodgy schemes on the go."

"And he's got Tamsin Spectacle to keep sweet. Bet she costs him a bob or two," offered Shapes, who continued in a more serious tone, "But that don't make him a cold blooded killer. I don't know as he's got what it takes to murder someone."

"You about to revisit your quest to pin it on one of the women?" asked Dykeman.

"No, I mean it," replied Shapes. "Do you reckon he's up to killing someone?"

"Don't reckon he's got the stomach for it," came back the instant response.

"That's what I think, sir. Happily nick the family silver and leave you without a penny to live on, but murder? I don't reckon so."

Dykeman looked sideways at his sergeant. "When did you last get it right, Shapes? Working out who did it, I mean."

The inspector knew his sergeant's recent record had not been impressive.

"My run of bad luck's got to come to an end some time," replied Shapes, sounding distinctly defensive. "And I reckon this is it. Want a couple of bob on it?"

"Nope. I haven't made my own mind up yet." Dykeman got to his feet and stretched. "Come on, let's get some fresh air. And I had a thought. We haven't worked out yet if there's anything been taken from the house. We ought to look into that."

The two men walked through a seemingly deserted house and out on to the terrace via the French doors in the dining room. For a moment it looked as though the house guests might have been in hiding, perhaps too afraid to show their faces. But way off on the far side of the garden could be seen two figures. Marie Macron and Daphne Collard were engaged in a game of tennis on the hard-surfaced court. Shapes strained to get a better view, but the distance was against him. A moment's frustration came and went.

"Oh, it's you two. I thought you were in the study," declared the housekeeper, who had approached the policemen from behind. Both felt an uncomfortable shiver run up their spines.

"Ah, it's you, Mrs Itchington," replied Dykeman, as he looked round.

"Well, I'm not the gardener, that much I know," replied the housekeeper. "Or were you thinking we are too alike to tell apart?"

The woman's acerbic tongue put both men on the defensive. Shapes even took half a step back, something not missed by Dykeman.

"Not many people out and about," prompted Dykeman.

"I imagine they're too scared to set foot outside their rooms in case someone comes along and does them in," answered the housekeeper. "Can hardly say that I blame them. Haven't you two worked out yet who the murderer is? You've had long enough."

Dykeman ground his teeth together, attempting to retain his composure or, at the very least, not give away how awkward the accusation made him feel. It seemed to him that growing familiarity with himself and Shapes was causing the housekeeper to lose whatever modicum of civility she had attempted to maintain up until then.

"Early days yet, Mrs Itchington. Early days," insisted the inspector.

"Yes," added Shapes. "Your average killer isn't too keen on being apprehended, not if they can help it. And they can be cunning bleeders. Good at covering their tracks. But we'll get him, don't you worry about that."

He did his best to sound upbeat, but had the distinct impression even before he'd finished talking that the sour-faced woman standing opposite wasn't buying what he had to sell.

"Well, if you say so. You're the so-called experts." Florence brushed the front of her apron and looked over at the two younger women running about the tennis court. "I suppose you know that Macron woman and the Reverend Sixpence were arguing the other day. Got very heated, it did."

Dykeman glanced at his sergeant, then back at Itchington. The housekeeper could suppose all she liked, but he hadn't heard any such thing and, from the look on his face, neither had Shapes.

"What were they arguing about?" he enquired.

"Oh, I don't know that," replied Florence. "They were too far away. Not that I was keen on hearing, you understand. I don't want you getting the impression I'm some kind of snoop."

"I'm sure you're not anything of the sort," replied Dykeman. "Probably impossible for you not to overhear a conversation every now and then, what with the job you do and all that."

Best butter the woman up, he decided. Obvious she went around listening in on every conversation she could. You could probably open any closed door in the house and, voila, there she would be, pretending she was dusting a skirting board or polishing a door handle. Still, if she had information then they needed to get it out of her.

"That's just how it is. Can't be helped if people are indiscreet. When I was a girl that kind of discussion was kept for behind closed doors but these days people don't seem to have any proper sense of privacy," insisted the housekeeper.

"Where was this argument?" asked Dykeman.

"They were in her bedroom. If they'd closed the door, I doubt I would have noticed them, but they left it ajar, you see. I was in Mr Dipping's room, cleaning up the mess he'd left in there. He's not got a thought for anyone but himself, that man. There were clothes everywhere and two glasses he'd taken upstairs from the lounge. Honestly, you'd think the man would show some consideration."

"Yes," said Dykeman, keen to get back on to the subject of the argument between Macron and Sixpence. "And you couldn't hear anything of the argument, not even a word or two?"

"No, not a word," asserted Florence, sounding a tad disappointed.

"That's a shame," commented Dykeman. "But helpful all the same, to know they were arguing, eh Shapes?"

"Certainly, sir. A real help."

"Of course, it could have been the same thing they've argued about before," added the housekeeper, effecting a casual air.

Dykeman scratched his head and attempted a smile, unable to fend off the feeling the housekeeper was deliberately making the most of things. People, he knew from experience, were prone to that kind of thing. They liked their moment in the sun, as it were, and he felt pretty confident Florence Itchington was a woman who liked more than her fair share. He also felt sure she was enjoying mucking the two of them about. Gave her a sense of control, maybe even superiority. Best start keeping his eyes peeled for an opportunity to put her right on that one.

"They've argued before, you say. And what would that have been about?" asked the inspector?

"She wouldn't leave the poor man alone. Obsessed, she was. Every time she saw him, she'd try to persuade him to marry her. Though that's hardly surprising."

The housekeeper looked again towards the figures on the tennis court and gave a little snort of disapproval.

"She was after Sixpence?" asked Shapes, both surprised and concerned at the suggestion Marie Macron had been trying to get shacked up with the vicar. "But she could... well, have her choice of any man she wants, you'd have thought. One with lots of dosh, is what I mean."

Dykeman too was surprised at what he'd just heard and something about the news nagged in the back of his mind.

But it was something else the housekeeper had said that caught his attention.

"Why do you say 'hardly surprising', Mrs Itchington?"

"Well, a woman like that. With her history and reputation. She could hardly do better than marry a vicar if she wants to restore her reputation. The Reverend Sixpence would have been the perfect match, for her," added Florence.

"And they've had words over this before, you say?" Dykeman asked.

"Oh, definitely. They had a disagreement the last time she was here. I was cleaning up in the dining room and they were out here. Sat over there, they were", she said, pointing. "What with the doors being open, I could hear every word. Very upset was the vicar that she wouldn't take no for an answer. Said his heart had been broken when he was a younger man and he couldn't face the prospect of loss again. Poor man, she hounded him something rotten."

"Why didn't he just tell her to clear off?" asked Shapes.

"Maybe he should have done," replied Florence, with a sigh. "I think he found it difficult, what with her being a family friend and all that. Her father was an officer in the same regiment as Mr Sixpence during the war. I'm sure he felt obligated, as any normal person would do. Mind you, it might have been because he was afraid of her. She'll tell anyone who'll listen that she's an expert shot with a gun, you know. If either Mrs Golightly or the Reverend had been shot dead, I'd point the finger of blame at the woman straight away."

"Good with a gun, you say," replied the inspector, mulling over what the housekeeper had just told them.

"Should imagine there's a few people here who can use a gun, of one sort or another, wouldn't you, Shapes?"

"Certainly, sir. All these toffs are born with a silver spoon in their mouths and a shot gun in one hand, I reckon. All I got was a whack on the backside and a life of hard graft. Don't seem fair."

"My heart bleeds for you, Shapes. Maybe one of these days I'll see some sign of all that hard graft you reckon you put in," Dykeman quipped, before turning his attention back to the housekeeper. "Was Sixpence ever married?"

"Oh, no. As I understand it, he was engaged during his thirties, but the young woman died in a road accident just a few weeks before the wedding. He told me once that he was too settled in his ways now to think about getting married. If only others would have listened to him and left him alone, well, we'd all be a lot better off, if you ask me."

"Well, don't you worry yourself, Mrs Itchington, we'll get this killer, sooner or later. We always do," replied Dykeman.

"I hope so, inspector," replied the housekeeper, pausing to look again at the women on the tennis court. "People always get their comeuppance, eventually, of that I'm sure."

The implication was not lost on Dykeman, who wondered just why the woman in front of him had got herself so upset about Marie Macron's pursuit of Sixpence. Maybe she was the possessive type, not happy at another woman sticking her nose in where it wasn't wanted. Or, perhaps, she was worried she might end up losing her job if Marie Macron had married Sixpence and saw fit to get rid of a housekeeper she apparently didn't much care for.

"There's one thing you can help us with, if you don't mind, Mrs Itchington," resumed Dykeman, keen to make the most of things while the housekeeper was so talkative.

"Well, so long as I've got time I'm willing to help, inspector. But it's a busy and demanding job, running this house, you know."

"It would be a big help if you could take a look through the vicar's things, to see if there's anything missing. I can't think of anyone better suited to such a job and we really ought to know if theft is part of the picture here. Best to concentrate on his valuables. Small things first. The sort of things someone could easily slip into a pocket or hide in their baggage."

"Oh, you think Reverend Sixpence found someone stealing things from his bedroom and they murdered him to keep him quiet?"

The housekeeper sounded distinctly animated, even excited. Dykeman felt sure he'd signed up a new confederate.

"Let's not go jumping to any conclusions now," answered Dykeman, a note of caution in his voice. "But it's possible. Definitely worth a look. And it would be best if you did this discretely. Wouldn't want to give the game away. Might give the murderer an opportunity to dump anything he's stolen, if that's what he did."

"Well, I'll do my best, inspector. But I wasn't in the habit of rummaging through the Reverend's belongings, you understand, so I won't be aware of everything of value he owned."

"Your best will be just fine, Mrs Itchington. And it will be a whole lot better than me or Shapes could do."

Dykeman had only just finished the last sentence when the figure of Edward Sweet came tearing round the side of the house. He looked to be in a state of some considerable agitation, his wide-open eyes suggesting he might have encountered something that was less than pleasant, and he was moving at a speed that would have made him a candidate for an Olympic gold medal in the hundred yard sprint. As soon as he clapped eyes on the two policemen, he made directly for them.

"What's wrong with Mr Sweet?" asked the housekeeper in an irritated voice as he closed on them.

"Looks to be in a right old hurry," added Shapes. "I've got a feeling it's not good news."

Dykeman wondered what on earth could have happened this time. Surely to God, there couldn't be any more dead bodies. He scratched the back of his head as Sweet jumped the steps on to the paving, nearly falling in the process, and covered the last dozen or so yards in admirably quick time.

"Fallen in a wasps' nest, have we?" asked Dykeman, hoping for the best.

Sweet stopped in front of the others, then dropped on to one of the chairs close by. He tried taking a few deep breaths but struggled to calm himself as quickly as he wanted. Looking up at Dykeman, he paused for a moment, took another breath, then delivered his news in a voice that was little more than a whisper. "It's Albert Collard. He's... he's dead. In the stables."

Chapter Fifteen

"You what?" asked Shapes, not sure he could trust his own ears.

"Good Lord," was all the housekeeper could manage.

"For heaven's sake," sighed Dykeman. "What is wrong with you people? Maybe me and Shapes should clear off back to the station and just let the rest of you sort yourselves out. Last man or woman standing and all that. You sure he's dead?"

"Yes," replied Sweet, now beginning to shake as shock took hold. "There's no pulse and... well, you need to see for yourself."

"In the stables you say. Come on Shapes, let's get round there. And where's that constable gone?" barked Dykeman.

The policemen took off in the direction of the stables at a sedate jog, having taken on board the lesson they'd just learned from Sweet that moving at too swift a pace would only leave them unpleasantly short of breath, which would definitely not be good for effective policing. In Dykeman's case, it was also very likely he wouldn't have been able to maintain a faster pace, even if he'd tried; not that he would have been keen to own up to any such thing.

Having skirted round the side of the house, they entered a cobbled yard lined on three sides with stable buildings. Those to their right and at the top end were clearly no longer used as horse accommodation since, even from the outside, it was possible to see they were packed with all manner of items deemed to be no longer deserving of a more luxurious home.

Shapes looked inside the first stable on the left and shook his head, before moving on to the second. A brief nod of the bonce confirmed it was the right one. He stepped away so his boss could claim the scene of this latest crime.

There was a horse in the stable. As Dykeman pushed open the half-height door and stepped over the threshold, the stink of manure wafted up his nostrils. He looked across at the all-black mare, who shook her head as they made eye contact, then took a step back.

"What a bloody stink," observed Shapes. "How do these horse riding types put up with it?"

He wafted a hand in front of his nose, hoping it would help fend off the stench. It didn't, much to his annoyance.

There was a scurry at the back of the stable, followed by a brief high-pitched squeak, before a large grey rodent shot across the floor and disappeared under a stack of hay bales at the far end of the building.

"Reckon that's our chief suspect, sir?" asked Shapes.

"Shapes," came the curt reply.

"Sir."

The wall to the left of them was largely filled with two neat rows of horse riding equipment and sundry other implements. On the cobbled ground beneath these lay the body of Albert Collard, flat on his stomach, his left arm tucked underneath him, the right one laid out to his side. It was possible, thought Dykeman, that Collard might have been taking a nap, albeit an uncomfortable one, if not for the fact there was a long-handled garden rake attached to the right-hand side of his head. The ground around the body was coated with a generous wash of blood. Dykeman crouched down next to the prostrate figure to take a closer look.

"Two of the metal prongs have pierced the side of his head, right by the temple. Likely he died on impact, I'd say."

Shapes stepped close to the body and surveyed the scene with care, before making his pronouncement, "Right-hander, I reckon." He put his hands together and swung an imaginary rake through the air towards an equally imaginary figure of Albert Collard.

"Mm," was all Dykeman made by way of a reply, before standing up and stepping his way round the body, making a careful study of both the dead man and the surrounding ground as he went. "Don't suppose we'll get any footprints here, not unless someone stepped in some of that horse muck."

As if recognising its cue, the horse whinnied and shook its head again. Dykeman wasn't entirely certain the beast wasn't attempting to communicate with him. There was little doubt she had seen what happened. Sadly, he didn't speak horse and she, he was pretty confident, didn't speak human.

"Looks like the rake came from up there," observed Dykeman gesturing towards an empty peg on the top row of implements hanging from the wall. "I suppose we'll have to assume the worst, for now, what with the other two deaths."

He scratched his chin, wondering just what might, in fact, have happened in the stable. He couldn't say, yet, just what it was, but something didn't seem, well, right. Was it really murder? Then he realised what it was that bothered him about the scene.

"You don't sound convinced," said Shapes.

"I'm not," replied the inspector. "You should try smelling his breath. Stinks of alcohol."

"An accident?" Shapes looked at the horse. "What, the horse tripped him?"

"Who knows. But I can tell you one thing, Shapes, the press are going to have a field day with this. I won't be able to show my face in town for weeks."

"Shouldn't bother about that, sir. Some other disaster will happen soon enough, then everyone will be talking about that. Won't be long until farmers start finding their crops or their animals are going missing in the night. As soon as that happens, we won't read another word about this in the papers."

"Might be a good time to take a little holiday," suggested Dykeman, looking down at the corpse.

"What do you reckon we should do now?" asked Shapes.

"Which constable we got on duty today?" Dykeman asked.

"Dartington, sir."

"He the one with the personal hygiene problems?"

"You mean the bad breath?" smiled Shapes.

"Yep."

"That's him, sir."

181

"Well, tell him to stop whatever it is he's doing and round up the rest of the guests; what's left of them. Oh, and give Doctor Delph a call. Tell her she's got more work to do here. She'll probably think you're having a laugh," added Dykeman.

Shapes was about to leave, to carry out his instructions, when a shadow fell across the entrance to the stable, followed, almost at once, by a shriek. Shapes turned round just in time to catch hold of the fainting figure of Daphne Collard.

"AT LEAST NOW YOU MUST know who the killer is," teased Dr Sheila Delph.

"Meaning?" replied a wary Dykeman, leaning against the lower half of the closed stable door as his friend inspected the latest body he had been so good as to provide her with.

"Well, there's hardly any guests left," she smiled, as she looked up at the grumpy policeman. "Surely the inevitable process of elimination has made it obvious who the killer is."

She was tempted to laugh. She certainly wanted to. But she could see her friend was already feeling depressed about this latest unwelcome development and she knew he'd be in for a hard time back at the station. She really ought to offer support rather than take the mickey.

"Ha, ha," he responded, ironically. "I'm getting right hacked off with this case. Three bodies and hardly a clue worth the name. Don't seem to be any connections, apart from the fact they've all been staying in this damn house."

"Well, clearly there is some sort of a connection. You just haven't uncovered it yet, though I'm sure you will. You always do," smiled Delph.

For the second time in as many days, Dykeman was grateful for the doctor's presence. She had a positive view of things, even when they looked dire to everyone else. It helped to lighten the growing mood of gloom that had descended on him. Perhaps, he thought, he ought to trade in Shapes and replace him with the doctor. Might be a hard one to get past his boss, but could be worth a go. Her conversation was certainly a cut above anything Shapes could manage. Her card play was better too.

"There are no other wounds," declared Delph, getting back on her feet. "And no signs of any other foul play, though, of course, I'll need to get the body back to base before I can be sure of that."

"Mm," was all Dykeman could manage by way of a response.

"What's on your mind? Something not right?" enquired Delph.

"I'm not convinced anyone else was involved here," said Dykeman, tapping the fingers of one hand against the door. "Doesn't look right to me. Taking a swing at someone with a garden rake? If it was me, I'd have gone for something more likely to do the job, like that axe over there."

"I hope you're not pointing the finger of blame at that lovely horse, Leslie."

"You been talking to Shapes?" asked the inspector.

"Not if I can help it. You're so easy to tease sometimes," she smiled.

"Can't help it. It's in my nature," replied Dykeman before adding, "I'm just a big softy, really."

"We already know that. Am I OK to have the body moved?" asked Delph.

"Might as well, Sheila. No point in keeping it here." He paused. "Have the local reporters been trying to speak to you?"

"You shouldn't let yourself get worried about a little press coverage," she replied, rubbing a hand up and down his left arm. "And, yes, they have."

"Vultures. I'm crossing them off my Christmas card list. What's wrong with sticking to covering village fêtes and the like?"

"It's the nationals now, as well as the locals," pointed out Delph as she took Dykeman by the arm and led him out into the sunlight. "Come on, let's get you a cup of tea, while I wait for the ambulance to arrive."

SHAPES AND PC DARTINGTON had assembled all the remaining guests in the lounge, as instructed. By the time Dykeman joined them, he had more or less recovered his composure, having drawn heavily at the well of his friendship with Sheila Delph. What would he do without that woman?

The small gaggle of people awaiting his arrival looked sombre and a dark mood hung over the room. Dykeman cast a quick eye over them. Richard Dipping was nervous, fidgeting ceaselessly and smoking in a manner that suggested he wasn't particularly enjoying things. Tamsin Spectacle sat in an armchair away from the others, silent, with her legs drawn up close to her chest. Marie Macron stood by one of the windows, looking up at the cloud-flecked sky, a sour, drawn look on her face. Daphne Collard had been offered the opportunity of forgoing the roll-call, but insisted on joining in; though why, she hadn't chosen to let Shapes know. She was perched on the edge of one of the settees, a hanky in one hand, her eyes still rimmed red from her tears. Upset, she might well be, but the inspector could make out what could only be described as a determined look in her eyes.

Edward Sweet was the only one of the surviving guests not to look stressed or scared. He sat, almost lay, on a settee, reading a copy of *The Times*. He appeared rather disinterested in proceedings. Dykeman had noticed him as soon as he entered the room and couldn't make up his mind whether Sweet really was nonplussed or putting on a show. The latter seemed more likely. If not, then it was a rapid recovery from the red-faced, short-breathed mess he'd been when he'd hurtled round the side of the house to announce the horrific discovery he'd made in the stables.

Dykeman caught Shapes's eye and nodded in the direction of the young man laying on the settee. Shapes walked across the room and swiped the newspaper from out of Sweet's hands. Sweet started to complain, then gave up the effort, muttering something inaudible under his breath.

"Right," barked Dykeman, taking up station in the middle of the room, the better to address his audience. "With all due deference to Mrs Collard, who, by the way, insisted on being here, it's about time you lot stopped fannying around and started co-operating. Fully co-operating. Because if you don't, I reckon another day or two and, the way things are going, there won't be any of you left."

The inspector paused for a moment, looking, in hope rather than expectation, for some sign of a reaction. Each and every one of them met his stare, apart from Richard Dipping, who found it necessary to inspect the end of his latest cigarette. The inspector made a mental note of that.

"Personally, I'd be happy enough to leave you all here overnight, then come back to clear up the mess tomorrow morning. Would save me a lot of trouble and stress. I'd be in the Chief Inspector's bad books for a while, I'll give you that, but he's hardly got the memory of an elephant. Next bit of naughty business that comes along and he'd forget all about what's happened here."

At last, noted Dykeman, they were actually paying attention, listening to him with something he could only view as respect. Perhaps for the first time since he and Shapes had arrived at the vicarage, he felt as though they might now have the upper hand. What he needed to do now was make the most of this happy situation, before it slipped through his eager fingers.

"One of you has been bumping off the other guests. Hardly a friendly thing to go and do. Worse still, you've also murdered your host and a man of the cloth at that. Tut, tut. I think someone's going to find themselves barred when they try to get in through those Pearly Gates."

Dykeman took a couple of steps towards an enormous, teak sideboard that covered a good portion of one wall.

There was a vast array of framed photos and small ornaments of all sorts scattered erratically along its surface. He picked up a photo of a young woman looking quite the thing in what he thought was a flapper outfit, then put it back, face down.

How long, he wondered, could he draw things out. Could he make it last long enough for someone to crack, for the guilty party to cave in? They must be under incredible stress by now. Two murders, at least, and the police crawling all over the house, there to nab you if you slip up even just the once. It was hard to imagine how anyone ever had the nerve to hold out for any decent length of time under such circumstances, but, there again, if they were cold-hearted enough to kill twice, then perhaps that wouldn't be such a difficult thing to do after all.

"For God's sake, man," Richard Dipping barked, stubbing out his cigarette with such force it snapped in half. "Get on with it. I doubt I'm the only one here who really would like you to work out who the hell has been killing us off."

He fired his words at Dykeman loudly and rapidly, causing most of the others to flinch. Interesting, thought the inspector, though no big surprise. The man on whom suspicion seemed determined to settle had snapped first. Did that mean anything? Maybe. The trouble was, now he'd broken the tension it meant the others were off the hook, so to speak. He ignored the outburst. Dipping shook his head then lit up another cigarette.

"Do you have to?" asked Tamsin Spectacle, blowing away the smoke that drifted across her face. Dipping ignored her.

"I think we'd all rather you got on with your job, inspector, and arrested the person responsible sooner rather than later." Marie Macron spoke in a calm, controlled manner. Shapes found it rather appealing and just what he would have expected of the woman. "Or perhaps you and your sergeant need help." Shapes felt his fondness for Macron ebb somewhat.

Dykeman picked up the small, sculpted figure of a naked woman from off the sideboard and ran a thumb over the contours of her body, impressed by the skill deployed to make it. They'd got the proportions spot on, at least as far as he was concerned. He placed the piece back on the sideboard and turned to face the others.

"What's been proving a little troublesome for me and Shapes is what connects the murders. Or, it would be more accurate to say, it has been bothering us up 'til now."

He took care to take in each of the faces looking back at him, but all he found there was expectation. He'd dangled the bait, but no one had taken it. Not a single solitary sign of worry, let alone panic. Perhaps the killer really was the kind of cold, confident operator he'd hoped they wouldn't be. That was a shame. The others were waiting for him to say more, but he wasn't ready just yet to give up on this attempt to unsettle or even unmask the killer.

"As of this morning, Shapes and I have been in possession of some new information which, we feel confident, will soon be followed by more. You will all be pleased to know this particular parcel of information will very likely allow us to identify which one of you is, in fact, the murderer."

Well, if that didn't do the job then they'd have to try an entirely different approach, most likely one that involved finding clues and such like. Not ideal, given their failure in that department to date, but beggars can't be choosers and all that.

"About ruddy time!" chimed in Edward Sweet, nodding his head vigorously. "I'm a young chap. Got years ahead of me. I really don't want to shuffle off this mortal coil for a good long time yet and I'd like to leave here in a taxi, not an ambulance."

Dykeman paused a while, studying a photograph of what appeared to be a family grouping. He was keen to let his last statement settle over the room like an enveloping fog, reaching into their bodies with a cold, threatening chill. Or, at least, that's how he hoped it would feel for one of them.

"There's a few hours to wait yet until we hear again from the station. In the meantime, Shapes here is going to take another round of statements as to your whereabouts today. Need to make sure we've got our facts all ship-shape."

Having given them one last, stony-faced stare, Dykeman turned and strode from the lounge in the manner of a man who was filled to the gunnels with confidence that his day would surely end a happy one. Every last one of them needed to be under no illusions that the time for unmasking the guilty party was almost upon them. The fact it wasn't anything of the sort was the last thing he wanted them to consider. No, the pressure needed to be turned up to maximum.

As he entered the study, Dykeman realised he was feeling a whole lot better than he had a mere half hour before, when the discovery of Albert Collard's body had left him tempted to run away screaming and never set foot inside the place again. But that sense of depression had lifted almost as quickly as it had descended.

He couldn't actually put his finger on just what it was, but there had been something about the atmosphere in the lounge that gave him the definite impression events were about to unfold in an altogether more helpful manner. Maybe it had been a look on someone's face, or perhaps something one of the surviving guests had said. He didn't know, but his gut told him something was going to happen; and he trusted his gut, because more often than not it was right.

He sat down behind the desk, leaned back and started to hum a Cole Porter number, while he waited for Shapes to join him. The sense of anticipation was a pleasant one and highly welcome. Yes, things were looking up, he was sure of that.

Chapter Sixteen

"Well, what you got for me?" asked Dykeman.

Shapes froze, temporarily caught out by his boss's upbeat mood. He'd reckoned on finding Dykeman still deep in a state of gloom. And why not, when the case had gone so disastrously wrong? He'd half expected the Chief Inspector to have replaced the two of them by now. But the old man's problem was that he had limited options available to him. If he and Dykeman didn't see the case through, who would? Wasn't as if they were a big station with dozens of officers to choose from. No, chances were he and his boss would have to see it out to the bitter end, like it or not.

One thing was for sure, they'd be carrying the can if no one was brought to book for the murders. There'd been three of those now. Three! He wasn't half so sure as Dykeman that Albert Collard had died as the result of a drink-related accident. Too much of a coincidence was that. And he, Shapes, didn't believe in coincidences. Never had and never would. Things like that were much too easy to set up so they looked like an accident.

Maybe his boss had lost it, gone doolally. Bit like those poor sods who'd been found in the North African desert during the war having being lost for days or weeks on end.

Most of the time they'd gone right out of their minds, imagining all sorts of peculiar things. They never recovered, so he'd heard. Had to be locked up at the funny farm. Perhaps Dykeman was going the same way, overwhelmed by the disaster their case had turned into. What a prospect.

"Dunno," replied Shapes, fishing in a pocket for a boiled sweet he'd put there the week before. "What were you hoping for? A confession?"

"That would do," replied Dykeman.

"Well, I don't have one. And don't reckon we're going to get one, either. Not unless we beat it out of them."

Shapes failed to find the sweet, then remembered he'd eaten it in the car on the way to the vicarage that morning. A little ripple of disappointment ran through him. He'd stash away two the next time he got his mits on some. He sat down on the nearest chair and waited to hear more.

"Reckon you're right there, of a sort." Dykeman grinned, stretching out his arms and bringing his hands together behind his head.

"What d'you mean?" asked Shapes, suspicious at once that his boss was up to something.

"Don't want to guess?" asked Dykeman, sounding positively playful.

"You been drinking?" Shapes asked.

The sergeant looked at his strangely and maddeningly upbeat boss. There was no doubt about it, he was up to something and a little game of read-my-mind had already started. And, anyway, what was all that rubbish about important information that would identify the killer?

"Not a drop of the alcoholic persuasion has passed my lips all day," smiled Dykeman.

"So, what's wrong with you? Five minutes ago you were ready to chuck in the towel and now, it's like... I don't know what it's like. You're far too happy for my liking. Something's going on. Ah," announced Shapes, sitting bolt upright, a grin the size of a Turkish moon on his face. "It's Delph, isn't it. Don't tell me you finally proposed and she accepted?"

In the blink of an eye, Shapes felt as excited as a little boy in a sweet shop. One with a lot of money to spend. He wagged a finger at his boss as if he was making an accusation.

"No, of course I didn't propose to Sheila, er, Delph," insisted Dykeman.

The inspector's demeanour took a minor and temporary downward beat at the mere suggestion of a marriage proposal. For God's sake, Shapes ought to know better than that. The day he popped the question would be the day after he'd left the force and he had no plans to do anything of the sort any time soon.

"No, don't suppose you would. Stupid idea," said Shapes.

The sergeant's mood changed in an instant as he sampled the bitter taste of disappointment. He rather fancied being Dykeman's best man. Had even made a few notes for a speech one cold dark evening while he was keeping an eye on a warehouse that had attracted more than its fair share of thefts.

Dykeman brought them back to the matter at hand. "No one is going to own up to killing Sixpence and Golightly, not in so many words..."

He left the sentence hanging, knowing it would irritate Shapes like a nasty rash, one he would be desperate to scratch. Ah, the joy of it. Itch, itch. Itch, itch.

"I'm not playing this game any more," complained Shapes. "Tell me what you're up to or I'm going to sit here and not say another word. What was all that stuff about us getting information that will identify the killer?"

Dykeman laughed, deeply satisfied he'd got one over on his sergeant, who had caved in with unusual ease. A rare treat and one to savour.

"I was feeling a tad down in the dumps about this case, it's true to say," declared the grinning inspector. "And I was still feeling that way when I walked into that room just now. But something happened in there. I don't know what it was that did it, but I got the distinct impression someone is about to do something stupid. Stupid, that is, from their point of view. Flipping marvellous from ours. All I did was tell a bit of a fib to help them along the way."

The happy inspector leaned forward as he spoke, his eyes like two little spotlights fixed on Shapes.

"It's your podge, isn't it?" suggested Shapes. "Your gut has been talking to you."

"Most certainly has," answered Dykeman. "And there's not a better copper on the whole force than my gut."

"Shame it can't tell us who's going to win the 12.15 at Newmarket. We'd make a right killing."

Shapes may have sounded a little sceptical, but in truth he was inclined to take note of Dykeman's gut, because its record wasn't half bad. Most recently, they'd collared a jewel thief who'd turned over a domestic premises. Dykeman's recently fed gut had told him the thief would try to sell the goods to a suspect individual who accompanied a travelling show that just happened to be in the area at the time. That was exactly what happened and they were ready and waiting when the thief showed up to sell the jewels.

"I'm working on it, Shapes. Can't hurry these things. They need to be nurtured, treated with love and respect."

"So, what we going to do now then, just sit here scratching our backsides until something happens?" asked Shapes, scratching at his chin.

"Pretty much," answered Dykeman. "I was going to tell that lot out there they were confined to their rooms. Would have been best for their own safety, no doubt. But I changed my mind. We need to leave the killer room to make their next move and I fully expect it to be a big one."

"But what if that move is to murder someone else? We'll be no better off and have another body on our hands. Well, I say we'll be no better off, but it would mean there'd be one less suspect," added Shapes, inspecting the little flake of skin he'd freed from his chin.

"There we go, Shapes, now you're taking a more positive view of things yourself," smiled Dykeman. "But don't worry, I'm not expecting another murder. I've got a hunch the killer is starting to feel the pressure. Can't tell you why, I just have."

"You'd better be right, sir, or we're going to be looking for new jobs and I don't fancy emptying bins for a living."

"No need to worry, Shapes. We'll be absolutely fine. Anyway, you haven't told me yet, did they all have an alibi for Albert Collard's so called murder? And what about witnesses? Anyone see anything suspicious?"

"Hard to be sure about alibis, not knowing exactly when Albert Collard was murdered..."

"Died, Shapes," interceded Dykeman. "When Albert Collard died."

"Have it your way, sir, not knowing when Albert Collard died," Shapes placed an emphasis on the last word. "Looks like they all have a pretty decent claim to an alibi. Before we saw him, Edward Sweet was writing some letters in the lounge. Mrs Itchington saw him there on two separate occasions. After that he says he went for a walk in the garden. Watched the ladies playing tennis for a bit, then wandered off to the stables to have a nose around."

"I don't think he did in Albert Collard," insisted Dykeman. "Either he's a brilliant actor or he was genuinely scared when he came running up to tell us what he'd found and I don't see him being able to act his way out of a paper bag."

"Don't trust him, I don't. He's got too jumped up an idea of himself. And he's a toff," added Shapes, with a snarl.

"I'm with you on that one," replied Dykeman.

"We saw Marie Macron and Daphne Collard playing tennis ourselves," continued Shapes. "They reckon they'd been out there half an hour before we showed up."

"What do you think about Daphne Collard topping her husband? She could have done the business before heading off to the tennis court," suggested Dykeman, who didn't sound any too convinced.

"That's an idea," replied Shapes, enthusiastically. "Wanted to get full control of his money. Yes, that would work."

"Can you really see her doing something like that, Shapes? And what's going to happen once she's spent all his money?"

"Maybe she's found someone new, with deeper pockets. She looks to me like the sort who'd dump one man for another one if it meant she was trading up," replied the sergeant, on something of a roll now.

"I suppose it's possible," observed Dykeman, still not convinced. "Go on. Who does that leave?"

"Richard Dipping and Tamsin Spectacle, who insist they stayed in their rooms until late, then went down to the lounge just as Sweet was leaving the room to go for a walk. He agreed with that part of their story."

"Which means if I'm wrong and Albert Collard was in fact murdered, then one of them is lying. On the other hand..."

"One of them is lying, sir," insisted Shapes.

Dykeman eyed his eager sergeant. "We'll see. You know, I've changed my mind about staying put and waiting for something to happen. Let's use some of the time to have another word with Marie Macron. I'd like to do a little digging into the relationship between her and Sixpence."

"I'll fetch her, shall I?" offered Shapes, at once.

"And do let her change out of her tennis gear first, Shapes."

"If you say so, sir," replied Shapes, sounding a little disappointed.

"WAS IT A MESS?" ASKED Marie Macron.

She was sat opposite Dykeman, still wearing her tennis gear. Shapes looked as he felt, a happy man.

"I've seen worse," replied the inspector.

"Poor Daphne, I don't know how the woman has managed to hold herself together so well. I doubt I'd be anything other than a complete wreck if I was in her position."

Marie Macron spoke with a degree of sympathy Dykeman hadn't been expecting from someone who had, up until then, been such a cold and unyielding individual. He wasn't sure if this should put him on his guard, so he opted to tread with caution.

"Quite a woman, that's for sure," he observed. "No doubt things will start to seep in more as time goes by. That's often the case."

"What can I do for you, inspector? I'm not sure there's much more I can tell you that I haven't already told your sergeant, but I'm happy to answer any questions you have."

Shapes sat in his now usual seat, off to one side of the others. He'd been delighted to find Marie Macron still in her tennis gear and took the opportunity to march her straight over to the study. The knee length, white cotton skirt she was wearing had ridden very appealingly up her shapely legs as she sat down. He found it hard not to stare and the room had begun to feel a bit on the warm side.

"I do have one or two rather personal questions I need to ask you. You should understand they are highly pertinent to our investigations," added Dykeman.

"If it helps you make progress then please don't feel inhibited, inspector. Like the others, I'd much rather you find the killer before I become their next victim."

"Good," responded Dykeman. "So I'll crack right on. We understand you had romantic desires towards the Reverend Sixpence, is that right?"

Marie Macron's mouth opened wide before she could stop herself. She shut it, then attempted a smile, keen to avoid giving the impression she was in any danger whatsoever of losing her self-control. That was something she most definitely did not want to do. She had done much, since the unpleasantness and chaos of her failed marriage and subsequent divorce, to project a new version of herself to the rest of the world. Appearing weak or erratic, let alone overly emotional, was to be avoided at all costs, whatever effort it required. She'd already let that mask slip once in recent days, pushed into losing her temper by Dykeman, and she was determined not to let that happen again.

"Oh dear, inspector, I'm afraid to say the gossips have got that one terribly wrong," she replied, with amusement.

"So there was nothing going on between the two of you?" persisted the inspector.

"There was not." She paused, before adding, "But that wasn't how George wanted things to be."

"Eh?" asked Dykeman, momentarily confused.

"You see, it wasn't me chasing after George. It was the other way around," replied Marie.

"Sixpence was chasing you?" Dykeman couldn't help sounding surprised.

"Yes. He'd had a thing for me for years, poor man," answered Marie Macron. "Practically every time we met he'd ask me to marry him. I'm afraid this weekend, I really had reached the end of my tether and had to tell him in the very clearest terms that if he didn't stop then we wouldn't be able to see each other any more. He is, was, a lovely man, but very definitely not the sort I want to spend the rest of my life with."

"Well, that makes a good deal of sense. Him chasing you, that is," added the inspector.

"Who told you it was me that was doing the chasing?" asked Marie.

There was that now familiar flash of steel in Marie Macron's eyes, which had Dykeman feeling pleased there was a large, heavy wooden desk between the two of them. She could probably move a whole lot quicker than he could and God knows what she was capable of doing to a man if she got a firm grip on him. Shapes might be keen on finding out, but he was not.

"I'm afraid that's something we can't share. By the way, is she any good with a tennis racquet? Daphne Collard, I mean."

There was a moment's silence before Marie Macron answered. It was obvious she was less than impressed with the inspector ducking her question.

"Yes, she's rather a better player than I am. Mind you, that isn't saying a great deal."

"You'll be a much better player than me or Shapes, that's for sure," smiled Dykeman. "Well, thank you for your time. We'll let you get changed now. I do apologise you didn't get a chance to do so beforehand. Shapes gets a little too eager sometimes."

"I quite understand, inspector."

As Marie Macron spoke, she turned and looked at the horrid little man sitting to her right, his eyes fixed on her legs. Quite what chance he thought he had of seducing a woman like her, she could hardly imagine. The housekeeper was more in his league, but even she would be sure to hesitate before allowing herself to become involved with such a man.

"RIGHT, LET'S HAVE A recap," barked Dykeman at his still dewy-eyed sergeant.

"If you like," replied Shapes, sounding mournful.

"We've got three bodies on our hands. A dead woman, who was bopped over the head. A vicious attack of the sort that tells me there was something personal about it and it was likely planned. So far the only person who stands to gain from her death is her arrogant, stuck-up nephew, who picks up plenty of money in her will."

"Sounds like a good enough reason to me. And he's the sort who'll reckon he won't get caught because he's too smart for the likes of you and me," commented Shapes.

"True enough," replied Dykeman, ambling over to the window. "Then we have a dead vicar, stabbed in the heart as he sat in a chair in his bedroom. He may or may not have been subject to the amorous and unwanted advances of Marie Macron. Other than that, there doesn't seem to be any reason why someone here would want him dead."

"Don't you believe her then, when she says it was him chasing her?" asked Shapes.

"Probably, Shapes, but we can't go making assumptions. Then we have Albert Collard, found with a garden rake attached to his head, lying on the ground in one of the stables. One witness, with a mane and a long tail, who won't tell us a thing."

"Shame that," chipped in Shapes.

"Again, as far as we can tell, there is no one who stands to gain from his death, apart from his wife. Trouble is, she also ends up losing her main source of income. And, anyway, I still reckon that one was an accident," insisted the inspector, as he stared out the window.

"We ought to see if she's got a bloke on the side, sir. It's hard to keep that sort of thing under wraps for long."

"You're right, Shapes. Let's add that one to our shopping list."

"Done," replied Shapes, scribbling on his notepad.

Dykeman rolled his lips together. "And the truth is, we can't properly account for the whereabouts of all the other guests for any of the three deaths. On every occasion there's at least one of 'em without a proper alibi."

Shapes stretched. "It's the connection between the killings that gets me. I can't see one. I've tried working it out but not got anywhere. I reckon if we can solve what they've got in common then we'll have our killer."

"It's always possible, Shapes, the deaths aren't connected. Like I said, Golighty's murder looks personal and planned. The vicar's, on the other hand, that looks different. His killer took a serious risk there, stabbing him when the place was crawling with coppers. I suppose he might have caught someone pilfering from his room and we still don't know if there are any valuables missing."

"Richard Dipping," piped up Shapes. "He's the only one here with a confirmed dodgy background. Wouldn't surprise me if he'd run into some trouble with the wrong people and ended up desperate enough to do some thieving."

"Possible, Shapes, and he looks far too nervous for my liking. As if he's got something to hide."

"His sort always do have something to hide, especially from the likes of you and me," said Shapes. "We should take him down the station. Really put the frighteners on. He don't look like he'd be able to hold out very long."

"We might just do that, Shapes. It's worth a try." Dykeman turned away from the window, towards his sergeant, and rubbed his hands together. "But before we do anything else, we're going to take a tour of the house or, more precisely, the upstairs rooms. Time we did a little digging in wardrobes and cabinets."

THE TWO POLICE OFFICERS spent an hour and a half carefully inspecting the guest bedrooms. None, thought Dykeman, were extravagantly furnished. In fact, it looked like some of them hadn't been decorated in a very long time. The familiar and unwelcome musty whiff of mothballs greeted them on several occasions. He also noticed the housekeeper kept all the rooms entirely free of dust, which merited a note of appreciation.

Though they searched in a careful and purposeful manner, they weren't sure in the slightest what they should be looking for, just that they should be searching. Both men knew from experience that important clues could turn up in the most curious of places and when you least expected anything of the sort. Better to be thorough and disappointed than to do nothing was their mantra.

The last room they entered was rather more homely than the others, bar that of the Reverend Sixpence. They soon realised it was the housekeeper's. Alone at one end of the landing, separated from the other rooms by the intersection of the landing with the stairs, it had the benefit of a little more privacy, noted Dykeman.

There would originally have been servants' rooms in the loft, all now storage space, according to Mrs Itchington, and this was where she would have been quartered once upon a time. No need for such rooms now there was only the one servant. Dykeman realised he hadn't given a thought before then to where the woman would be lodged. It didn't seem relevant to their investigations.

They'd barely started rummaging through Florence Itchington's room when Shapes found a drawer filled with her collection of plain and, to his mind, unappealing stockings. It made him twitch, worried mere contact with the undergarments would be harmful to his health. He slammed the drawer shut almost as soon as he'd opened it. Should be a warning notice on there, he decided.

Whilst Shapes dealt with the stockings, his boss poked around in a cavernous, walnut veneer wardrobe, trying his best not to be overwhelmed by the stiff pong of mothballs.

He too was unimpressed by the housekeeper's bland attire, but decided a woman in her line of work didn't have much call for ballgowns and tennis clothes. No, what she needed was solid, practical stuff that could survive the rough and tumble of a hard day's work.

Having left behind the hideous stockings, Shapes found himself drawn to a collection of framed photographs on the bedside cabinet. He fingered his way over a motley cast of faces, young, old and many in-between. One photograph in particular took his fancy and he picked it up to look more closely. It showed what appeared to be a small family group and he was sure the one woman pictured was the housekeeper, though a fair few years younger. If he was right, it seemed reasonable to conclude the man was her husband and the teenage boy their son. It was tricky to estimate when the photo was taken, but Shapes guessed it was at least ten years old, based on his assessment of the housekeeper's age. Mind you, he thought to himself, the outfits she knocked around in at the vicarage didn't do her any favours; it was quite possible she was years younger than she looked.

"Look at this, sir," called out Shapes.

"What you got there, Shapes?" asked Dykeman, extricating himself from the wardrobe.

"Photos, sir. This one looks interesting," replied Shapes, holding up the one in his hand.

Dykeman walked across the room and took the proffered portrait. He studied it for a moment, looking with care at all three faces, before offering his own conclusions.

"It's the housekeeper. Reckon that's her old man, do you?" he asked.

"I do," replied Shapes. "And what about the boy?"

"Their son, maybe," suggested Dykeman as he looked again. "Looks like a family group to me. Wonder what happened to the husband? You'd have to think he can't be around any more, otherwise she wouldn't be working here all on her lonesome."

"Yeah, that's what I was wondering. But it's not that what's got me interested," Shapes said, prodding an eager finger at the photo. "I've seen that boy somewhere else. Not in the flesh, I mean. I've seen his face in another photo."

"Oh, and where's that then?" asked Dykeman.

"Don't know," responded Shapes, sounding a tad frustrated.

"Well, that's not a fat lot of use, is it?" quipped Dykeman. "Do you think it matters? To our investigation, I mean?"

"Don't know that either. But I reckon if I try not to think about it too much then it'll come back to me, where I've seen his face before."

"Well, in the meantime, Shapes, how about you put this photo back where you found it and get on with some useful detecting?"

Dykeman shoved the frame back in to his sergeant's hands and returned to the wardrobe, muttering under his breath. They didn't want to go spending their time on things that didn't matter. Focus was what they needed and lots of it.

Shapes placed the picture back where it he had found it. He was frustrated. He hated that feeling you get when you know you've seen or heard something before but just can't put your finger on where it was. It spoke of loose ends and there really was little he disliked more than loose ends.

THEIR RUMMAGE THROUGH the vicarage bedrooms having revealed nothing to help identify the killer, the two policemen decided to take a well-earned break and so retired to the terrace, where they took up residence at one of the little tables overlooking the garden. Mrs Itchington had obliged by making them a pot of tea and rustling up a few custard creams. A stiff breeze had picked up, but, as it was coming from the front of the house, the policemen found themselves largely protected from it its embrace.

The two men were deep in discussion, debating the competing merits of steak and kidney pie, on the one hand, and chicken and mushroom pie on the other, when the excitable figure of PC Dartington hove into view, tumbling on to the terrace through the open dining room doors.

"Sir," he announced a little short of breath and with a healthy glow to his cheeks.

"Yes, Dartington," responded Shapes, annoyed the pie debate had been interrupted before they'd been able to reach a conclusion.

"It's Richard Dipping, sir," said Dartington.

"What about him?" asked Shapes.

"He's done a runner," replied the constable.

Chapter Seventeen

Shapes looked at Dykeman, but was surprised to find his boss looking supremely relaxed, even going so far as to pick up his cup and take another sip of tea.

"When did this happen, Dartington? And," went on Shapes, turning his beady gaze back on the PC. "more to the point, how did he manage to leg it, when I was under the obviously misplaced impression you were keeping a close eye on our house guests?"

"Well, there's a few of them, sir, and it's a bit tricky keeping an eye on all of them at the same time," replied the constable.

"It's alright," butted in Dykeman. "I was expecting something of the sort to happen. Remember what I said to you earlier, Shapes, about having a feeling something was afoot? Well, it looks like this here gut of mine was right again. Must remember to give it a reward later. Maybe a bit of apple crumble and custard."

Dartington looked at Shapes, a question mark writ large on his slender face. Shapes looked to the skies and shook his head.

"Right, sir," said Dartington, not at all sure what he was supposed to say or do next. "So, you knew he was going to leg it?"

"No, I wasn't certain it was going to be Dipping. True, he would have been odds-on favourite, but I thought Edward Sweet was almost as likely a candidate." Dykeman placed his cup back on its saucer with care and precision. "Taken his car, has he?"

"Yes, sir," answered Dartington. "Looks like he left about ten minutes ago, as far as I can tell."

"What about Miss Spectacle? He taken her with him?" asked Dykeman.

The inspector's tone suggested he didn't expect the answer to be a positive one.

"No, sir. She's still in the house. Seems a bit upset about things."

"I bet she is," smirked Shapes. "Probably reckoned she was on top in that relationship. Bit of a surprise for her there."

"Yes, sadly you're right, Shapes," added Dykeman. "A man like Dipping won't want any form of baggage with him, not when he's set on doing a disappearing act. Shouldn't imagine it's the first time he's done something of the sort. And I'll bet it's not always been the police he's been looking to hide from."

"Shouldn't we be getting after him, sir? In the police car, I mean," prompted Dartington, sounding rather hopeful that was exactly what they were about to do. He rather fancied a car chase.

"Nope," replied Dykeman, easing himself to his feet, then stretching his back. "Come on, Shapes. We've got a phone call to make. Then we'll tootle back to the station. Dartington, you remain here and try not to let any of the other guests escape, not that I'm expecting any of them will try."

"As you say, sir," replied the disappointed constable.

ALTHOUGH HE DIDN'T like to say so, Shapes had been intrigued, as well as a bit irritated, by the relaxed way in which Dykeman had responded to the news of Dipping's departure, even if he had, as he claimed, been expecting something of the sort. After all, if Dipping did have form when it came to that sort of thing, then, to his mind, they ought to get their act sorted out and pronto. But his boss was behaving as if they had all the time in the world. The way things were going, he wouldn't be surprised if Dykeman suggested they stop at a tea shop for afternoon tiffin on their way back to the station. What the heck, he wanted to know, was going on?

Dykeman had led them back to the study, where he made a call to the police station, asking for road blocks to be set up on the few main roads out of the area. This, thought Shapes, was a good thing, though he wasn't feeling as confident as his boss that said road blocks would ensnare the fugitive. Chances were, he'd not take the main roads, but stick to the maze of lanes that covered the area. Lord only knows how they'd find him then. He did his best to match his boss's relaxed demeanour by attempting an air of casual disinterest, but it was a bit of a struggle.

The phone call made and chairs returned to their rightful places, Dykeman led them out into the hallway, making for their car. But they'd not got as far as the front door when they were intercepted by Marie Macron.

She looked a little agitated and was, it transpired, keen to talk to them. Shapes was, as ever, also keen to talk to her. Dykeman, alert to the situation, stepped in front of Shapes so that he became a temporary barrier between his sergeant and the attractive house guest.

"It looks as though I'm just in time," announced Macron.

"In time for what?" asked Dykeman, instantly curious.

"You appear to be heading out the door. Are you going back to the police station?" Macron asked.

"We are," replied the inspector, as his irritated sergeant manoeuvred himself into a new position, free of any obstruction.

"I would imagine I'm not wrong in assuming you're off to track down Richard. I hear he left unannounced and in rather a hurry," said Macron.

As she spoke, Marie Macron brought her right hand up to pinch together the top of her blouse, having noticed the trouble her cleavage was causing the observant sergeant.

"He has indeed," replied Dykeman. "Though I don't imagine he'll get very far."

If the inspector sounded confident, it's because he was. In fact, if there had been a chance of placing a bet on it, he would have put down every penny he could get his hands on.

"I was wondering, is this an indication that he killed Eleanor and George?" asked Marie Macron. "It does look rather suspicious, wouldn't you say?"

"It's possible he's our killer, though I don't want to go jumping to any conclusions. He might be running because he's scared, worried he's next for the chop," replied Dykeman.

"Well, I have some news for you that might help you make your mind up," said Marie Macron, the merest hint of a smile on her immaculately made-up face.

"In that case, we'd better hear it," responded Dykeman, clicking his fingers in the general direction of Shapes, who promptly pulled notepad and pencil out of a jacket pocket.

"While I'm not one for idle gossip, there are times when something one sees really can't be ignored and, given the circumstances, there is something I saw earlier this afternoon which I really need to tell you about," began Macron. "I made my way down to the lounge, thinking I might take a look at one of the newspapers. There's not an awful lot else to do here at the moment. As soon as I walked into the room, I saw I wasn't alone. Richard was lying face down on one of the settees, the one nearest the fireplace. But he wasn't alone. There was a woman with him, or, I should say, under him and they were..." she hesitated, before adding, "getting intimate. So much so, they didn't appear to notice me."

"I've got a feeling you're going to tell me it wasn't Tamsin Spectacle that Dipping was with," said Dykeman.

"Not unless she's aged a considerable amount, inspector. No, he was with Daphne Collard."

"Daphne Collard," repeated Shapes, in a louder voice than he had intended.

"And just how intimate are we talking here?" asked Dykeman.

"Oh, they still had their clothes on, but they were in what you might describe as a passionate embrace. She seemed rather eager; that would be a polite way of putting it. I'm afraid I can't tell you how things developed, because I chose to turn right around and leave the room. I'm quite sure they still hadn't noticed me when I left."

"Her old man's not been buried yet," chipped in Shapes. "And what would Dipping want with her when he's got Tamsin Spectacle to spend his time with?"

If Shapes sounded incredulous it was because he was just that. Why Dipping would want to get 'intimate' with an old bossy boots like Daphne Collard when he could spend all his time fondling Tamsin Spectacle seemed plain mad.

"That's true enough," added Dykeman. "Seems a bit odd."

He glanced at his watch, weighing up the merits of interviewing Daphne Collard before they set off for the police station. This certainly was an interesting development and one that had obvious implications for the death of Albert Collard. Why couldn't Marie Macron have found them a bit sooner? Damn it, now he was in a bit of a bind.

"I think you'll find Tamsin is something of a tease, inspector," said Marie Macron, with the merest hint of contempt in her voice. "Her sort are invariably very good at stringing a man along, until they get what they want and then they simply leave. I believe they are referred to as gold diggers and she has a very big shovel indeed."

Dykeman couldn't fail to notice the little dance of delight that filled Marie Macron's eyes as she made her pronouncement on the character of the younger woman. The two hadn't appeared keen on each other from the off and this latest exchange only went to confirm that impression. But the suggested lack of morality in Tamsin Spectacle's behaviour was not the important thing on this occasion; it was the behaviour of her partner, Richard Dipping.

"You were quite right to tell us what you saw, Mrs Macron. It certainly muddies an already murky pond. I would ask that you don't say anything about this to Daphne Collard or Richard Dipping, if he happens to return to the vicarage. We shall want to speak to both of them about this later and it's best if they've not had time to, erm, prepare."

"Of course, inspector. I quite understand," smiled Marie Macron.

"THAT WAS A TURN-UP for the books, sir," observed Shapes as the two men at last stepped out the front door.

"You can say that again, Shapes."

"Reckon he's after her money? Putting himself in pole position as soon as he's seen an opening? Wouldn't surprise me with someone of his sort," Shapes declared, eagerly.

"I wouldn't put it past him at all, Shapes. In fact, I wouldn't be surprised to find out it's the sort of thing he's done before."

They crunched their way across the gravel to their car, which was parked in the shade of an enormous ash tree. Shapes produced the keys from a pocket and unlocked the vehicle.

"You reckon we can trust her, then?" asked Dykeman, as he opened the passenger door.

"Who? Daphne Collard?" asked Shapes.

"No, Marie Macron," replied Dykeman, sliding into the car without waiting for an answer.

Shapes paused, staring at the roof of the car; he hadn't thought about that.

Chapter Eighteen

Dykeman and Shapes hadn't been ensconced at the police station for more than ten minutes when a call came through to say that Richard Dipping had crashed off the road and into a ditch on the Banbury to Oxford road. The only part of the report that genuinely surprised Dykeman was the news that Dipping had been heading south, since north seemed the more obvious choice as it presented him with an opportunity to lose himself in any one of numerous Midlands towns and cities. But, there again, perhaps the man hadn't been thinking entirely clearly.

Fortunately, Dipping had survived the crash in more or less one piece and the ambulance had taken him to Banbury Hospital, a short drive across town for the two police officers. Neither of them, as it happened, were all that keen on hospitals; they smelled of disinfectant and reminded them of death or, if not that, then hideous, life-threatening illnesses. And there was always the chance you could arrive at one fit as a fiddle and leave having unknowingly picked up some foul disease that would floor you within a day or two. If not for the fact Dipping had suffered some meaningful injuries, they would have had him shipped over to the police station, so as to save themselves a trip to the hospital.

Dipping had been given a room all of his own and a constable to keep watch over him. It was quite a nice room, for a hospital, thought Dykeman. Clean, bright and airy; in fact, probably a bit too airy, but nurses liked it that way, in his limited experience.

"Quite the hotel, you've got here," remarked Dykeman in a cheery tone as Shapes closed the door to the room behind them. "Bit drastic though, don't you think, getting yourself all smashed up like that just so you can get yourself a room here?"

He looked down at the laid out figure of Richard Dipping, tucked into his bed so tightly he could barely move, not that he much wanted to. The matron on duty had told the two policemen that Dipping had broken his right arm, cracked two ribs and generally bashed himself around a good deal. She wasn't filled with an immense amount of sympathy, though it wasn't clear if this was a result of the police interest or was simply her normal bedside manner. She had made the two officers wait for half an hour while a doctor attended to Dipping's more serious injuries, or those which they could. It would be a while before they'd be able to set the broken arm.

"The room service isn't up to much," grimaced Dipping as he turned his head towards the two policemen.

"Just wait until you see what's on the menu," chuckled Shapes. "And if you don't eat it all up they force feed you. Did you know that?"

"Matron tells me you've got a few scratches and bruises, but apart from that you're alright," suggested Dykeman. "You're a lucky man. There are ditches on that road so deep you can hide a car in them. If you'd gone off into one of those we'd probably be visiting you in the mortuary."

"Seems I'm blessed," said Dipping, in little more than a whisper.

Richard Dipping's face was covered with cuts of varying degrees of severity and they caused him a good deal of discomfort, itching and burning by turns. It had already occurred to him that he was likely to end up with a good many scars; not something he looked forward to, given the ease with which he had, until then, been able to seduce pretty much any woman that took his fancy. He wasn't feeling sorry for himself just yet for the simple reason he was in too much pain, but it was only a matter of time. The arrival of the two idiotic policemen hadn't improved matters.

"We'd have brought you some grapes, but we didn't have time, I'm afraid. Anyway, Shapes would only have eaten the lot. Right gannet, he is," said Dykeman.

"Never mind," came the weak reply from Dipping.

"Didn't work out too well for you, did it?" prompted Dykeman, keen to get down to business. "Something to hide, have you? Worried we were on to you?"

Dipping looked away, towards the window. He could see the tops of some large trees looming up over the roof of one of the hospital buildings and, up above that, a block of cloud-filled sky. The room started to feel something like a prison cell, somewhere he felt sure he would soon be spending a long stretch of time. Not a happy prospect. He wanted to sleep, but even if the police hadn't been there firing questions at him, he was sure the pain in his battered body would have kept him awake. Damn it, why did things have to go so badly wrong? What had he done to deserve this?

"Bloody tractor," replied Dipping. "Pulled out in front of me as if I wasn't even there. Had no time to stop."

"They're like that, tractors," chipped in Shapes. "Get quite a few of them round here, what with it being the countryside."

"We thought you might have nipped out to pick up fish and chips for everyone," suggested Dykeman, his voice heavy with sarcasm. "But I'm thinking that wasn't the case, was it? Especially as I'd gone out of my way to tell you all to remain in the house."

"Or the garden, sir," corrected Shapes.

"Quite so, Shapes. House or garden. But you did a runner, didn't you? And that has me and Shapes asking ourselves why. An obvious question, I'll grant you, but an important one all the same."

"Makes you wonder if he hasn't realised we'd nearly worked out it's him who did the killings," suggested Shapes. "Thought he might be able to get away before we tidied up the loose ends."

"You could be right there, Shapes. The hangman's noose probably getting a bit too close for comfort."

Dykeman's voice had taken on something of a menacing tone, one he felt was entirely appropriate for the situation. In fact, he felt pretty pleased with himself, switching it on just like that. Quite the skilful practitioner, he was. He doubted it would take much more to have Dipping singing like the proverbial canary.

Dipping went to shake his head, but stopped as pain flared there. "No, inspector, I didn't kill anyone. I promise you I didn't kill anyone."

"Heard that before," snapped Shapes. "They all say that. Don't want to be caught, do they? Makes me sick."

"No, it wasn't the killings. I didn't run because of those," grimaced Dipping.

He was already in a lot of pain and things weren't helped by the sudden bout of panic brought on by the accusation that had been levelled at him. He wanted to jump right up and run as far away as he could, but, of course, that wasn't possible. The situation was beginning to look desperate.

"Go on," prompted Dykeman, sticking his hands in his coat pockets.

"I thought you'd worked out what I was up to," replied Dipping. "I lost my nerve."

"We worked out that much," said Dykeman. "Keep going."

"Not all my business affairs are exactly above board. I'd sold a large batch of stolen watches to a dealer in London recently and he'd worked out they weren't legit," admitted Dipping.

"So, he was after you, was he? Wanted his money back and you'd already spent it? Familiar story," observed Dykeman.

"Not exactly," replied Dipping, wincing as he tried to shift himself just a little, so as to relieve the pressure he was feeling in his lower back. "He found out I'd pinched the watches from an East End crook, who'd already nicked them himself. It's the crook I've been hiding from."

"You're pulling my leg," laughed Shapes, his eyes lighting up with joy. "What a laugh."

"Wish I was," sighed Dipping, grateful to have managed to shift his body about half an inch.

A series of high-pitched screams from somewhere nearby caught the attention of all three men. Shapes winced, feeling the pain of the unseen victim. A few seconds later the pitter-patter of running feet scuttled along the corridor outside the room. Dykeman looked at Shapes; Shapes looked at Dykeman. Richard Dipping tried his best to ignore the whole thing.

"That might be enough to get you off a charge of murder, once we've verified what you've said," commented Dykeman. "But that's not an end to things. We have a witness who saw you getting intimate with Daphne Collard in the lounge at the vicarage."

Richard Dipping felt the last wafer-thin vestiges of resistance evaporate from within. Who the hell had seen him with Daphne? They'd not been in there all that long. Well, ten minutes, perhaps. Had that really been long enough for someone to stumble upon them? Good God, just what had they seen? Idiot! He knew he should have bided his time, strung her along until it was safe. But then he might have missed his opportunity.

"It's not my day, is it?" he asked.

"Looking to get your leg over with the merry widow so soon, were we? Don't imagine all that money she's about to get control of had anything to do with it, do you Shapes?" Dykeman winked at his sergeant, warming to the occasion.

"No, sir, he wouldn't do a thing like that. He's far too much the gent."

"OK, I admit to kissing the woman, but believe me, it wasn't me who chased her. She threw herself at me. I just... got on with it," added Dipping, closing his eyes.

"I bet you did," suggested Shapes. "See her again later, did you? Somewhere more private, I'll bet."

"No, no. Honestly, it was just the once. God almighty, I made a mistake," admitted Dipping.

He tried again to shake his head and, just as before, stopped as yet more pain surged through his battered body.

Dykeman thought Richard Dipping looked as though he might cry. He might have felt sorry for him, except he didn't like the man, so tough. No sympathy. He scratched an itch on his backside, as he contemplated his next move. He knew he couldn't trust Dipping, but he also had a definite feeling the man had told them the truth; at least in part. They would need to follow up this interview by speaking again to Daphne Collard and checking out Dipping's claims about the stolen watches. But perhaps he wasn't their killer after all. An interesting thought, because if, as he suspected, it wasn't Dipping, then who was it?

"Look," gasped Richard Dipping as he attempted to lift his head so he could make more of an impact when he spoke. "I might break the law every now and again, but I didn't murder anyone. I wouldn't have the nerve to do that. Lock me up if you must, but the killer will still be on the loose."

"Well, I don't reckon you'll be going anywhere soon," replied Dykeman. "Which leaves time for me and Shapes to check out your claims."

"I'm looking forward to asking Daphne Collard how well she reckons you snog," quipped a smiling Shapes.

"HONESTLY, INSPECTOR, how on earth could you believe such a man? If you ask me, he's the one you should be speaking to about the murders of Eleanor and the Reverend Sixpence. I doubt very much I have ever encountered a more obvious criminal in my life. My husband's not yet buried and yet here you are accusing me of all manner of inappropriate things."

Daphne Collard was alone in the lounge when Dykeman found her. Indeed, she was sitting on the very settee that Marie Macron claimed she had been using while kissing Richard Dipping. The irony did not escape his notice, and, though not certain about it, he thought he saw a little hint of embarrassment flush briefly into Daphne Collard's cheeks. If it did, she quickly had it under control and it was subdued before it had a chance to flourish.

Shapes had left his boss to it while he went in search of the housekeeper. The two policemen intended to spend the night at the vicarage and he wanted to make whatever arrangements were necessary. Most important of all, Shapes wanted to ensure he got a superior bedroom to the one Dykeman was allocated, preferably close to the one being used by Marie Macron. Better still if it was next door to hers and had an adjoining door.

Dykeman had to admit to himself that Daphne Collard did look drawn and tired. Her eyes had lost their lustre and her previously immaculate deportment had left her. She certainly didn't look to him like a woman who was feeling frisky enough to launch herself on to another man at the earliest opportunity.

"The problem there, Mrs Collard, is that it isn't only Richard Dipping who says the two of you had a right old snog. On that very settee, by all accounts."

Daphne Collard ran a hand over the material of the settee, a little pang of guilt flaring up from within as she did her best to maintain her composure.

"What do you mean by that? Is the house filled with spies, is that what you are saying?" she asked, though it sounded almost like an accusation.

"Nothing of the sort. Only wish it was. That way, this whole mess would have been sorted out as soon as we'd shown up. Nice and tidy," declared Dykeman. "No, the two of you were seen by another guest. You were seen very clearly and, we were told, you looked to be very... keen."

There was silence for a while as Dykeman waited for an answer, determined he wasn't going to be the one to speak next.

"I... I don't know what came over me," Daphne gasped, before collapsing in a flood of tears.

Dykeman didn't possess a clean hanky, so he whipped a small, heavily patterned cover off the back of his chair and handed it to her. She didn't seem to notice what she'd been given and blew her nose into it all the same.

"So, you made advances towards Richard Dipping? Not him towards you?"asked the inspector.

"Yes," she whimpered, nodding her head.

Dykeman was surprised at the speed with which the woman had caved in. He'd expected more and was sure that if it had been Marie Macron sitting in front of him, he would have had a much harder time of it. Funny how people are, he mused. Often turn out different to what you'd expect.

"I... just got the urge to, well... I really don't know what came over me," bleated Daphne Collard, struggling to stem the tears. "I needed comforting."

Don't look to me for any sympathy, thought Dykeman. You made your bed, now you've got to lie in it. Despite the widow's state, Dykeman still considered it an odd way to react to the death of your husband. And just what was she alluding to when she said 'comforting'? It was hard to be certain, given that Marie Macron hadn't hung around to see how things developed. Shapes would have, there was absolutely no doubt about that. He'd have seen it right through to the end, whatever that might have been.

"Some might say it looks highly suspicious, you and Dipping getting so 'friendly' like that, when your husband had only just died. And in mysterious circumstances," pointed out Dykeman.

Daphne looked up at him, her mascara smeared across half her face and her hands twitching nervously in her lap.

It was clear that she didn't immediately understand the implications of what he had said and it took a moment for it to sink in.

"No, inspector," she replied, her lips quivering. "I didn't murder my husband. How on earth can you say a thing like that. How could you..."

The inspector looked on as Daphne Collard gave her nose another blow. It was a shame, really, that it hadn't been Dipping who'd launched himself on her, rather than the other way around. It was hard to picture Daphne Collard sinking that rake into her husband's head, but he wouldn't altogether put it past Dipping, despite what he'd said at the hospital. If there was money in it and he was desperate, then, at a push, a chancer like Dipping might resort to murder.

There again, he was still yet to be convinced that the death of Albert Collard wasn't a drink-related accident. Put that death to one side and they were back to just the two murders. Just the two! One was bad enough. And, worse still, one was a vicar.

"You'll appreciate that, until we've confirmed what happened to your husband, you'll remain a suspect, Mrs Collard. You all do, in fact. And, for that matter, you all remain suspects for the two other deaths too. Well, I'll leave you to tidy up now. I need to speak to my sergeant," added Dykeman.

Daphne Collard didn't say anything else to Dykeman before he left the room. Instead, she had another little sob, too upset, it seemed, to say or do much else.

"AH, THERE YOU ARE SHAPES. We all sorted on the accommodation front, are we?"

"Of a sorts, sir," answered Shapes, with a frown.

"What's that mean, 'of a sorts'?" asked Dykeman.

"There aren't two spare bedrooms. Well, not ones we can use. The vicar's bedroom is a crime scene, of course, so we can't use that. And that just leaves the bedroom used by Mrs Golightly. The housekeeper is changing the sheets now," replied Shapes.

The sergeant fidgeted as he spoke, knowing full well what was coming, and he didn't like it.

"Well, that's no problem. You're sleeping on one of the settees in there," announced Dykeman pointing at the lounge door. "They look comfy enough for a decent night's kip. And I'll have the bedroom."

"Pulling rank are we, sir?"

"Yep, I certainly am." Dykeman laughed and slapped a hand on Shapes's shoulder. "Come on, time for a cup of tea and I'll tell you all about the little chat I've just had with Daphne Collard. Very interesting it was, too."

"She jump on you too, did she?" asked Shapes, sounding hopeful.

"Didn't give her the chance. Kept plenty of daylight between the two of us," answered Dykeman.

"I'm guessing you don't reckon she murdered her husband, do you?"

"You're right," said Dykeman.

"Why not?"

"Because, like I said before, I don't reckon anyone murdered him," insisted the inspector.

Shapes shook his head and made a face. "But you can't be sure about that. We ought to be thinking it's three murders, not two, otherwise we're going to miss something important. They're all connected. It's just we haven't worked out how yet."

"Ah, but if we reckon on it being three murders, then we're going to get ourselves all confused trying to work out how Albert Collard's death is connected to the other two, when it isn't. Then we'll end up chasing our own tails. Come on, I want that cup of tea," insisted Dykeman.

"I'm not giving up on this one so easily," grumbled Shapes, as the two men began the walk to the kitchen.

"I know," replied Dykeman, shaking his head.

Chapter Nineteen

Dinner was at six-thirty precisely and it was a quiet affair. All the remaining guests were in attendance. Dykeman surveyed them with interest. Tamsin Spectacle appeared to have heard about Richard Dipping's little encounter with Daphne Collard, as a result of which the two women sat at opposite ends of the table, the younger one largely silent and surly. The widow still had red rims round her eyes and showed little interest in the meal, sticking almost entirely to a large gin and tonic. She too said little of note.

Marie Macron, on the other hand, gave the appearance of being in a rather jolly mood. She certainly had no trouble tucking into the meal and made polite if sporadic conversation. Dykeman got the distinct impression she had taken a good deal of delight in telling Tamsin Spectacle all about the scene she had witnessed in the lounge.

Edward Sweet was keen to hear what progress the police had made during the course of the day.

"Well, you jolly well must have found out something," he said, at one point, irritated they weren't being told more. "Just why did Richard run off like that? Can't imagine it was for any good reason."

"It's a police matter, Mr Sweet," answered Dykeman, pausing between mouthfuls of sherry trifle. "Like I said before, we can't go telling all and sundry what happened, or what Richard Dipping said to us; though, needless to say, it had a bearing on the case at hand."

"Well, you've not arrested any of us, so I'd say it's not looking at all good for him," persisted Sweet. "We've all heard what he and Daphne were getting up to in the lounge. Not exactly the act of a grieving widow and a concerned friend, is it now?"

There was an unpleasant smirk on his face and, observed Dykeman, an edge to his voice that suggested he was really rather enjoying the discomfort he knew he would be causing Daphne Collard. It didn't exactly make him any more endearing.

The obvious provocation caused Shapes to glance at Daphne Collard and Tamsin Spectacle in turn, expecting either or both of them to respond, but neither so much as twitched a muscle. It was, in fact, Marie Macron who replied.

"I doubt very much that someone, who's still at school, has much of an idea what it's like to feel real loss, let alone the way it can tear a person to pieces. You really should stick to talking about things you understand, Edward, and that appears to be very little."

"So speaks the bitter and twisted divorcee," snapped back Sweet.

"They do say that children should be seen and not heard," countered Macron, with all the hiss of a snake. "Such a sensible suggestion."

"Can't stand to hear the truth, is that it? Afraid I might hit a little too close to home? Or just jealous you're too old and wrinkled to nab Richard Dipping for yourself?" Sweet smiled.

Dykeman would have laughed at the spectacle being played out before him, but he held back, keen not to risk bringing things to a premature end; it was too much fun for that. Instead, he helped himself to a second portion of trifle, which, he noticed happily, only he and Shapes seemed to be enjoying. Fussy lot, some people. Well, waste not, want not.

"Edward, please," came the plea from Tamsin Spectacle. "Can we not fall out any more than we already have. Not now. Not when so many terrible things have happened."

There was a moment's hesitation before Sweet responded. It was as if, thought Dykeman, he was keen to do the right thing but also reluctant to bring an end to his fun. It seemed to the amused inspector that the young man needed to make some sort of a choice. Interesting.

"Of course, Tamsin. I do apologise, to you, for causing any upset. Very careless of me. I do believe recent events are making things difficult for us all."

Shapes looked at Dykeman, who was sitting opposite him, and raised an eyebrow, as if to suggest that something of note had just occurred. Dykeman winked back, not in the least bit bothered if anyone else noticed.

"Will you be wanting coffee, ladies and gentlemen?"

Mrs Itchington had slipped into the room unnoticed by any of the diners. Shapes felt a nervous twitch flare in one shoulder.

"Absolutely," replied Sweet. "Can't miss out on that, can we now?"

"I'll take it through to the lounge. Why don't you go straight through," prompted the housekeeper, already beginning to clear the table.

As the depleted party shuffled out of the room and down the hall, Shapes sidled up to his boss and whispered, "If you ask me, that Sweet could be said to be making a damn good job at steering our attention towards everyone else but himself. The question is, why would he want to do that?"

"He does seem to have cheered up," responded Dykeman. "Maybe he really does think we've got Dipping in the bag for murder, twice over. And that suits us just fine. Whichever one of that lot is the real killer might let their guard down if they reckon we've already got our man."

The two men were disconcerted to find that Florence Itchington had appeared behind them, as if she'd materialised out of thin air.

"If you don't mind moving to the lounge," she said. "I need to get on with tidying things away."

It was a command, not a suggestion, and both men did as they were told, without any further hesitation, too fearful to disobey.

DYKEMAN LAY IN HIS bed unable to sleep. The sherry trifle was keeping him awake. He'd spent nearly an hour reading half a dozen pages of a copy of *Frankenstein* he'd found in a little stack of books that were piled up next to the bed. Ordinarily, any half-decent book would have had him off to sleep in no time at all, but indigestion was not to be overcome by any amount of reading. He knew if he didn't get to sleep soon he'd pay the price the next day, and that would be far from ideal for a policeman working on a murder case, especially one he felt sure was close to being solved.

The house was silent, not so much as an irritable water pipe or a ticking clock could be heard. Even the world outside seemed to be devoid of any noticeable signs of life. If he'd had access to a couple of bottles of brown ale, Dykeman would have downed them swiftly, certain that would have solved the trifle problem, but he didn't even have a glass of water. Maybe he'd find something in the kitchen if he could drag himself out of bed and down the stairs, but he couldn't be bothered, preferring to lay where he was and grumble. Still, at least he could console himself with the knowledge that he had a bed and all Shapes had was a settee. It wasn't all gloom and doom.

It was eleven-fourteen when Dykeman heard the kerfuffle. He knew that because, like any good policeman, he checked his watch. It was a woman's scream he heard first. It appeared to come from either the landing or the downstairs hallway and was followed at once by an erratic series of knocks and bangs. Unfortunately for Dykeman, he much preferred to sleep in the nude, which meant he had to pull on some clothes before he could head off to investigate. The resulting ensemble of trousers and jumper was basic but functional. It did, at least, cover his modesty.

As he trotted out of the bedroom and into the murky gloom of the poorly lit hallway, Dykeman could hear stirrings in at least two of the other bedrooms. It seemed he wasn't the only one awake and keen to investigate. With no immediate sign of what had caused the commotion, he strode on along the hall until he reached the top of the stairs, whereupon all was revealed.

The stairs took a dog-leg about three-quarters of the way up and where they turned was a small, rectangular section of landing. Ordinarily, a tall, narrow, wooden plant-holder stood in the far corner, but now it lay like a drunken man across the very bottom of the stairs. The reason for its little trip was clear to see. There, on the small landing, lay the dishevelled figure of the housekeeper. She was shaking and a thin trickle of blood ran down the side of her face, coming from a cut above her right eye. Already on the scene and attempting to establish the extent of the housekeeper's injuries was Edward Sweet. His natty, red velvet dressing gown was something of a step up from the outfit Dykeman was wearing, which caused the policeman some irritation.

As Dykeman took in the scene before him, the door to the lounge swung open and out skipped Shapes, whose long johns and vest combo perked up his boss no end. He looked up at the little scene on the landing and asked the obvious question, "What's happened?"

"It seems Mrs Itchington has fallen down the stairs," replied Sweet as he produced a starched white hanky from a pocket in his dressing gown and dabbed at the blood on the housekeeper's face.

Dykeman heard feet padding along the hall behind him and turned to see Marie Macron approaching. Holding up a hand to indicate she should stay back, he made his way down the first short run of stairs to join the gathering on the middle landing.

"Is she seriously hurt? Can you tell?" He asked Sweet.

"I'm no doctor, so I wouldn't rely on what I say, but she appears to be nothing more than badly shaken," answered Sweet, stuffing the soiled hanky back in his pocket. "Shock is the problem now, I'd suggest."

Dykeman turned back towards the stairs down which he'd just descended and studied each one in turn, all the way up to where the runner joined the carpet on the landing. There appeared to be nothing that a person might trip on. A stumble perhaps. Marie Macron stood at the top of the stairs, her arms crossed so as to keep her lightweight, silk dressing gown fully wrapped around her. Her face was impassive.

"Missed your step, did you Mrs Itchington?" asked Dykeman. "Easily done."

"No," came back the shaky reply and the housekeeper shook her head to emphasise her answer. "Someone pushed me."

"Someone pushed you?" repeated Dykeman. "Are you sure about that? That's a serious accusation."

The housekeeper's face was drawn and her hair a tangled mess, but, despite her loss of composure, she still had the strength of character to assert herself. "I was pushed," she insisted, in a firm but quiet voice. "I felt a hand in my back as I was about to take the first step."

"I don't suppose you saw who was behind you?" asked Dykeman, certain what the answer would be even before he asked the question.

"No," came the reply, again with a little shake of the head.

Shapes had advanced halfway up the main flight of stairs and he had a question of his own, "First on the scene were you, sir?" he asked Edward Sweet, the implication clear in his voice.

"I think that is self-evident," answered the younger man. "And if by that you are implying that means I must be the one who pushed Mrs Itchington then you can jolly well think again. I hardly imagine I would have hung around so you could take a cheap shot like that."

If Sweet sounded annoyed then it was because he was. How dare the obnoxious little man imply such a thing. A chap shows up first on the scene and what does he get for his troubles? An accusation that he pushed the housekeeper down the stairs. True enough, he'd give a pat on the back to whoever had done the deed, since the housekeeper had treated them all with remarkable disdain, but there really was no good reason for anyone to go around telling the world he'd done it.

"Or you didn't have time to leg it back to your room before we all showed up," came back the sharp-edged response from Shapes.

"Really, inspector, can't you keep your little man here under proper control. Or perhaps he'd prefer to find himself on the end of a claim for slander," hissed Sweet.

Dykeman was every bit as suspicious as his sergeant, but first things first; there was an injured woman lying on the landing who really ought to get some medical attention. The accusations and questioning could wait.

"We'll talk about this later," he replied. "Right now we need to get Mrs Itchington back up to her room. Shapes, wake up the local doctor and tell him to get his backside over here right away."

As the sergeant disappeared back down the stairs and into the study, Dykeman and Sweet helped the housekeeper to her feet and steered her back up the short flight of stairs and on to her bedroom, where they sat her up in her bed. Marie Macron had volunteered to head down to the kitchen to make a cup of tea for the injured and still shaky servant, while Tamsin Spectacle watched events in silence from her own bedroom doorway.

"The doc will be here in about twenty minutes," announced Shapes, as he entered the housekeeper's room.

Dykeman was sitting in a high-backed, floral-patterned armchair, his legs stretched out before him and his hands folded together in front of his face. He looked across at Shapes. "Good. One of us will have to keep an eye on the patient all night, you realise."

"Already thought of that. Got Dartington coming over, so he can have a sleepless night. It'll earn him some overtime money to spend on that baby his wife is about to squeeze out, so he oughtn't to be too grumpy about it."

"And there I was thinking all you are is a pretty face," replied Dykeman.

"She sleeping?" Shapes tilted his head towards the housekeeper.

"Looks like it," replied Dykeman, sitting up and leaning across to take a closer look at the apparently slumbering woman.

"Want me to have a word with our happy house guests? Try to work out who might have pushed her?" asked Shapes.

"Might as well, though something tells me a crystal ball will give you more chance of working that one out."

HALF AN HOUR LATER Shapes and Dykeman were heading for their respective beds. The doctor had been and gone, having pronounced that Florence Itchington had suffered no more damage than a cut above the eye plus some bruising to her legs and ribs. Since she was still suffering from shock, he had sedated her to ensure she would get a good night's sleep. If she did need any more assistance during the night or the following morning, all they needed to do was give him a call and he'd make his way over at once. All in all, thought Dykeman, Dr Hendrick had been both helpful and well-mannered, not a combination the police officer was used to finding in members of the medical profession, Dr Sheila Delph apart, of course.

As Dykeman had expected, Shapes got nowhere in his efforts to identify a likely culprit. None of the guests had seen anything suspicious, let alone seen anything of each other, since they'd all been tucked up in their beds. Edward Sweet insisted the only reason he'd reached the housekeeper so quickly was because his room was nearest to the stairs and, like Dykeman, he'd not been able to get to sleep by the time he heard Mrs Itchington's scream. He did add that, given how quickly he'd reacted, he was somewhat surprised he hadn't seen anything of the culprit, but none of the bedrooms were all that far from the stairs, so it wasn't beyond the bounds of possibility that whoever pushed the housekeeper had managed to scuttle back to their room before he appeared on the landing.

Of course, that did imply that it was one of the three female guests who had done the deed. What's more, since, in Shapes's eyes, there was no way Marie Macron would do anything of the sort, that potentially reduced the number of likely suspects even further. But Dykeman was having none of that. As far as he was concerned, all four of the remaining guests were equally as suspect, unless and until proven otherwise.

PC Dartington's arrival had put an end to any further discussions and, as he settled down with a cup of tea and a newspaper in the same chair Dykeman had been using in the housekeeper's room, the other two policemen made for their beds. Or, in Shapes' case, made for their settee. Both men had a strong expectation that the following day would bring things to a head.

DYKEMAN ARRIVED IN the dining room the next morning to find Shapes already there, tucking into a large fried breakfast. He looked like a man who couldn't possibly have been any happier, a sparkle in his eyes and the occasional shimmy in his shoulders. The wonderful smell of bacon wafted up Dykeman's nostrils and his stomach began to scream at him to join in the fun.

"Take a seat," suggested Shapes, as he chewed his way through a lump of sausage. "Mrs Itchington will come and take your order. We should have stayed here from the start. Could have eaten one of these every morning."

"She's back on her feet, then?" asked Dykeman.

"Yep. Looks like nothing ever happened to her. They make her sort tough."

"Well, I'm not going to say no to a fry-up," said the inspector, rubbing his hands together.

As if on cue, the sturdy figure of the housekeeper walked purposefully into the room.

"Good morning, inspector. Will you be having the same as your sergeant?"

"Couldn't think of a better way to start the day, Florence."

Dykeman pulled out a chair opposite his sergeant and sat down.

"Here's some fresh tea for the two of you," said the housekeeper, replacing the old pot with a new one. "How do you like your eggs?"

"Runny," replied Dykeman, all sweetness and light. "The runnier the better."

As soon as the housekeeper had left the room, Shapes took a pause in his eating and looked directly at Dykeman, keen to ensure he had his attention.

"If it's alright with you, sir, I'm off back to the station after I've finished this."

"Something up?" asked the inspector.

"Don't know. Maybe. Remember those photos we found in Mrs Itchington's room?"

"On the bedside table," observed Dykeman.

"That's them. Well, there's something about one of them, the one with Itchington, her old man and the son, that's been bothering me."

"And you reckon you're going to find the answer back at the station?" asked the inspector.

"Don't know. Possible. But I need to have a look, because it's really getting on my wick."

"That's alright with me, Shapes. The station sending someone over to replace Dartington are they?"

"Yes, I called them earlier. Should have another PC here by nine. Dartington's taking the job so seriously he's sitting in the kitchen right now, so he can keep an eye on Itchington."

"Worried someone's going to sneak in and finish her off with one of her own kitchen knives, is he?" chuckled Dykeman.

"Would do a better job than pushing her halfway down the stairs," replied Shapes, before slipping half a mushroom and a few baked beans into his mouth.

"That is very true, Shapes. I must have a word with Dartington. Give him a pat on the back for his dedication to the job. Fresh cup of tea?"

"Go on then."

"Anyone else been down yet?" asked Dykeman, surveying the empty room.

"Nope, not a soul. I've been up and about since half-seven. Couldn't sleep any too well on that settee, you'll not be surprised to hear. There's been no sign of anyone else since then. Probably too scared to leave their rooms in case they too have an unpleasant accident."

"I'm going to give Eleanor Golightly's solicitor a call this morning," said Dykeman. "Want to find out what's in her will. Should have spoken to him already, if I'm being honest."

"She's not worth all that much, is she? Not the sort of money someone would kill for?" asked Shapes.

"I don't know, Shapes. But appearances can be deceptive. For all we know, she could have some serious money stashed away in the bank, for a rainy day."

"But it's only Edward Sweet who's likely to get something out of the old bird, isn't it? He seems to reckon there's money coming his way and I can't see why she'd leave anything to the rest of them," added the sergeant.

"Apart from Sixpence. Remember, Shapes, they've been friends for years. I wouldn't be surprised if she left him a few bob."

"But who the hell gets their hands on his money now he's gone to meet his maker?" asked Shapes before shovelling another forkful of beans into his mouth.

"Don't know, Shapes. After I've spoken to Golightly's solicitor, I'm going to speak to Sixpence's. I'll tell you one thing, though; whoever benefits, they won't get this house. It belongs to the Church."

"I didn't know that, sir. Someone's going to be disappointed if they're expecting to move in here, on account of being his nearest and dearest."

"You know what, Shapes? I'm starting to have my suspicions that these murders have got nothing to do with money. It just doesn't add up when you think that neither victim was exactly flush with the stuff."

Dykeman poured two cups of tea, then put milk and two sugars in his own. He pushed Shapes's across the table. As he well knew, his sergeant preferred to add his own milk and sugar.

"What do you think it's all about, then? And it's three murders, not two." Shapes added.

"If it's not money, then how about sex or maybe revenge."

"Sex and a vicar," mused Shapes. "Should look good in the papers."

"And something else," continued the inspector. There could be more than one motive at play here."

"Maybe," said Shapes, chasing a mushroom around the plate. "We still don't know for sure if all three murders are connected."

"Assuming I'm right about Albert Collard's death being accidental, then I reckon it's safe to say the other two are connected. It might not be obvious what that is right now, but I bet we'll be kicking ourselves when we do find out."

"If we find out," muttered Shapes.

"We will. Now, how's that housekeeper getting on with my breakfast?"

THE REST OF THE MORNING passed without incident. Dykeman made his calls to the two solicitors, plus one to the hospital to see how Richard Dipping was getting on. He was told the injured man would likely be ready to leave the hospital in two days' time, once they'd assured themselves he hadn't suffered any internal damage or head injuries they'd not yet identified. Just to be on the safe side, Dykeman asked if Dipping might have sneaked out of the hospital in the middle of the night, but the ward sister was insistent he had remained in situ the whole time. Indeed, she didn't find Dykeman's line of questioning all that amusing and ended the call rather abruptly.

After making his calls, Dykeman had studiously ignored the rest of the house guests and taken the time to read the newspaper, followed by a little turn round the gardens. Sadly, the hot, sun-drenched days they had been enjoying seemed to have come to an end, at least for now, because he found the sky filled with grey clouds and a strong, erratic wind was blowing in from the south.

It was just before twelve when, looking out the study window, he saw Shapes pull into the driveway in their car. His sergeant practically jumped out of the vehicle and scuttled across the gravel driveway with uncharacteristic haste, which immediately piqued the inspector's interest. Shapes, it was clear, had discovered something of importance.

"Well, what you got then?" asked Dykeman, as soon as his sergeant set foot in the study.

Shapes wore a broad grin and delivered his news without hesitation, "I was right about recognising one of those faces in that photo, but it wasn't the son, it was the housekeeper's husband."

"Mr Itchington?" queried Dykeman.

"Not exactly," retorted Shapes, his grin growing broader by the second.

"Eh?" Dykeman was now confused.

"I'll explain in a bit. I went through all those folders I put together at the start of the case and there he was, in a photo I found in Eleanor Golightly's notes. So, I looked him up. Took a few calls, but what I found out was very interesting. Turns out Mr Golightly, now deceased, as we know, owned a fireworks factory in Coventry. Been in the family for years. And who do reckon was a manager there?"

"Mrs Itchington's husband?" suggested Dykeman.

"Yep. Only he was called Humphreys. One day there's an accident. A load of fireworks being stored in a building away from the main factory caught fire and the whole place blew up. People living nearby thought it was the Blitz all over again, it made such a noise. There were two deaths and half a dozen injured."

"Itchington's husband was one of the dead ones, I'm guessing?" cut in the inspector.

"He was. But it got worse. An investigation found that safety standards on the site weren't up to scratch. All sorts of shortcomings were identified. And guess who the manager responsible for safety was? Yep, the housekeeper's old man. Bit ironic that."

"But you're not suggesting, Shapes, that Florence popped down here to kill Golightly and, for whatever reason, the vicar, when it was her old man who was responsible for his own death?"

"Don't know about that. Could be. But there was more. When the case went before the pathologist's court, Mr

Golightly blamed everything full square on Itchington's husband. Then, for good measure, he refused to cough up any compensation, saying as her husband was to blame for what happened she could hardly expect the company to make a pay out. Well, she didn't take all that any too good. Had a breakdown and had to be shipped off to a mental institution near Peterborough. She was there for eight years."

"So, you reckon she's turned up here to get her revenge, eh, Shapes? And what about her name? You suggesting she changed it?"

"You said yourself all murders boil down to either sex, money or revenge."

"I did," replied Dykeman.

"And yes, she changed her name. Her married name was Humphreys," answered Shapes.

"But why didn't Golightly recognise her?" asked Dykeman.

"We don't know for sure that she didn't. And, anyway, all this happened over nine years ago. She could have changed a bit since then. She could have dyed her hair, put on some weight, that sort of thing to make it harder for Golightly to recognise her."

"But why stick a knife in Sixpence? What's that got to do with it?"

Dykeman, scratched at his chin as he mulled over the startling news his sergeant had just delivered. It almost added up, but no more than almost. It still seemed to leave the killing of Sixpence unexplained. Or maybe they needed to look again. One thing was for sure, he had to admit Shapes had done a spot-on job, though perhaps he'd not go saying so just yet. Didn't want his sergeant getting all big-headed and lax when they might be on to something.

"Who knows? Maybe he saw something. Like they say..."

But Shapes didn't get to complete his sentence. From the hallway, came the sound of what appeared to be something metallic falling to the floor. The policemen looked at each other, before Shapes turned and made for the partially open door. As he swung it fully open, he saw Tamsin Spectacle coming out of the lounge with a cup and saucer in one hand. There was no spoon on the saucer, but when Shapes looked down at the floor by the study doorway he saw one lying there.

"Yours?" he asked Tamsin Spectacle as he bent down to pick it up.

"No, I don't take sugar, sergeant. It's not good for the hips."

Shapes looked along the hallway and up the stairs.

"See anyone else out here just now?"

"No. I think we opened our respective doors at more or less the same moment. I'm pretty certain I saw only what you saw. Is there something wrong?" asked Tamsin.

"Seems not," replied Shapes, before retreating back into the study, taking care to fully close the door this time.

"Well?" asked Dykeman.

"Just Tamsin Spectacle coming out of the lounge. Said she doesn't take sugar, so I don't know who dropped this on the floor," he said with concern, as he held up the teaspoon.

"I think it's time we had another chat with the housekeeper. It seems she's not been entirely honest with us," observed Dykeman.

Chapter Twenty

Florence Itchington was busy chopping mushrooms when her attention was caught by a loud *meow*. She looked down to see a large, long-haired brown and white cat give a regale flick of the tail before it rubbed itself against her leg. She smiled and placed her knife on the chopping board.

"Oh, there you are Lancelot. You're late today. What have you been getting up to?" she asked, in a motherly manner

She bent down and scooped up the waiting cat. As she held it to her chest, the cat rubbed the side of its face against her neck and began to purr loudly.

"Aren't you the handsome one?" she said, stroking the animal's belly. "I suppose you want some breakfast of your own."

She slipped Lancelot back on to the floor, then took a slice of cooked bacon, which she cut it into thin pieces and dropped into a small dish, which she placed on the ground in a corner of the room. The cat launched itself at the food at once and Florence smiled as she watched her favourite companion tuck into his breakfast. She was still standing there when the two policemen appeared in the doorway.

The kitchen was, mused Dykeman, a feast for both the eyes and the nose, filled with a whole pallet of delightful foodie smells and boasting a selection of appetising breakfast delicacies. Clearly, the housekeeper was expecting a serious increase in demand at any moment. A not unreasonable thing, given even the fearful and nervous had to eat, sooner or later. Their empty bellies would drive them down the stairs before long.

The other thing that immediately struck both detectives was how impressively tidy the place was, especially bearing in mind that everything was being done by just the one individual. It reminded Shapes of the kitchen his mum maintained when he was in his youth; spotless, ordered and not to be messed up by him or his sister. In fact, being there in the centre of Mrs Itchington's kitchen while she was so busy left him feeling uncomfortable, something like the naughty boy he'd often been in his younger days. He wondered if Itchington might tell him off and send him up to his room for getting in the way and causing trouble. He fiddled with his tie.

"Yes, something you want?" barked the guardian of the kitchen, who had by now noticed them. "I'm very busy right now. Can't it wait?"

Just as Shapes feared, the dragon of the kitchen didn't sound exactly thrilled to see them there. He took half a step back.

"As it happens, it's not food we want, it's you we've come to see," replied Dykeman.

His boss was showing absolutely no signs of being intimidated, noticed Shapes, which gave him the courage to take back the half-step he'd just given up. He hoped Dykeman hadn't noticed the initial retreat.

"Well, I'm busy," came the curt response. "Always am at this time of the day. The rest of the guests will be down soon and I don't like to keep people waiting."

Mrs Itchington fixed her hands on her on hips and gave the two officers a stiff stare. The message was clear.

"We need to speak to you and we need to do so now," insisted Dykeman, folding his arms across his chest.

"Well, you'd better make it quick, is all I'm saying. What do you want?" The housekeeper continued about her business as she spoke.

"You know it occurred to us, we've been a little neglectful up to now in failing to ask you if you saw anything amiss at any time over the last few days," prompted Dykeman, not yet keen to give away the fact they were there to find out more about her own movements.

"If I'd had anything to tell you, inspector, believe me, I would have told you by now. I wouldn't have waited for you to ask, if that's what you were thinking."

"Well, let's take the murder of Eleanor Golightly, shall we? Would I be right in assuming you weren't taking part in the game of hide-and-seek?" questioned the persistent inspector.

"In case you hadn't noticed, inspector, I'm the one who does all the work round here. I don't have time for playing games."

The housekeeper took a long, black-handled knife to a sink and wiped it over before placing it in an empty slot in a large wooden block that stood on one of the worktops.

"But you must have seen people coming and going. Where were you, for example, when Golightly's body was found?" asked Dykeman.

"I don't keep a note of everything I do and everywhere I go," she replied, clearly irritated. "I imagine I was in here. It's where I spend a lot of my time. Or maybe cleaning the bedrooms or the lounge or the study or the dining room. Or I might have been setting the fire or cleaning up the fireplace. Or perhaps I was sweeping out the yard outside."

Itchington gave Dykeman a piercing stare that suggested he ought to leave, then picked up a bowl of chopped mushrooms and walked the few paces to the stove.

Dykeman ignored the veiled threats and heavy sarcasm. He was too battle-hardened to be bothered by such things and, anyhow, the woman's explanations as to her whereabouts at the time of the two murders was a serious matter. He wanted answers.

"Did anyone see you, wherever you happened to be?" He pressed.

"I really couldn't say. Maybe you ought to ask them."

"And what about the murder of Reverend Sixpence?"

"Look, inspector, if you want to know what I was doing and where I was, you'll have to invent a time machine so you can go take a look for yourself. I'm far too busy to be making notes of where I've been all day, every day. Now, if you don't mind, I have work to do."

The housekeeper jabbed a rigid finger in the direction of the hall door, then began to toss mushrooms into an enormous frying pan, which fizzed and steamed in response.

The policemen exchanged glances. There was a look in Dykeman's eyes that left Shapes confused, but he said nothing. He'd learned from experience that saying nothing was often the very best thing to do in circumstances where he had little idea what was going on in his boss's head.

"That'll be all, for now," declared Dykeman at last. "But we'll be back. Come on Shapes, we need to talk."

Stopping only a short way outside the kitchen doorway, Dykeman turned to his sergeant and, in a voice that was louder by far than it needed to be, summed up what he believed had just occurred.

"Well, she's not done herself any favours in there. If you ask me, she was damn evasive and that has me wondering why. Maybe she's got something to hide."

His back to the kitchen, Dykeman gave Shapes a wink. The sergeant had already realised there was a game of some sort being played and the wink from his boss confirmed it, ensuring he picked up the thread without any confusion or delay.

"I'm with you there. I bet she runs this place to a strict routine. Bit like being in the army. It's the only way she can cope with everything that needs doing."

"You think she might be protecting someone, Shapes? Maybe she saw something she wasn't supposed to and has her reasons for not wanting to let on."

"Or worse," suggested Shapes.

"Yes, or worse," repeated Dykeman, glancing across his shoulder in the direction of the kitchen.

THE DETECTIVES RETURNED once again to the retreat that was the study. Dykeman sat down at the desk and pulled his notepad out of a coat pocket.

"Don't tell me you've been using that," said Shapes, with amusement. His boss so rarely used his notepad it was a wonder he still knew how or, even, where it was.

"I like to give it a little outing every now and then, Shapes, just to keep my hand in. I didn't tell you what those solicitors told me earlier," he added, flipping through the pages of the pad until he found the one he was looking for.

"You didn't. Something juicy, I hope," replied Shapes, parking himself on the edge of the desk.

"Some of it is. Sixpence hasn't left much of an estate. House is nice enough, but not his, and the pay for a village vicar isn't what it used to be, so there's not a whole lot in his bank account. There was an older brother, who moved to Australia before the war. He's dead, but there are a couple of nephews who will get what little Sixpence has left behind."

"No one here gets their mits on any of his loot then?" asked Shapes.

"Nope, not a penny. But that's not the case with Golightly's estate."

"Sounds better."

Shapes rubbed his hands together, filled with a growing sense of anticipation at what his boss had heard from the solicitors. Mind you, what was Dykeman doing not having already told him all of this. Holding out on his own sergeant? They'd have to talk about this later.

"She owns her house and still has shares in the family business. According to her bank manager, she's always been pretty frugal with her money. I think we know there's at least one exception to that and he's been staying here the last few days."

"Edward Sweet," observed Shapes with a grin.

"That's him. He gets a tidy little payout from the will. Interestingly, the solicitor reckons Sweet has some pretty hefty bills outstanding. Seems he's continually over-spending and his sensible parents refuse to keep bailing him out."

"That's more like it. Someone with a reason to bump off the old woman."

Shapes was brimming with excitement now, confident they were on the brink of fingering their murderer and, joy of joys, things were looking properly bad for that stuck up toff, Edward Sweet.

"Could be, but we're talking twenty-five thousand here, not a million quid. Is he really going to top the woman for that kind of money?" asked Dykeman.

"I reckon he would if he's desperate enough. He might have bigger debts than the solicitor knows about. And he might have borrowed money from people he shouldn't have. That happens often enough and those sort don't have a lot of patience."

"Would you do it?" asked Dykeman.

"What?"

"Top your old auntie for twenty-five grand?"

"Haven't got any old aunties left alive. No, not even if I was desperate. But I'm not Edward Sweet. He's a toff and an arrogant little one at that; I'm not," asserted Shapes.

"Well, maybe he did it and maybe he didn't," said Dykeman, closing his notepad. "At least he has a motive. Let's put him through the wringer one more time and see what comes out the other side. You can take the lead this time, if you fancy it."

"About time. Come on then, I'm up for this and no point in hanging around," declared Shapes.

IN THE EVENT, THE POLICEMEN allowed Edward Sweet to eat before presenting himself for a fresh grilling in the study. Shapes managed to string out this latest interview with Sweet to a whole twenty minutes. It irritated the young man, who was keen on walking out of the room after the first two minutes, but it amused Dykeman no end to see the stamina and persistence that his sergeant was able to display. It felt as if the man had actually been paying attention over the course of the years they'd been working together.

Unfortunately, it didn't uncover anything even remotely new. Sweet was offended at the suggestion he would bump off anyone for as little as twenty-five thousand pounds and unconcerned about the debts that were outstanding against his name. For one thing, he replied, he had good reason to anticipate a sizeable bequest from his now deceased aunt, since she had herself told him so. Now he knew how much that actually was, he seemed a little disappointed. In any case, he went on, he now had less than a year left at university and could always find himself some paid employment after that, even if that would interfere with his travelling plans.

Dykeman wasn't impressed by the young man's arrogance, even if it was in keeping with his previous behaviour, but that in itself didn't mean he was responsible for anyone's death, more's the pity. It was hard to maintain a belief that Sweet had killed either Golightly or Sixpence, however much he tried. What's more, even if he did tell himself it was Sweet who murdered Golightly so he could get his hands on her cash, then what possible reason did he have for killing the vicar?

They now had motives and genuine suspects but Dykeman's earlier confidence was teetering a smidge; a little undermined by the thought that perhaps all the killer had to do to remain undetected was keep their nerve. They were close, he knew that. The thought they might lose the killer at such a late stage hovered over him like a dark and growing cloud. He needed to ignore it and push on regardless. That was the thing to do. Push on.

He was still adamant that Albert Collard's death was an accident, but without a statement from the horse, he couldn't be absolutely certain about that. It was, he had to admit, a tad awkward. The attack on the housekeeper also confused matters, as did the lack of a clear connection between the murders of Golightly and Sixpence.

It had occurred to him earlier in the day that what might be needed was some sort of scheme that would flush the killer out into the open, but what form that might take was proving hard to work out. Perhaps he needed to taunt the others like he had the housekeeper. If only a little more inspiration would come his way.

Having dismissed Sweet from their presence and compared notes with his boss, Shapes went in search of tea and biscuits, as much to give himself a change of scenery as anything else. But when he returned to the study, he was empty handed. Instead, he had news.

"PC Smalling told me Mrs Itchington's gone off on a bike to pick up some supplies. I've put the kettle on, but couldn't find the biscuits."

Dykeman glanced up, saying nothing, then looked at his watch before returning his gaze to Shapes.

"When did she go?" he asked.

"Itchington?"

"No, Gracie Fields," came the sarcastic response.

"Don't know. Does it matter?"

"Ask Smalling if he noticed," instructed Dykeman.

Shapes was back with an answer little more than a minute later. "She left about twenty-five minutes ago, maybe a bit longer. Why's that?"

Dykeman was on his feet with uncharacteristic haste and reaching for his jacket as he answered. "Might be nothing, but there was a grocery delivery van here early this morning. I saw it heading out through the gate. Makes you wonder why she needs to make a trip out for more goods. Come on, let's see what she's up to. Not much to hang around here for right now."

"GOOD TO BE BACK IN the car," observed Shapes, as he pushed his right foot to the floor, causing the engine to roar with delight.

"Having fun, are we?" asked Dykeman, grabbing hold of the side of his seat and flinching as the car bucked and bumped over the pothole-riddled road.

"Yep," grinned Shapes. "Hope she's gone for a long ride. All the more driving for me."

Leaves on the trees they passed fluttered erratically in the wind, while cows and sheep munched with their usual determination and detachment in the surrounding fields. Here and there they passed a grassy field where the old ridge-and-furrow system could still be made out. If they'd been able to hear anything except the car engine, the policemen could have savoured birdsong that warbled melodically from many quarters. It was an almost perfect rural scene. Perfect, that is, except for the racing police car, which did its very best to act as a sizeable blot on the landscape.

They called in on the nearby village grocer, only to be told there had been no sign of Mrs Itchington all morning. The shopkeeper suggested they might like to try the grocer in the next village, as he stocked one or two additional lines. But that too resulted in a blank, by which stage Dykeman's initial mild interest had developed into something rather more concerned.

"You reckon she's doing a runner, sir?" asked Shapes as he ran the car round a long, sweeping bend, causing a flurry of dirt to kick up behind them.

"Makes you wonder," replied Dykeman, a nervous edge to his voice. "But I guess we'll never get to find out if you end up killing us before we reach the town."

"Can't hang around, sir. She might get away. Wouldn't want that, would we?"

Shapes was having fun even if his boss wasn't. What's more, it was starting to look like they were on to something. He might have spared a moment to wonder why the housekeeper could have turned into a bloodthirsty killer, if that's what she had in fact done, but he was far too busy keeping the car on the road to have the capacity to do so. Anyway, they'd soon enough find out what was going on, once they caught the woman.

"Just keep the car on the road, Shapes. And the road is in front of you, not over here on the verge."

"Relax, sir. I could race round these roads all day long and not so much as squash a rabbit, worse luck."

They stopped at a public phone box in the next village they came to and put through a call to the police station, asking that all officers be on the look-out for the vanished housekeeper. There was little doubt she'd been gone long enough to have reached Banbury and, if she was making a run for it, the sensible thing to do would be to head for either the railway station or the bus depot. A constable was being deployed to each, just in case. After a brief discussion, Dykeman and Shapes had decided to head for the railway station, on the basis that it offered Itchington the best chance of getting far away as quickly as possible.

As they turned on to the Banbury Road, Shapes slowing only as much as he felt he had to, they faced at least another ten minutes of driving before they'd get to the railway station, which the increasingly excited sergeant seemed intent on reaching in half that time. They shot past a line of three slower moving cars in one go, then found themselves stuck for half-a-mile behind a large lorry, busy hogging the middle of the road. Shapes eventually managed to swing round it, then back across to their own side of the road just in time to avoid a car heading in the opposite direction.

Dykeman's face grew more and more pale with each passing minute and his stomach began to complain in a manner that suggested his breakfast was becoming a little unsettled. He looked at his watch, struggling to make out the time as the car bumped and bucked at every opportunity.

At last, just when Dykeman was beginning to think he might have to ask Shapes to pull over and stop so he could be ill in a roadside ditch, they came to the outskirts of the town and even the flying sergeant was forced to abate his speed, though not without a groan or two of disappointment.

They entered Banbury on the Southam Road, passing the limestone finery of the Puritan's Head Hotel and the more modern extravaganza of the Neon Cinema, which accounted for much of the town's social life for anyone under the age of twenty-five. As they reached the crossroads at the Banbury Cross, Shapes flung the car left into the High Street, only to find himself forced to slow even more as they encountered a scattering of both moving and parked vehicles on what was one of the town's main shopping thoroughfares.

It was fortunate it was not a market day, otherwise Market Place would have been packed and almost impossible to navigate. Instead, they went straight through, passing along Bridge Street as it rose up over the Oxford Canal and the River Cherwell. Finally, with a deeply-felt sense of relief on Dykeman's part, they turned right into the short stretch of road that led down to the town's Victorian railway station.

"Thank God for that," remarked Dykeman, as the tension began to ebb from his body.

"I was enjoying that," replied Shapes as he drew the car up outside the main entrance to the station.

"I should hope so. God knows how we didn't crash. Come on. She can't be far ahead of us, assuming she's here."

They decided, with some reluctance on the part of Dykeman, that it was necessary to break into something akin to a modest run, which attracted some inquisitive looks from the half-dozen people waiting to purchase tickets. By the time they reached the top of the staircase that took them up, over and down to the platforms, Dykeman was already breathing heavily, much to Shapes's amusement.

"That little flight of stairs worn you out, has it, sir?"

"Less of your lip," replied Dykeman, trying to catch his breath. "Which one is the London bound platform?"

Shapes looked up at the boards hanging from the high ceiling. "Platform two, right here," he said, pointing at the long, straight flight of stairs that led down to the nearest platform.

"Good," replied Dykeman, breathing heavily. "At the bottom, you go left and I'll go right. She's only a woman so we ought not to have any trouble, but if she does put up a fight you've got my permission to use force if you have to."

"Hit a woman? Me? If you say so, sir."

The two detectives came down on to something like the middle of a platform that was several hundred yards long, most of it benefiting from the shelter provided by a weather-worn metal and wood-framed roof. A smattering of passengers were waiting for the arrival of the next London bound train, due in eleven minutes. Some of these lounged on the wooden benches that were scattered along the platform, whilst others stood stiffly to attention alongside their luggage.

A member of the station staff, his sleeves rolled up to his elbows and his hat tilted at a jaunty angle, stood by with a furled red flag in one hand. He seemed to be watching a young woman sitting alone on a bench a little way along from where he stood.

Two sets of rails ran alongside the platform, one for northbound traffic, the other for southbound. Beyond these was another platform, this one all but deserted. Sunlight broke through the cloud here and there, glinting on the rails, polished to a glossy finish by the regular passing of train wheels. From somewhere off to the south came the sound of industrial works, which didn't seem to be bothering the gently cooing pigeons that loitered here and there in the hope of picking up scraps of food. The smell of smoke from the last train to pass through still lingered in the air.

Shapes and Dykeman exchanged a brief look before going their separate ways. Shapes slipped by one of the thick columns that supported the roof, then began working his way towards the back of the platform so he could approach his section with less chance of being noticed. That still assumed, of course, that Florence Itchington was indeed to be found at the station.

But Shapes had made very little progress when he heard a shout from Dykeman, one that caused him to immediately turn around and head back the way he'd just come. As he stepped out from behind the wall of the waiting room, Shapes could see Dykeman about seventy or eighty yards further along the platform, gesturing repeatedly across the tracks at the other platform. It didn't take Shapes more than a moment to see what had attracted his boss's attention.

Clambering up on to the far platform from the tracks was the figure of a woman. She had already shoved a small suitcase on to the platform and, although wearing a calf-length coat and a wide-brimmed hat, it was clearly Florence Itchington. Given the height of the platform from the ground, Shapes was properly impressed as he watched the middle-aged woman haul herself up.

The sergeant broke into a sprint and had reduced the distance by half when he saw Dykeman lower himself on to his bottom with his legs dangling over the edge of the platform, before dropping on to the tracks. Unfortunately, he managed to land in a heap, which gave the housekeeper just enough time to get back on her feet and grab her luggage.

Itchington took a step forward, as if to continue her flight, then stopped, turned back to face Dykeman and shouted across the tracks at him. He wanted to reply, to ask questions, maybe even bring her to her senses and stop this nonsense, but the brief exchange was over before he got the chance to do so and the housekeeper made off, albeit at something short of an actual sprint.

Having got back to his feet, Dykeman glanced up at the advancing Shapes, now barely more than twenty yards away.

"Not this way, Shapes," he shouted. "Get back up the stairs and stop her from getting out that way," he added, jabbing a finger in the direction of the covered bridge.

Shapes paused, looked up, then turned and hurtled down the platform. He was on the stairs and gone before the housekeeper had even reached the stairs on her own platform. She stopped and looked around. Dykeman was by now picking his way over the rails towards her. Unable to see any other way out of her predicament, Florence Itchington, suitcase still in hand, began to run down the platform. She thundered past a somewhat startled Dykeman, as he struggled to drag himself up on to the platform, and had reached the end of the little row of station buildings by the time he was back on his feet.

From up above him, Dykeman heard a worried shout. It was Shapes, now on top of the bridge and looking through the railings at the fleeing figure of the housekeeper. The sergeant had to admire her determination and stamina, but that didn't mean he was keen on seeing her escape.

"The fence. The fence up there is broken and there's a big gap she can get through," he shouted.

"Got it," yelled Dykeman, before setting off after his quarry as quickly as he could manage, which wasn't a particularly impressive speed.

He saw the housekeeper disappear round the corner of a small building and out of his sight. Then, entirely to his surprise, she almost immediately reappeared, once more at track level, this time running back across the two sets of lines towards the far side of the station. He huffed and puffed his way to the end of the platform and found she had taken advantage of a set of steps to make her way down. God the woman was persistent. If she managed to keep going for another couple of minutes and get through the gap in the fence then it might be enough to throw him off her trail. Best hope Shapes still had plenty of energy left.

What neither the hunter nor the hunted had yet noticed was a goods train approaching from the south, it's heavy rolling rattle not loud enough yet to attract their attention. Until, that was, it got close enough for the sound of its approach to be amplified as it echoed off the station buildings.

As Dykeman looked on, he saw the determined housekeeper step on to the northbound track seemingly certain to be hit by the advancing train, which gave out a long, ear-splitting blast on its whistle. Dykeman winced at the prospect of what would be left of the woman. It looked like it might be a long and tricky clean up operation.

To his surprise, the train continued on its way, rattling on through the station without any hint of slowing down. And there, just visible through the flickering gaps between the passing rolling stock, he could see the still fleeing figure of Florence Itchington, picking her way across the remaining sets of tracks.

Frustrated at having to wait for the goods train to pass, Dykeman looked back up at the bridge to find Shapes was no longer there. A surge of hope and expectation ran through him. Shapes was no mug. There was little doubt he'd seen what was happening and had made his way down the far side of the bridge with the intention of cutting off the housekeeper's escape. Good man.

His ears still ringing from the close passing of the goods train and his lungs objecting to the unaccustomed exercise, Dykeman recommenced his own pursuit, doing his best not to stumble on the uneven ground. Someone on the platform to his right, where a crowd had now gathered, roared on encouragement to the fleeing woman. Idiot, thought the advancing inspector.

On the far side of the station there was another single set of tracks, the purpose of which was to give non-stopping express trains a means of unfettered progress through the station. The fleeing housekeeper skipped almost gazelle-like, thought Dykeman, towards this set of tracks, while he plodded along in a manner that felt akin to a hippopotamus. The contrast would have been embarrassing if he'd had time to linger on it.

Things were looking distinctly dicey to Dykeman's eyes. There was a very serious possibility now that Itchington was going to escape the confines of the railway station and, if she did, there was no guarantee they'd be able to catch up with her in the maze of streets that lay beyond. He was worried, and all the more so as there was, as yet, no further sign of Shapes.

Just as it looked as though the housekeeper was going to make a clean getaway, she stopped and looked to her left, appearing to freeze on the spot. As if from nowhere, the London express now roared into the station at a speed that took Dykeman's breath away. In a total blur, the train screamed past him, a maddening, dashing animal that moved so fast at close quarters he could hardly believe it possible.

Florence Itchington had disappeared from his field of view, leaving him with a sickening feeling that she'd repeated her trick of a moment ago with the goods train and was now picking her way through the gap in the fence. It was then he heard the screams go up from the people clustered on the nearest platform and noticed the looks of horror that appeared on their faces. As the express blasted its way out the other end of the station there was no sign now of the fleeing woman. None whatsoever.

With some reluctance, Dykeman pressed on, in the general direction of where he'd last seen the figure of Florence Itchington until he could see, on the far side of the little strip of scrubland that ran along that edge of the station, a crumpled, misshapen heap. It was the battered and deformed body of the housekeeper. There was no doubt at all that she was dead. No human-being could be left in such a sickening state and still be alive.

A few yards before he reached the remains of the housekeeper, Dykeman found the small suitcase she had been carrying. He bent down and released the two metal catches that held it closed. There, laid out on top of a pile of neatly packed clothes, was the framed family photo of Itchington, her husband and their son that Shapes had noticed on the bedside table at the vicarage. He closed the suitcase, glanced again at the woman's remains, then turned to face the on-rushing Shapes.

Shapes was breathing heavily, his face redder than normal. "Well?"

"She's dead. Not a pretty sight," added Dykeman, pointing towards the house-keeper's remains.

"Strewth." Shapes eyes bulged as he saw Itchington's corpse for the first time. "Glad I'm not the one having to deal with that. What a mess."

"You can say that again. Don't reckon I've seen worse."

"So, it looks like she did it then, killed Golightly and Sixpence?"

"She did," replied Dykeman quietly. "She shouted across the platform at me that Golightly deserved it, after what her husband did."

"The factory accident, you mean?" said the heavily breathing Shapes.

"Seems so. It was all the revenge that was left to her. Apparently Sixpence worked out it was her, so he had to go too."

"Stupid old sod, he should have told us," said Shapes. "I bet he told her, thinking he could save her soul or something like that."

"She must have been waiting for her chance all these years. Talk about bitter and twisted. I suppose, since she couldn't get back at Mr Golightly, she went for the next best thing: his wife."

"She didn't own up to killing Albert Collard, I suppose?" asked Shapes, leaning forward, his hands on his knees.

"It wasn't exactly a lengthy chat we had, Shapes, but no, there was nothing about Collard."

"Guess you were right about that one after all. It was a drink-fuelled accident. You want me to call for an ambulance?"

"Might as well. Someone will need to take the body away. What's left of it. I'll keep an eye on things. Oh, and pick me up a cup of tea from the cafe, will you, Shapes? Think I could do with one."

Chapter Twenty-One

The following day, Dykeman and Shapes found themselves once more at the hospital, standing outside the back entrance. The sun had returned in all its glory and, despite the fact it was only mid-morning, it was warm enough for the two policemen to have removed their jackets. They stood in the shade cast by a tall, spreading oak tree, watching in silence as hospital life went on all around them.

They had both enjoyed the benefit of a decent night's sleep after the stress and strains of the previous day. Much though he'd tried to resist it, Dykeman had been forced to join the Chief Inspector first thing in the morning for another stint in front of the press, answering their pointed questions and open criticisms of his handling of the case. Apparently, now it was all very much after the event, it was universally agreed that it had been obvious from the start where he and Shapes should have been looking for their killer. What a shame, he'd been told more than once, that three people had died before the police had, at long last, identified the killer. Dykeman had bridled at the criticisms the idiots had levelled at him and Shapes, but the Chief Inspector had made it very clear beforehand that this press conference needed to go without a hitch.

It had taken Dykeman much of the rest of the morning to calm down enough for Shapes to go anywhere near him. He couldn't blame his sergeant; the man knew only too well how bad-tempered he could be in such situations. Best, he'd decided, to lay low until the storm had blown over.

Their visit to the hospital had been prompted by the news that Richard Dipping's doctor had pronounced him sufficiently recovered to make the trip to London in an ambulance, where he was scheduled to be handed over to the Metropolitan Police. They were very keen to have several words with him, about watches, sundry unpleasant crooks and the various other ways in which they were sure he could help them with their enquiries. Given the somewhat tricky nature of his situation, Dipping had decided co-operation was his best route to some sort of safety.

At two minutes past eleven, the double-doors the policemen were keeping half an eye on swung open and a young porter looking, thought the inspector, as though he felt he'd got the day's plum job, pushed a wheel-mounted stretcher out into the open air. On the stretcher lay Richard Dipping. As the sunlight flooded over his face, he shut his eyes, thereby failing to notice the small party of two well-wishers who had been waiting to see him off.

An ambulance driver and his mate climbed down from the cab of their waiting vehicle and helped the porter lift the stretcher off its temporary wheels. Once they were happy it was properly fixed in place in the back of the ambulance, the porter withdrew. The driver returned to the cab and started up the engine as his mate climbed in the back with Dipping and closed the rear doors.

Thought had been given to the notion of assigning a constable to escort Dipping down to London, but, in the end, his total inability to effect any kind of an escape had resulted in the obvious conclusion that it was an unnecessary use of limited police resources. All the same, the two heftiest ambulance crew that Dykeman could find were assigned the job as some sort of a precaution.

"No Tamsin Spectacle here to wave him off then," remarked Shapes, with a smirk on his face as the ambulance pulled away and made off towards the Oxford Road. "Didn't waste any time changing horses, did she?"

"No big surprise there, Shapes. A woman like her is never going to hang around when her man finds his future options suddenly blighted."

"Yep, and I bet the lure of that money Edward Sweet is going to collect was just too much to resist. Stupid sod. Give her twelve months and I reckon most of that cash will be gone," observed Shapes.

"And so will she. Sweet's a stepping-stone, if ever there was one," added Dykeman.

"Can't say he doesn't deserve it, mind," said Shapes. "Stuck up toff."

"He wouldn't pay a blind bit of notice if someone did try to warn him. The fool probably thinks he's going to be wearing the trousers in that relationship." Dykeman almost laughed.

"I wouldn't mind paying him a visit in, say, a year's time. See how he's getting on," said Shapes.

"You didn't get an offer of dinner from Marie Macron, then, before she left?" asked Dykeman, affecting an air of innocence.

"No. Would you believe it, she barely said a word. Not even thanks. And after all I'd done for her," smiled Shapes. "Her loss, not mine."

"If you say so, Shapes."

"They released Albert Collard's body yet?"

"This afternoon, I'm told. His wife's decided on a cremation. Takes place next week. Think I should feel sorry for her, but I can't. Didn't like any of them, not really. At least Florence Itchington had a reason for doing what she did. The rest of them were just..." Dykeman tailed off, unable to come up with the right word.

"Toffs?" suggested Shapes.

"That's been your favourite word these last few days, hasn't it?"

"Well, it's spot on, if you ask me, sir."

The hospital doors opened again and a familiar figure walked out.

"Oh, there you are Leslie. The Duty Sergeant told me you would be here, somewhere."

Dr Shelia Delph walked up to the two men. Her face was radiant in the sunlight, decided Dykeman. In fact, she was looking like a right corker. He tried not to gawp, but felt sure that was exactly what he was doing.

"Sheila, what a nice surprise," replied Dykeman, grinning from ear-to-ear. "On your way out somewhere?"

"No, I was looking for you, Leslie. I'm hoping you might take me out to lunch, if you can spare the time."

She smiled softly and, to Dykeman, if no other, her eyes seemed to sparkle with more radiance than the sun. He rustled up a cough, so as to disguise his feelings and give himself a moment to regain his composure.

"Are you now? Well, I think I can manage that." He scratched at an ear and moved his weight to his other foot. "Poor old Shapes here has got some paperwork to finish off back at the station, haven't you, Shapes? Which means I'm free as a bird."

Shapes hesitated, for a moment, wondering if he should avail himself of some fun at Dykeman's expense. It was tempting, very tempting. But he couldn't bring himself to do it. The poor sod was love-struck; any fool could see that. Couldn't they? Surely Dr Delph had realised that by now. Or had she? She must have. How could she miss it?

"Well, Shapes?" Dykeman poked his sergeant in the ribs.

"If you say so, sir. Can't get enough of that paperwork, I can't."

As Shapes lingered under the tree, the other two wandered off towards the road, in search of a bus and as he watched them go a grin grew on his face. They might not realise it yet themselves, but those two were as likely to end up a married couple as any he'd ever seen. A best man's speech began to shape itself in his head and he chuckled a little at the prospect. He certainly had lots of material about Dykeman to make use of in any speech. Plenty of laughs there.

Reaching into the inside pocket of his jacket, he pulled out a small, rectangular photo and took a moment or two to admire it, his shoulders sagging just a little. It was a portrait of Marie Macron that had been sent on to the station at his request by the police in Nottingham, where she had grown up. She looked at least ten years younger, and no less beautiful for that.

It had been such a long time since he'd enjoyed the love of a woman that he'd started to think it would never happen again. Perhaps he was going to see out the rest of his days alone, with only the fellas down the pub to talk to from time-to-time. Dykeman getting married would only make matters worse. Perhaps, after all, he'd better start working on plans to undermine Dykeman's growing relationship with Delph, before it was too late.

As he set off back to the police station, he tore up the photo of Marie Macron and dropped it in the first bin he came to. What was he thinking, trying to chat up a woman with a stupid name like that?

The End

The Club of Death

If you've enjoyed reading *The Hide and Seek Murders* then why not take a look at the second story in the series *The Club of Death*.

https://benwesterham.com/books/book-details-the-club-of-death/

Free Book

IF YOU ENJOYED MEETING Dykeman and Shapes then why not find out how it all began as they investigate their very first murder case together. Download your free copy of *Murder at Stockton Farm*, sit back, relax and enjoy yourself as bruised egos and repeated misunderstandings ensure that solving the case isn't the only challenge the two policemen will need to overcome before the day is done.

https://benwesterham.com/bookoffer/

THE HIDE AND SEEK MURDERS

If you enjoyed this book then please consider leaving a
review at the store you bought it from.
Many thanks,
Ben Westerham

From The David Good private investigator series

From 'Good Investigations'

"MR GOOD," SHE PURRED like a hungry cat meeting a blind mouse, "and I do hope you will be." She slid beautifully, effortlessly in to the knackered old punter's chair, and I swear the thing wrapped itself lovingly around her sexy, lithe frame. Then she tempted me with those dark bewitching eyes, calling me closer, closer, closer

From 'Good Girl Gone Bad'

IF YOU ASK ME, GOOD girls can be the baddest there are, if the fancy takes them. Maybe it's because they save it all up for one big splurge, then go mad bad. I don't know, but what I do know is that anyone who tries telling you some little darling of theirs' wouldn't say boo to a goose is either stupid, misinformed or both. Any goody two shoes type should carry a health warning, 'Danger, Good Girl. May go bad at any moment'.

From the Alexander Templeman espionage series

From 'The House of Spies'

MY FINGERS WERE TINGLING from the force of the blow and my head pounding as my heart beat madly. I was exhilarated. There is no other way to put it, such was my sense of excitement at what I had just done. But there was also an edge of fear now over what I had started and the knowledge that there was no going back, no means of trying to explain away my assault as some sort of unfortunate accident. I was committed to a course of action, with no guarantee of success and no real idea of the consequences of failure, other than they would not be good.

BEN WESTERHAM

You can find out more about Ben Westerham here
www.benwesterham.com[1].

---

1. http://www.benwesterham.com/